Raven

Raven

Mys

A NOVEL

Mike Lundy

Lyle Stuart Inc.   Secaucus, New Jersey

Published by Lyle Stuart Inc.
120 Enterprise Ave., Secaucus, N.J. 07094
In Canada: Musson Book Company
A division of General Publishing Co. Limited.
Don Mills, Ontario

Queries regarding rights and permissions should be
addressed to: Lyle Stuart, 120 Enterprise Avenue,
Secaucus, N.J. 07094

Manufactured in the United States of America

Library of Congress Cataloging in Publication Data

Lundy, Mike.
  Raven.

  I. Title.
PS3562.U58R38   1985   813'.54   85-12001
ISBN 0-8184-0377-2

Raven

One

"I thought it was dumb," Bill Lamps said, referring to *Rosemary's Baby*, a movie he and his girlfriend, Pat Knees, had seen earlier in the evening.

"I liked it," Pat said. "It was scary."

He slipped his arm over her shoulder and pulled her close. The car's interior was warmed by the heater, and the windshield wipers rhythmically removed a light snow.

The radio was tuned to a rock station; "Cheap Thrills" by Big Brother and the Holding Company came to an end and a newscast started with news of America's latest setback in Vietnam.

"Dumb war," Lamps said. "I'd never go."

"My father got mad when you said that," Knees said.

"He's like the others..."

She silenced him with a gentle kiss on his lips, then increased the pressure. They turned to face each other, and Lamps dropped his hand to her breast. He could feel the outline of her nipple through her pink sweater. He turned off the ignition.

"We'll freeze," she said as his hands went behind and fumbled with the bra snap.

"Better than dying of carbon monoxide," he said.

"I hate winter," she said as his hands went behind and fumbled with the bra snap.

"I always have trouble with this damn thing."

She giggled, reached behind and deftly undid the snap. "You're all thumbs," she said as he pulled the bra away and tossed it on the seat behind her.

"Just because I don't wear one of those stupid things," he said as both hands kneaded the silky, pliant softness of her. The world outside the car disappeared behind a light layer of snow and the steam they created inside... The car was a gray-white cocoon on Van Cortlandt Park's "Lovers' Lane."

Two

A Rockland County patrol car pulled up to the emergency entrance of Nyack Hospital, turned around and backed up against the receiving dock. Two officers opened the rear doors. A nurse and a medical technician dressed in white peered inside.

Huddled in the back of the patrol car was William Lamps. He was shrouded in a greasy gray blanket one of the officers had given him from the trunk. Lamps was naked beneath the blanket and he shook uncontrollably despite the blast of hot air from the car's heater.

"Exposure," one of the cops said to the nurse.

She shivered in the fifteen-degree weather.

"Let's get him inside," the technician said, "before we all catch it." He laughed and helped Lamps into a wheelchair. One of the officers followed them inside to a treatment room where Lamps was placed on a table. The nurse stripped the blanket from him, exposing his blue body.

Minutes later, after having been given an injection, he was made to sit up and his hands were placed in a blue plastic tub filled with a warm solution. Three electric blankets were wrapped around his body. The nurse plugged in a hairdryer and directed a stream of warm air onto his feet.

Lamps started to moan.

"Give him another," a resident said. The nurse injected another needle into his arm.

"How are you feeling?" the resident asked.

Lamps started to say something but had trouble with the words. As his body began to return to a more normal temperature, his pain intensified. He tried to focus on the faces surrounding him, distorted gray shapes that blurred as they moved in and out of a harsh white light.

"Let's get him into a room," the resident said. They returned him to the wheelchair and rolled him into the hall where the officer stood.

"What's the story on him?" the nurse asked.

"Killed his girlfriend," the cop said.

Lamps heard him and tried to respond but was whisked away to a private room, put in bed, given another shot and had an I.V. inserted into the crook of his right arm.

An hour later, Lamps awoke. The nurse was adjusting the I.V. On the other side of the bed stood a man with a round, ruddy face. A thick black cigar protruded from his mouth, and he exhaled a cloud of smoke that stung Lamps's eyes and nostrils. There was whiskey on his breath. He wore a three-quarter tan down jacket over a blue suit, and heavy rubber boots with buckles he hadn't bothered to latch.

"Let me have him for a couple a minutes," the man said to the nurse.

When she was gone, he said to Lamps, "Joe Mayer, homicide, Rockland County P.D."

"Is Pat dead?" Lamps asked in a hoarse voice.

"Your girlfriend? Yeah, she's dead. Want to tell me about it?"

Lamps pressed his eyes tightly shut against tears that had formed. "Shit," he said.

"That's all you got to say to me?"

14

Lamps opened his eyes, looked up into Mayer's face. No emotion. His blue eyes were bloodshot and he kept them narrow against the smoke. "I don't know what to say," Lamps said. "We went together—we were in Van Cortlandt Park...necking. We went there a couple of times a week to be alone and..."

"Fuck?"

"No, we..."

"Yeah, yeah, go on."

"We were there and all of a sudden these guys showed up...they had guns, a shotgun...they took us someplace and..."

"Someplace? What place?"

"I don't know. They blindfolded me and..."

"What'd they do at this 'someplace'?"

"They chained me in a basement, I think, and they took Pat and...I could hear her...they raped her...then they took my clothes and locked me in the trunk and we drove...then we hit a tree and they left, I guess...I got out and went to this house and..."

Mayer directed another stream of smoke into Lamps's face. "You know what I think, Mr. Lamps? I think you're full a shit. This is grownup time now, baby, no kiddy shit, you understand?"

"That's what happened."

"Bullshit, that's what it is, and you know it, your dead girlfriend knows it and I know it. You killed the cunt, ran out of gas on the way to wherever the fuck you decided to dump her and came up with this cute story. You don't kid me. You're under arrest for murder. You'll get your rights read at New City." He clamped one end of a pair of handcuffs on Lamps's wrist, the other around the bed's metal framework.

"I didn't do anything," Lamps said.

"Shut up," Mayer said. "I'll be back."

Three

A New York telephone truck eased into a space in front of a fire hydrant directly across from the Forty-Sixth Precinct in the Bronx. Detective Fred Raven flipped down a sign on the visor— *Police Department Official Business*. His partner, Leroy Higgins, rubbed his eyes and asked, "What do you figure they called us back for?"

"Beats the shit out of me," Raven said, getting out of the truck and slamming the door.

They entered the precinct building and went to the second floor where the Bronx Boro Detective Office was situated. A clerk said, "What took you so long? He's been bitching all morning."

Raven and Higgins shrugged and looked through a glass door at Chief Warren Bratten, who was behind his desk, a phone wedged against one ear, a thick file of papers in his hands. Higgins knocked. Bratten looked up, scowled and waved them in.

"...and so I don't give a rat's ass what some goddamn community do-gooder group says, the order holds. Goodbye!" Bratten slammed down the phone, tossed the file on a desk already stacked high with papers, leaned back and laced his fingers behind his head. "Nice of you to stop by," he said.

"We couldn't just pull out," Raven said. "The guy was getting close to dealing. We figured..."

"I don't care what anybody figures around here," Bratten said. His nasty tone was unusual. Bratten was a good boss, easygoing and a gentleman most all the time. His detectives respected him.

"I'm pulling you off the narcotics case. Get up to the Fiftieth and see Lieutenant West. He's into a homicide from last night and needs help. Check it out with him and call me, let me know what's falling. By the way, this came through the commissioner, by way of chief of detectives. Don't fuck up."

Raven and Higgins looked at each other.

"And don't give me that precious 'What's he talking about' crap. Get back to me."

They got into Raven's white Imperial and headed for the Fiftieth Precinct, unofficially known as a country club where detectives were retired on full pay. It took in Van Cortlandt Park, which generated little crime of importance. The 50th's detectives had the reputation of eating and drinking in the best joints, exercising in gyms on precinct time and screwing the Bronx's best. It was a prime assignment; it took a good hook to get it.

"West's ass must be in a sling," Higgins said as they parked in front of the precinct house. They'd been discussing that as they drove. No squad boss liked to admit he needed outside help, and calling in detectives from another precinct indicated something was fouled up.

There was another detective in West's office when Raven and Higgins walked in—John Smith. A big reputation. With only five hundred detectives out of a force of thirty thousand men, the good ones floated to the surface fast.

"What's up?" Raven asked after preliminary chit-chat was out of the way.

"John," Lieutenant West said, looking at Smith.

"All right," Smith said, shifting on his hard chair and crossing one leg over the other. "We've got a homicide with twists. There's a guy, one William Lamps, whose been charged with murdering his girlfriend, one Patricia Knees. Lamps works for Con Ed. He claims he was necking in his car in Van Cortlandt Park with the girlfriend when a couple of guys show up. One has a shotgun. They put bags with draw strings over both their heads and shove 'em in the trunk, drive for about a half hour until they get to some unidentified place. Lamps says they took him into a basement, stripped him naked, chained him to a pipe and gave him a bench to sit on.

"They take the girl upstairs and rape her. Lamps says he could hear her screaming. An hour, hour and a half later, they come back to the basement, unchain him and dump him naked into the trunk again. This time the girl's not in there with him. They drive... Lamps says for about forty-five minutes, then they stop, put Lamps in the trunk of his own car, take off again, stop.... Lamps says they roll his car down a hill into trees. He claims he waits five minutes, then finds a book of matches with two matches left, lights one, finds an open-end wrench and goes to work on the trunk lock bolts. The match goes out. He lights the other and finishes the job, gets out in the snow and looks in the car window. His girlfriend is dead on the back seat. He can't get in, he says, because the car ended up in a clump of trees. He climbs the hill, goes to the first house he sees and they take him in, give him coffee and call the Rockland police, who don't buy his story and charge him with murdering Patricia Knees. That's about it."

Raven liked Smith's concise replay of the events. He asked, "Where do we fit in?"

Lieutenant West said, "We don't think he's guilty."

"Lamps?"

"Right. About four months ago, a guy and a girl came in and said they'd been kidnapped from Van Cortlandt Park by a couple of guys with shotguns. The girl was raped after a long drive, then they were brought back to the park and warned not to tell anybody. They made the complaint but we came up a triple zero. Then, after Lamps was arrested, I dug in the files and came up with thirteen similar cases, the same M.O. over a two-year period. I called the Rockland D.A. and told him what we had. He was concerned with jurisdiction—they end up with the girl's body and Lamps in Rockland, which makes it their business—but Lamps claims its happened down here, in the Bronx, which makes it our business, if he's telling the truth. Which I think he is, at least about *where* it occurred. I told the D.A. I wanted to interview Lamps, and he agreed to it. He's got his re-election coming up and doesn't need to burn an innocent man."

"I still don't know what this has to do with us," Raven said.

"We're shorthanded here," West said. "I'm having Smitty and Bowers stake out the scene for the next month. I need somebody to get what we can from Lamps, to re-interview previous victims to see if we can paint a complete picture and to do some tail and wire work. When we pick up a suspicious car in the park, we want it wired. Chances are we won't come up with enough justification for a legal order, so we'll do it on our own. Bratten says you two can wire a car pretty good."

Raven laughed. "I've never illegally wired a car in my life."

"Me neither," said Higgins.

"Good," said West. "One thing I don't need are cops doing anything illegal in my precinct. Look, unless you hear different, you two are mine on this case."

"Says who?" Raven asked.

"Says the commissioner and chief of detectives," West replied. "Don't ask me why because I don't have the answers, but bet your pension that Lamps has a rabbi somewhere who has the commissioner's ear. Don't fight it, just help me out. I understand from Bratten you two pretty much go your own way. You've got the same loose leash here. I'm heavy into bottom line these days. Let's nail the fuckers."

Four

Lamps hadn't slept all night. He'd yelled out for someone to talk to and was told by a prisoner in the next cell to shut up. He'd vomited during the night, and it was still in a corner the next morning. Outside the cell, a video camera slowly scanned the cellblock.

He'd spent much of the night going over the bizarre events leading to his arrest. It was like a nightmare; fragmented images kept appearing in front of him, then broke up into undulating patterns of cruel color until, as he squinted to keep them in focus, they floated away like vapor he couldn't grasp.

He'd met Patricia Knees at a party at a friend's house and had immediately fallen in love. At least, that's what he told her on their first date. She'd giggled, which made him feel foolish. But then, she slipped across the front seat of his car and kissed him gently on the cheek. He'd felt instantly better. That's the way Pat Knees was, a warm, sensitive girl who inevitably made those around her feel comfortable.

Lamps had spent most of their relationship being insecure. He knew he wasn't handsome—he was painfully thin, and had feet that were unusually large for his body. His teenage years had left his face pockmarked. He'd tried to grow a beard to cover it but finally decided that the beard looked worse than his pitted skin. He settled for a moustache, a formless, straggly red one that drooped over his upper lip no matter how often he trimmed it.

Pat was short and chunky. She had an olive complexion and thick black hair that she wore short. Lamps was not especially experienced sexually, but he was certain that her breasts were the most beautiful in the world. Of all the aspects of their sexual activity together, it was the fondling and kissing of her breasts that he enjoyed most.

They were in love, and planned to be married.

* * *

Lamps was escorted at noon to a waiting patrol car at the rear of police headquarters, then driven across the street to the courthouse. A wide leather belt was strapped around his waist. Handcuffs secured his hands to the belt. "I'm hungry" he said. He was ignored.

There was a knot of reporters and photographers waiting at the courthouse. They shouted questions at him as he was led from the car. All he could think of was that people would see him and know what had happened. "Don't," he managed to say to the reporters before he was ushered across a lobby with a marble floor and through heavy mahogany doors into the courtroom.

He was seated on a long wooden bench. The judge was an older man with white hair and half-glasses. The detective from the hospital conferred with another man next to the bench. The other man said to the judge loud enough for Lamps to hear, "Judge, if you're agreeable, we'd like to call a case out of sequence. Detective Mayer has been up all night on it and would appreciate this courtesy."

The judge looked around the courtroom. "I don't think anyone will object. Call the case."

Lamps was led to the bench. He said to the man who'd asked that the case be heard, "What's going on? I don't know what's happening to me. I want to go home. She's dead—where are the ones who killed her?"

The man whispered in his ear, "If you can't do the time, kid, don't do the crime." He then looked up at the judge and said, "Your honor, this is case Number 34254 on the record—William Lamps charged with homicide as spelled out in the complaint. He has been advised of his rights and is not represented by counsel."

The judge peered at Lamps over his glasses and, it seemed to Lamps, made a face as though he'd been sucking lemon rind. "Mr. Lamps, you have been charged with the crime of homicide. Do you understand the seriousness of this charge? Do you have a lawyer?"

Lamp's face reflected his desperation. He looked around the courtroom, then up at the judge. "I don't know what's happening," he said in a voice that broke. "I'm all tied up here and I don't know why."

The judge looked at the man who'd called the case and said, "Mr. Roth, I suggest you get someone from Legal Aid to represent the defendant. Obviously, he's confused and has no understanding of the charge for which he's being arraigned."

Roth said, "Your honor, Legal Aid has been contacted, but no one is presently available."

The judge looked at the assistant district attorney, a pretty young woman in a tailored gray suit named Arlene Nidel, who was prosecuting cases that morning. "Miss Nidel, we really can't proceed unless the young man has legal counsel."

She said, "Judge, if you will appoint someone for the arraignment, the state will offer no objection."

The judge looked at an obese attorney sitting at the side of the room with two scruffy-looking defendants. "Mr. Wolleski, would you be kind enough to represent this defendant for the purpose of arraignment on the specified charge?"

Wolleski blinked, stood and said in a husky voice, "It'll be okay, your honor, as long as the court and the state take notice that the appearance is only for the purpose of arraignment, and that counsel will be released immediately thereafter." He belched. "Excuse me."

Roth, the court bailiff, led Lamps to the side where he handed Wolleski a copy of the detective's complaint. Wolleski pulled out glasses from his pocket and scowled as he read it, handed it back to Roth, looked at Lamps with disdain and said, "You're charged with murder. You understand that?"

"I didn't kill anybody," Lamps said.

"It says you killed your girlfriend."

"No, that's not true, I..."

"Yeah, yeah, I know. It doesn't matter. This is all a formality, but I suggest you get yourself one hell of a good lawyer. You're going to need it."

"I..."

"Let's go," Wolleski said. "We stand in front of the judge and I'll handle things. Keep your mouth shut, understand? Don't shoot it off because he can be a mean cocksucker when he's pushed. Got it?"

Wolleski walked to the bench, looked back and angrily waved for Lamps to follow him. They stood together as Wolleski said in a monotone, "Your honor, I have conferred with my client and have filed my notice of appearance on this case for arraignment purposes only. My client waives the reading of the indictment and pleads not guilty to the crime charged and wishes to obtain counsel of his own choosing. He has informed me that he is financially capable of such an act. I also request that your honor set bail in this case as the facts are in dispute, and my client assures me that he has never been in trouble with the law before, and I am aware that no yellow sheets have been returned in this matter. I request that bail be set in an amount that is reasonable."

Assistant district attorney Nidel said, "Your honor, while the defendant has no prior criminal record, I recommend that he be held over in No Bail, pending presentation of the case to the grand jury."

The judge sharply rapped his gavel on its block and looked down at Lamps. "So be it, William Lamps. You have been charged with the serious crime of homicide, your rights have been read to you and you have been adequately represented by legal counsel. You will be held over pending a hearing by a grand jury. Bailiff, incarcerate the defendant." He looked at Miss Nidel and asked, "How long do you think you'll need?"

"About six weeks, sir, but there is a jurisdictional question here. The crime is reported to have taken place in the Bronx."

"That's not at issue here, Miss Nidel. The defendant is appearing in my court, in Rockland County. Any jurisdictional disputes can be handled outside of this court. Six weeks? Fine." He told the bailiff to mark it on the calendar. "Next case," he barked.

"I didn't do anything," Lamps yelled as he was led from the courtroom. "Nobody asked me whether I was guilty or innocent. Who killed her?...I can't believe this shit...."

The judge removed his glasses, leaned back and rubbed his eyes. Wolleski told one of his defendants at the side of the courtroom not to shoot off his mouth like the last clown. Assistant district attorney Nidel searched for the file folder concerning Wolleski's clients, and William Lamps was driven across the street and returned to his cell.

Five

Detectives Fred Raven and Leroy Higgins decided to put off talking to William Lamps until they'd had a chance to interview the other couples who'd filed similar complaints. Raven had learned a long time ago never to ask a question unless you already knew the answer, and he wanted as much information in his pocket as possible before going to Rockland County. A team headed by John Smith had established the stake-out at Lovers' Lane in Van Cortlandt Park and had arranged to report to Raven on a regular basis.

The first couple—Joseph Pearson and Louise Toombs—had reported a crime with the same M.O. two years earlier. Pearson was stocky and had black curly hair. Toombs was slender and blond, pretty but unkempt. Raven noticed that her nailpolish was chipped. Her hair hung straight and looked as though it hadn't been recently washed or cut. They were nervous; they hadn't seen each other in over a year and talked in hushed, animated whispers until being led into a small room the 50th had given over to Raven and Higgins.

They sat next to each other in stiff wooden chairs across a battered desk from Raven. Raven wore a new brown suit with a muted check, a pale green shirt and a brown tie with a small pattern in it. He'd gotten a haircut recently; his hair was salt-and-pepper and had the consistency of a wire brush. His hairline hadn't receded at all, thanks to good family genes on his mother's side.

Higgins wore what had become almost a standard uniform for him—gray tweed jacket, blue button-down shirt and red paisley tie. The genes on *his* mother's side weren't as good as Raven's, and Raven often kidded him about his creeping loss of hair. He stood by a grimy window through which winter sun tried to push its way through and ignored the couple.

Raven said, "My name's Detective Raven. We've brought you in to talk about what happened a couple of years ago in Van Cortlandt Park. I want honest answers from you. If you remember, fine, but don't make anything up. Got that?"

The young man nodded. The girl asked with wide eyes, "Did you get the guys?"

"No, not yet, but we're working on it. That's why you're here. Okay, tell me what happened two years ago."

They looked at each other before he said, "We were in the park necking, I guess you could say, and these men came up and pointed shotguns at us. They took us out of the car, put bags over our heads and we were put in the car trunk. They took us someplace, stripped off our clothes and..." He glanced at her. She looked away. "They chained me in a basement and they took Louise upstairs."

Raven looked at the girl. "What'd they do to you upstairs?"

"They... I couldn't really see much because the bag was over my head. All I could see was by looking straight down. There was a wooden floor, I remember, and then..." She concluded her sentence rapidly. "They raped me."

Raven decided to split them up. She obviously didn't feel free to talk in front of her ex-boyfriend. It might have been different if they were still going together, but the fact was they weren't. "Why don't you wait outside, Raven told him. Pearson stood, looked at her, then hurriedly left the room.

"Okay, Miss Toombs," Raven said, "did you tell your boyfriend everything that happened to you that night?"

"Yes."

"Everything?"

"Yes."

"Listen, honey, let me tell you something. What happened to you that night has happened to a lot of other girls and it's still happening. I'm going to ask you some straight questions and I want straight answers so that we can nail these bums. Got it?"

"Yes."

"Let me tell you something else. We've been doing this a long time and nothing shocks us. We're both married, which means we've been laid, so you don't have to blush."

She blushed. "All right."

"How many guys were there?"

"Three."

"How do you know?"

"I heard them talking, and I know two of them held my arms while one of them did it."

"Did they all rape you? Take turns?"

"Yes."

"How do you know?"

"I just know."

"Yeah, but how?"

She paused, looked up at Higgins, who continued to stare out the window, and said, "After each guy came, he got soft, and then a new guy would be hard and go in me."

"How else do you know?"

"That's it."

"Hey, honey, I thought we were going to be truthful today."

"I am being truthful," she said.

"You ever been down on a guy?"

Another pause. Eyes to the floor. "Yes."

"So then you sucked off all three, right?"

"I really don't know why..."She looked up at the ceiling and kept her eyes there while saying, "Yes, they made me."

"So that's how you know there were three of them."

"Yes, I guess so."

"What else?"

"What else do you want to know?"

"How did it start? Did they rip your clothes off or did you take them off?"

"I took them off."

"Why?"

"Because they said they would hurt me if I didn't. I was afraid." Her voice now heralded the possibility of tears.

"Tell me what happened then."

"One of them told me to look down through the bottom of the bag. He was holding a big pair of scissors, like the kind you use to cut the hedge with."

"Shears, you mean."

"Yes, shears. He pressed them against my breasts and said that if I didn't do what they wanted he'd cut off my nipples."

"Go on."

"I felt sick. I wanted to throw up, but I didn't. I told them I would do anything they wanted if they didn't hurt me."

There was a silence until Raven said, "Keep going, you're doing fine."

She drew in a deep breath and wiped tears from her cheek. "One of the guys picked me up and put me on this table and..."

"How much do you weigh, Miss Toombs?"

"About a hundred and forty-five pounds."

"And one guy picked you up?"

"That's right, like I weighed nothing."

"You say he put you on a table. What kind of table?"

"It was slanted and smooth."

"A slanted, smooth table."

"Yes, it tilted to one side."

Again, silence. Raven prompted her.

"And then one of them raped me while the other two held my arms. And then the other two raped me. They took me off the table and made me get on my knees."

"On what?"

"On my knees."

"No, no, I mean on the floor or what?"

28

"On the floor."

"What kind of floor?"

"It was wooden. I know that."

"Parquet?"

"No, it was just old wood and kind of rough."

"And then?"

"And then I had to do each of them in my mouth. They pulled the bag off just enough. They wouldn't let me stop til I made them come again. It took a long time and I got sick and couldn't finish one guy, but then they put the scissors on my breasts again and I did it." She started to cry.

"Take it easy, honey. I know this is rough but if we're going to nail these bastards, it's your kind of cooperation that'll help. Remember anything else?"

She pulled a Kleenex from her purse and dabbed at her large, green eyes, took deep breaths until she was under control and said, "While I was kneeling down, one of them asked me if I was Catholic. I told him yes. He told me to go to confession. I promised I would and he said something strange."

"Strange how?"

"He said I had to go to confession right then. He made me confess to him like he was a priest. While I was doing it he started to talk Latin. When I was done, he told me I was absolved of all sin and made me say ten Hail Mary's and the act of contrition. I did it and they let me get up. I remember one of the other guys said that he had access to police reports and that if I told the police they would come and kill me."

Higgins turned and uttered his first words of the interview. "Weren't you afraid to come in and make your report?"

"Yes, I was very afraid, but Joe made me do it. I moved out of my apartment the next day so they couldn't find me."

Raven said, "You've been very helpful, Miss Toombs, and I want you to know how much we appreciate it. Anything else you can remember that would help us identify them, or where they took you?"

She thought for a moment before saying, "One of them wore a blue work suit, the kind men who work at gas stations wear."

"How do you know that?" Higgins asked. "You still had the bag over your head, right?"

"That's right, but I looked out the bottom."

They interviewed her boyfriend separately but he had nothing additional to offer. When they were gone, Raven took a tape recorder out of the desk drawer that had been running, put the tape in a box and marked the date, time and place of the interview. Higgins took one of the chairs vacated by the couple and said, "Big help."

"Yeah, maybe it was. Look." He quickly scribbled a list on a blank piece of paper and shoved it across the desk.

Three men—maybe a former priest—possible gas station attendant with blue work suit—possible former cop.
Place unknown, with old rough wooden floors.
One table—slanted.
One strong guy.
One guy speaks Latin.
One pair of shears.
Two shotguns.
Canvas bags.
Chains in a cellar.

* * *

The next person to be interviewed was a woman, Mary Scher. Her boyfriend at the time had left the state and she had no idea where he was. She was made up of a series of squares—square face, square body, square hands—but had languid, sexy brown eyes and a sensual, full mouth.

Raven started off assuring her that she could be candid and that nothing she said would offend them. Unlike the demure first interview subject, this one said in a loud voice, "Hey, don't worry about me. If you catch those shits, call me first so I can cut their balls off."

Higgins, who'd assumed his casual stance by the window, turned and smiled at Raven. Raven quickly and quietly slid the desk drawer open to make sure the tape recorder was running.

"How old are you?" he asked.

"Twenty-six, but I was twenty-five when it happened?"

"How come you don't know where your boyfriend is?"

"He wasn't my boyfriend. I only had a couple of dates with him. He was...he was like a friend, you know."

"I see," Raven said. "Go on, tell me what happened that night in the park."

She shrugged and chewed on her cheek for a second before answering. "I don't know, we were in the park in his car and I was giving him head and all of a sudden he pushed me away."

"Why would he do that?" Raven asked, a smile in his voice.

"These two guys were outside. They had shotguns pointed at us through the windows." She laughed. "It sure softboiled his hard-on—it went down in two seconds."

"Uh huh, go on."

She shrugged again. "They put bags over our heads and took us for about a twenty-minute ride." She proceeded to replay what the first girl had said.

"How many guys were there?"

"Two, but when we go to where we were going there was this third guy." She directed a stream of breath at an curl that had fallen over her forehead. "Damn, when I heard the third guy I knew I was about to get my ass fucked off." She talked about the shears being pressed to her breasts and the threat of her nipples being cut off, and how she assured her abductors that she wouldn't give them any trouble. She said she was put up on a table that slanted and each took his turn.

"They didn't ask you to blow them?" Higgins asked from the window.

"Sure they did, but not right away."

"Let's go back," Raven said. "You say the table was slanted."

"That's right. I kept sliding toward the edge and they kept pulling me back. When they were done screwing me, they spread my legs far apart. I tried to close them but they gave me the shears routine again."

"This was before you went down on them,"

"Yeah. They had my legs apart and I felt them putting something inside me."

"Where?"

"In my vagina."

"Did you see what it was?"

"I sure did."

"What was it?"

"A golf ball."

"A golf ball?" Higgins asked.

"Yeah."

"How did you know that?" Higgins asked.

"I could see through the bottom of the bag. I saw him put it in me, and then he did it with another, too."

"Hmmmmm," Raven said. "How many times did he do it? How many did he put in?"

It was the first time she halted in her statement. She said, "Three, maybe four."

"Maybe more?" Higgins said.

She laughed. "Come on, gimme a break."

"And then?"

"Then . . . they made me get down on my knees and suck them all off."

"All three?"

"Yeah, all three. When I was done, they told me to press down and make the balls come out."

"Did you?"

"Yes."

"What did it feel like?" Higgins asked.

She looked up at him and said, "What the hell are you trying to do, get your rocks off on me?"

Higgins said, "No offense, lady, but it's always the things you forget to ask that screws things up."

She paused, then said, "Actually, it felt kind of good, especially when they were coming out."

She had little else to offer concerning the actual sexual acts she was made to perform. She told them that one of the rapists asked if she were Catholic. When she said no, one of them poured water over her head and said, "I now baptize you in the name of the Father, the Son and the Holy Ghost." She told Raven, "He made me confess all my sins while he talked in Italian or Latin or something."

"You don't know the difference between Latin and Italian?" Higgins asked.

"Not all the time."

32

"Okay, then what?"

"One of the guys told me he was a cop and if I made a report he'd kill me."

"So, how come you made the report?" Higgins asked.

"I figured fuck them. I'm here, right?"

Higgins laughed. "Yeah, you sure are."

"Anything else?" Raven asked.

"Not really. They let me use the bathroom once, and I saw it had green tiles on the floor."

Raven had been adding to the original list he'd come up with after the first interview: *One bathroom, green tiles—golf balls (maybe golf course was location, or assailant was golfer).*

"How did you get here today?" Higgins asked.

"I took a taxi."

"Come on, I'll give you a lift home."

*   *   *

Higgins bought Mary Scher lunch. She had two scotch and sodas before lunch and another with dessert. Twenty minutes after they left the restaurant they'd checked into a motel that featured waterbeds, mirrored ceilings and triple-XXX movies.

Higgins couldn't get his clothes off fast enough to please her. He was still wearing his shorts when she pushed him back on the bed, pulled his erection through the opening in his boxer shorts and started sucking him. He pushed her off before he came, got out of his shorts and rolled her on her back.

"Come on, baby, deep and hard," she said, a crooked smile on her face. She was very slippery; he entered her easily and pumped for five minutes until he became bored. He rolled off, took his erection in his hand and said, "Come on, baby, finish me in your mouth." She did. After she'd spit his semen into a Kleenex from her purse, she looked at him and said, "What about me. I didn't get off yet."

Higgins, who was still relatively hard, started to mount her again but she pushed him away.

"What's the matter?" he asked.

"Go down on me, baby. I didn't feel nothing the other way."

Higgins' initial reaction was to hit her. He said instead, "You're like the Queens Midtown Tunnel. What have you had, lots of kids?"

"I'm not so big," Mary said. "You're long enough but you're too skinny."

"Maybe I should have brought golf balls," he said.

She laughed. "You got any in the car?"

He decided not to argue with her. He lowered his face between her heavy thighs and worked on her with his tongue until she climaxed.

Six

Raven cursed everybody in Westchester County's government as he hit an icy patch and almost lost control of his Imperial. It had been days since it snowed but the roads were still a mess. Not like the city. The roads there were clear. "For the taxes they collect they could electric wire every goddamn road and still have money left over," he muttered as he turned into his driveway. Two snow forts his kids had built still stood, and a full-scale neighborhood war was in progress. Raven's three kids were in one fort. The other was occupied by a dozen neighborhood kids, including a couple of teenage ringers.

"Daddy's home, Daddy's home," his kids shouted as they bolted from their fort and ran toward him, taking a barrage of snowballs on the way. He tried to hold them all as they leaped on him but they were too bundled up for that. His youngest, Rachelle, fell into a snow drift and almost disappeared. The oldest, Laura, had a stranglehold around his neck, and his son,

Freddie, punched his midsection and kept screaming, "Daddy, Daddy."

He managed to extricate himself and asked who was winning the war.

"Freddie's a baby," Laura said. "Every time he gets hit he cries and runs in to Mommy."

"Is that true?" Raven asked his son.

The boy looked at his sister as though she'd given away his darkest secret. He was on the verge of tears as he said, "They cheat. They throw ice and it hurts."

Raven looked across the front yard to "the enemy," who stood in and around the fort, every fist holding a snowball. "I'll fight you all," Raven yelled.

"All *right*," they yelled.

"You guys, too," he said to his kids. "Me against everybody."

The girls ran to the other fort, but Freddie stayed at his side. "I wanna be with you."

"No fair," Laura shouted.

"Let him stay with me," Raven said. "If I get killed I've got to have somebody to mark the grave."

The fight lasted only a few minutes. After taking some direct hits in the face, including an iceball, Raven ended up on his back in the snow, a ton of kids on top. One of the teenagers shoved an icy mass into his face and he briefly considered killing the kid. "Get off me," he growled. They did. "Where's Mommy?" he asked Laura.

"Inside."

"Go tell her I died and need medicine to live again."

"Huh?"

"Tell her I need a big dose of 'Manhattan' medicine right away."

"Okay."

"Gimme a kiss," he said as he slowly got to his feet and brushed away the snow from his clothes.

"I don't kiss dead people," she said, giggling and running toward the house.

"Did we win?" Freddie asked.

"You did, Freddie. I died. That makes you the general."

His seven-year-old face lit up. "What time do generals go to bed?" he asked as they walked hand-in-hand to the house.

"Ask the supreme commander."

"Who's that?"

"Your mother."

"She's no fun. She don't even play."

"Yeah, well, you tell her when I died I talked to God and he said you can stay up an extra half hour tonight just because you're a general."

The house's warmth was welcome as they stripped off their outer garments in the foyer. "Is Mommy higher than God?" Freddie asked.

"Sometimes," Raven answered.

"I can stay up, I can stay up," Freddie shouted as he ran toward the kitchen, and Raven knew the next phase of the war would soon begin—the girls raising hell because their brother would be up as late as they were.

He started upstairs when Joy, their maid, came from the kitchen carrying a perfect Manhattan. She was Jamaican. They'd met her while on vacation there two years ago. He'd tipped her generously in the nightclub where she worked as a waitress, and she'd called him Mr. Muck de Muck—big spender. Raven and his wife asked if she'd like to come to the States to work for them. She readily agreed. They posted the necessary bond and papers and she'd been with them ever since. He turned three small rooms on the basement level into an apartment for her, complete with tiny kitchen, bath, color TV and her own phone. He paid her eighty dollars a week and usually threw in an extra twenty.

"Here's your medicine, Mr. Muck de Muck," she said.

"Thanks. What's new, kiddo?"

"Nothing. Life goes on. I called home a few times because my aunt, she very sick. You tell me how much calls are and I pay you."

"No sweat," Raven said, tasting the drink. They always went through the game, and he wondered why she bothered. She'd call home, offer to pay, be told to forget it and go through the same routine again. He asked, "How sick is your aunt?"

"Very sick, very bad."

"Yeah, well, I'm sorry. If you think you have to go home for a couple of days, let me know."

"I might have to," she said.

"Okay. I'll set it up for you. If you do, call Harry at the travel agency. He'll know about it."

He went to the bedroom and stripped down to his shorts, called the travel agency and told Harry to give Joy a ticket anytime she needed it, and to charge it to his account. He downed the rest of the Manhattan and looked at himself in a full-length mirror. He liked what he saw. He'd stayed in good shape over the years, his 205 pounds nicely spread over a six-feet, two-inch frame. He'd been signed to play professional baseball in the Yankee system when he was seventeen but decided not to go because he was making too much money making book in the Gas House section of Manhattan's Lower East Side. He'd put in a stint with the Army, then joined the N.Y.P.D. where he'd quickly moved up through the ranks to detective status.

He'd been paired with Lee Higgins for almost seven years, and together they'd established themselves as one of the most successful teams in the department. Higgins also kept in tip-top physical shape. He wasn't as big as Raven—five-eleven, 180 pounds—but there was nobody tougher, nobody Raven trusted more when the chips were down and it was time to stand back-to-back.

Higgins had been a boxing champion in the Navy. He came out of New York City's Hell's Kitchen, on the west side, as poor a section as where Raven had grown up. Maybe that was one of the reasons they worked together so well—they understood each other, where they'd come from and how each of them viewed the world around them.

The Raven-Higgins team operated under one simple rule: Anything goes. Do the work, take the money and live good.

His wife, Mary, came into the bedroom. "Hey, babe," Raven said, kissing her. "What's new?"

"What's new? Jesus, you're gone almost three days, you walk in and want to know what's new. Got five hours?"

"Skip the bullshit, Mary, and touch the highlights. That should take a minute and a half if you string it out."

38

She laughed and shook her head. "The conquering hero returns. Lee called. He's in some bar on Staten Island and wants you to get back to him right away. I never understand it. You spend day and night with him, then you have to call him the minute you get home." She held out a slip of paper with the number on it and left the room.

He sat on the king-size bed and dialed the number she'd given him. A bartender answered and put Higgins on the line. "What's up?" Raven asked.

"I forgot to ask you to have Dr. Rappaport call the house with the needle bit. I don't trust that bimbo I fucked this afternoon, and I sure as hell don't want to drag something home."

Raven said, "Like little living green things in her snatch?" He laughed.

"Yeah, that's what I mean."

"Go home and gargle."

"Fuck you, too, Raven. Just do it, huh. I'm leaving now. What'd you do, walk home?"

"The roads were bad."

"Oh. You've got the tapes, right?"

"Yeah, in my locker. I'll call Eddie. He's on."

"Thanks. See you at eight, and for chrissake, make the call fast, before I get home."

"Yeah, don't worry."

Mary returned as he hung up on Higgins. She sat next to him on the bed and leaned her head on his broad, naked shoulder. She was wearing a fuzzy yellow sweater and a loose tan skirt. She was barefoot; she hated shoes.

He rolled her sweater up and undid her bra from the back. He gave her shoulders a little shake and her breasts fell free. He looked admiringly at them and thought how right the sage had been who said size didn't matter as long as they were big. He pushed her back on the bed, lowered his face and began sucking on her nipples, from one to the other. She protested—but not strenuously—that the children might come in. "Are you listening?" she asked as he continued to suck on the now hard nipples, and ran his hand up under her skirt where he squeezed her inner thigh.

"Yeah, I'm listening," he said. "They're in my mouth, not my ears."

She laughed. There was a knock on the door. "Fuck," he said. "Come in," Mary said, lowering her sweater. All three kids bounded into the room. Mary sat on her bra and tried to look casual. Raven crossed his legs to hide his erection that pushed out through the bottom of his jockey shorts. The kids wanted to talk about Freddie being allowed to stay up later.

"I don't want to talk about it," Raven said. "Go on, get out. Your mother and me will be down in a minute."

When they were gone and the door was closed behind them, Raven said, "Just let me stick it in fast."

"Nope," she said, jumping up from the bed, snapping the bra in place and checking herself in the mirror. "Come on, dinner's ready."

"I got one more phone call to make. Be down in a minute. Tell Joy I need a refill on the medicine."

* * *

Eddie Coontz had been the clerk in the Bronx Boro Detective Office for years. After receiving Raven's call, he went to Raven's locker, dialed the necessary three digits, opened the door, reached up to the top shelf and removed a box marked *Tapes*. He took one out that read *Hospital*, grabbed a battery-powered cassette recorder from his desk and went into Chief Bratten's empty office, telling the desk sergeant to leave him alone for ten minutes.

He dialed Leroy Higgins's home number. Janet Higgins answered. Eddie pushed a button that started the tape, and through the recorder's speaker came the background sounds of a busy hospital emergency room.

"Mrs. Higgins?" Coontz said.

"Yes."

"Is your husband home?"

"No. Who's calling?"

"This is Dr. Seymour Rappaport from the police surgeon's office. I'm calling from Bronx General Hospital, Mrs. Higgins."

"Are you... is anything wrong?" Her voice mirrored her sudden fear.

"Nothing too serious, Mrs. Higgins. What I wanted to

speak to your husband about was..." He stopped to allow the sound from the recorder to be heard by her. A female voice through a loudspeaker blared, "*Dr. Rappaport, please call extension 211. Dr. Seymour Rappaport, please call extension 211.*" Eddie said to Janet Higgins, "Excuse me for a moment, Mrs. Higgins, I'm being paged. He pushed the hold button on the phone, came back moments later and asked, "Are you still there, Mrs. Higgins?"

"Yes."

"Good. Sorry. I might as well give you the message, Mrs. Higgins. Your husband arrested a man today on a narcotics charge. The man had a needle in his possession, and it pricked your husband as he was making the arrest. The man your husband arrested shows some preliminary signs of having hepatitis which, as you know, can be highly contagious, depending upon its type. We really won't know for certain for a week or ten days, but we're going to begin treatment of your husband as a precaution. I suggest that you segregate his dishes and utensils for ten days and... well, I'd avoid any sexual contact over that same period of time."

"Yes, of course. What about the children?"

Eddie gave her his best Marcus Welby laugh. "Don't worry about them, Mrs. Higgins. Your husband can play with them all he wants. Just keep the dishes separate—wash them separately in extremely hot water—and no sex. Okay?"

"Yes, thank you, Doctor. I'll tell Leroy the minute he comes in."

"Good. I'll be in touch with him in the morning at headquarters. Good night, Mrs. Higgins."

"Good night, Doctor."

Eddie Coontz hung up and returned the tape to the box in Raven's locker, sliding it in next to other tapes that read: *Street noises, Airport, Jail, Bar-and-Grill* and a dozen others covering virtually every setting from which someone might make a call. He returned to his desk, put his feet up and smiled. He'd been at the top of his form.

* * *

Leroy Higgins stormed into his house and yelled for his sixteen-year-old son, Leroy, Jr. His wife Janet, came from the kitchen. "Where is he?" Leroy asked.

41

"Upstairs taking a nap. He's sick."

"Sick, my ass. I told him three days ago to shovel the goddamn driveway and walk and he still hasn't done it. The snow's all packed down—it's like a skating rink.

Higgins' father appeared from the living room. "I was going to do it but Janet wouldn't let me," he said.

"Of course not," Leroy yelled at him. "You had a heart attack, for chrissake. You're not supposed to shovel snow."

Leroy, Jr., appeared at the head of the stairs.

"Get your clothes on and shovel the walk and driveway. Put salt on everything and shovel it up when it melts."

"It's all ice."

"Of course it's all ice, you idiot. Go on, get out there."

"I got a cold."

"I don't..."

"He's sick," Janet Higgins said.

Leroy looked up the stairs at his son. "You go to practice today?"

"Yeah, but..."

"You hang around after school?"

"Yeah, and..."

"You go to Carrie's house?"

"Yeah."

"You shoveled her walk, didn't you?"

The boy looked at his mother. "Yeah, I helped a little a couple a days ago and..."

"You didn't tell me that," Janet said.

"Get it done," Higgins snarled.

He and Janet stood alone in the kitchen. She told him of the call from Dr. Rappaport. "Where did you get stuck?" she asked.

"My hand. It's small, you can't even see it, but I guess it doesn't pay to mess around. What'd he say—sterilize the plates and no sex?"

"Yes." She used her index finger to get him to keep his voice down. "Your father."

"He doesn't know about sex?"

"I just don't like..."

"Yeah, yeah, I know. What's for dinner?"

"Spaghetti."

42

"Good."

Leroy, Jr., came in from outside. "It's cold," he said. "I don't feel so good."

"You'll feel worse when I break your fucking head. You're a lazy piece of shit and I'm tired of it. Get out there now!"

An hour later the boy returned. "It's done," he said sullenly and went to his room.

"Why do you have to be so hard on him?" Janet asked as she put dishes in the dishwasher.

"Because I'm sending the lazy bastard for the sanitation department test and I want to see if he can shovel snow, that's why. Shit. I'm going to bed."

Later, in bed, Janet said, "The doctor said ten days."

"Big deal. Ten days is nothing."

Which he knew was true for her. They had sex as an accommodation to him, nothing more. He rolled over and closed his eyes. Next time he'd avoid strange stuff like Mary Scher. You could pull the Dr. Rappaport routine only so often.

Seven

They continued interviewing couples over the next three days. The third couple on their list couldn't be located, and the fourth and fifth told substantially the same story as the previous ones.

Then, the sixth couple arrived at the Fiftieth. The girl, Karen Bennett, was nineteen; her boyfriend, Herb Brody, was twenty. Brody told them that because there was a full moon that night, he had had a good look at one of the assailants—male, white, in his mid-twenties, blond hair, cleanshaven and wearing sport clothes.

"Did you see the second guy?" Raven asked.

"No, he was on the other side of the car."

"Anything else you can tell us?"

"Yeah, the second guy drove their car."

Raven leaned forward. "What do you mean the second guy drove *their* car?"

"The one I didn't see. I know he drove because I got a glimpse of the blond guy getting into the right seat."

"I don't care about that," Raven said impatiently. "They took you in *their* car?"

"Right. I have two snow tires and a spare in my trunk, plus tools and fishing gear. It wasn't my car we were in."

After the couple left, Raven made a note to check back with other victims to see if they knew which car had been used.

The next girl to be interviewed, Jennifer Caruso, had sparkling pale blue eyes set in an oval Mediterranean face. The result was visually pleasing. She could have been a high school cheerleader, but she didn't talk like one. Raven's first question was, "Tell us what happened that night in the park."

She spoke rapidly and was very animated. "I met this guy in a bar and we decided to make it that night, you know, so we went to a couple of motels but they were booked up so, like, we went to the park."

"Who is this guy you were with?" Higgins asked.

She shrugged. "I think his name was Marty, but I'm not sure. I never saw him again after that night."

"Okay, so you went to the park," Raven said. "Were you in the front or the back?"

"The front."

"What were you doing?"

"We were kissing."

"You mean necking?"

"Yeah... sort of."

"What does that mean?"

"Well, like, I was kissing him down there, if you know what I mean."

"I know what you mean. Did you see any of the people who grabbed you?"

"No. They put the bag over my head before I ever got out of the car. Then, I ended up in the trunk."

"Whose car did they put you in, yours or theirs?"

She didn't hesitate. "Theirs."

"How can you be sure?"

"When they put me into the trunk, they lifted me up feet first. I could see under the bag and I knew it wasn't my date's car."

"What about the car? Anything you can tell us about it?"

"Sure. It was a red Plymouth."

Raven glanced up at Higgins, who gave him a quizzical look in return. In none of the previous reports had a red Plymouth been mentioned by the 50th's dectectives who'd interviewed the victims.

Higgins asked the girl, "How do you know it was a red Plymouth?"

She looked at him as though he were an idiot. "It was red. I can tell red from green. Besides, my father has the same kind of car with the same emblem on the hood."

Raven asked, "What kind of car does your father own?"

"A Plymouth Fury."

"This was the same?"

"Yes."

Higgins asked her what happened next.

"They drove us to a junk yard or something."

"Wait a minute," Raven said, waving his hand in the air, "how do you know it was a junk yard?"

"Because I was looking out the bottom of the bag and, like, we were walking on boards that were set in the ground. It was like a walkway, you know, like the junk yards put down after it snows or rains. They put boards down so you can walk. When I was a kid I lived near a junk yard. I know."

"Okay, then what?"

"Then we went down into a cellar, eight steps down."

"How do you know how many steps?" Higgins asked.

Again, disbelief on her pretty face. "Because I counted them."

"Why the hell would you count steps?" Raven asked.

"Jesus!"

"All right, so you counted the steps. Then what?"

"They used a key and opened a door. We were in some kind of cellar. It had a dirt floor. They told Marty to take off his clothes and I heard one of them say, 'Put him on the bench and chain him to the pipe.'"

"What then?"

"They took me up two flights of stairs to a room."

Higgins asked with mockery in his voice, "How many steps?"

46

"Eight, then thirteen. There were no lights on the steps because when I looked down under the bag it was dark, and they kept cursing and stumbling while they were pushing me up."

"What did they do then?"

"They told me to take off my clothes. When I did, they put a pair of scissors on my tits and told me they'd cut them off unless I did everything they wanted me to do. They put me on a wooden bench or bed or something and told me to open my legs. Then they shoved something inside me."

"What and where?"

"You know, like, in my... in my pussy."

"What did they put in you?"

"It felt like marbles."

Higgins said, "Marbles. Maybe you mean golf balls."

She laughed and shook her head. "What are you, crazy? Golf balls? Jesus!"

"He's not kidding," Raven said. "Do you think it might have been golf balls?"

She shook her head. "No, they were small, like marbles, and there were a lot of them because they kept jamming 'em in and one guy said, 'Save the puries for last.' I remember him laughing when he said it."

Higgins asked, "Do you know what a purie is?"

"No. What is it?"

"It doesn't matter. What did they do then?"

"They turned me over and made love to me."

"With the marbles in you?"

"Yes. They did it in the back of me. It hurt."

"They screwed you anally."

"Yeah, that's right. After that, they made me kneel on the floor and do each of them in my mouth."

"How many guys were there?"

"Two."

Higgins and Raven glanced at each other before Raven asked her if she was sure about the number.

"Sure I'm sure. I heard them talking. There were just two of them."

"Sure there weren't three?"

"No way."

She continued: "While they had me kneeling there, one of them told me to go to confession. He said I was being a bad girl and wouldn't get to heaven."

"Did he talk Latin, or Italian?"

"Latin, like a priest."

"How do you know what Latin is?"

"Because I used to go to confession every Saturday and Mass on Sunday. They used to speak Latin then. That's how I know."

"Okay, okay, calm down. What about the marbles?"

"They told me to take them out myself."

"And?"

"I did."

"What did you do with them?"

"I dropped them on the floor."

"Did they use the word marbles?" Higgins asked.

She thought for a moment, then said, "No, I don't think they did."

"What did they say?" Raven asked.

"They just told me that I should take the things out of my cunt."

"Just like that?"

"Just like that."

"Okay, the marbles are out. Then what?"

"I got dressed and they drove us back to the park. They put us in the back seat of our car and told us to take the bags off our heads but not to look at them. We gave them the bags and they left. Once they were gone, we called the police."

The final bit of information she could give was that one of the men was very strong and had a lot of hair on his body. She also said his penis was unusually large.

"White or colored?" Higgins asked.

"White."

Later in the day, the other couples previously interviewed were contacted and said they weren't sure which car they were abducted in. Raven came to the conclusion that it probably was the car belonging to the attackers. "Hell, if they were stopped by the police they wouldn't be able to produce registration with the other cars," he told Higgins. "Make sense?"

Higgins nodded and said, "We got another couple out there. You feel up to it?"

"Yeah, as soon as I change the tape."

As the succession of interviews continued, two things became increasingly evident—that the detectives who'd done the initial questioning at the time of the attacks had done a lousy, slipshod job; and, that whoever the assailants were, they weren't content with getting their sexual jollies in the normal way. They'd had the girls insert not only golf balls and marbles, but rope, and Coke bottles; on one occasion, sand was poured into the girl's vagina. She ended up in a hospital for almost a week. Always, there was the order to go to confession and the warning that the men had access to police records, allowing them to know whether the police had been notified.

One of the young men called in for questioning threw a curve at them concerning the type of automobile. He was an auto mechanic and said he was positive it was a Willis Jeep. He even commented that it needed a new clutch; he could sense it slipping while they were driving.

The final interviewee proved puzzling to both Raven and Higgins. Her name was Margaret Watts. She was beautiful in a plain, placid way, and was hesitant in all her answers. They tried different approaches with her—sweet and considerate, harsh and angry, the whole spectrum of interrogation techniques, but none of them seemed to elicit the forthright answers they were looking for. They left her sitting in the small office and went into the hall.

"Freddie, I know what's up with that girl," Higgins said.

"Yeah? Tell me."

"I think she's a nun, maybe, or used to be. Look at her—the short hair, no makeup, no nailpolish, clean complexion, no swearing, always looking up at heaven before she answers. Hell, you notice her hands, always folded in her lap."

Raven smiled, opened the door and said, "Sister?"

The woman spun around and her face turned crimson.

It took a half-hour to calm her down and to encourage her to tell them what happened that night in the park. She told them she'd gone there with a man she'd known for quite a while. They'd gone there to talk, she assured them, just to talk. But then, they were staring into shotguns and, as she put it, "Money bags were put over our heads and we were placed in the trunk of a car."

"Money bags?" Higgins asked. "How do you know?"

"Because they were the same kind we use at church to take the collection to the bank. They even had a cord to pull them tight, and a little metal hasp for the lock."

"Lock? Why a lock?"

"We always locked the bags before we took the collection to the bank."

Raven asked what happened next.

"We seemed to drive in circles for a few minutes and then we went quite straight for another fifteen or twenty minutes."

Higgins asked, "How can you be so sure of the time?"

A pleasant, satisfied smile came over her face. "When you teach school, you can tell the time without looking at a clock. Believe me, we were in the car for twenty minutes after making circles."

It took some convincing to get her to be as direct as possible in recounting what happened once she was taken upstairs. She said she'd try, and after a few false starts, she blurted out, "They took my clothes from me and held a pair of garden shears against my breasts. They said they would cut them off if I didn't cooperate. They put me on a slanted wooden table and each of them raped me, one after the other."

Raven knew how uncomfortable she was and squirmed in his seat. He didn't want to continue but knew he had to. He thought for a moment, then said, "Sister, in each of the other incidents these men placed something inside the girl, either the front or back. Did that happen to you?"

She narrowed her eyes and said, "Yes."

"What did they do? What did they put in you?"

"They placed a cord with knots in it in my..." She'd been looking directly at Raven. Now, she raised her eyes and said, "Between my glutei maximi."

"What?" Higgins said.

"That's the proper way to say..." Raven decided not to explain it to his partner and asked her to do it.

"In my anus," she said to Higgins.

"Oh."

She turned bright red again and avoided their eyes. Raven and Higgins wondered what thought had suddenly crossed her mind to cause such embarrassment. Raven asked.

"I don't know how to say this, and I am so terribly ashamed of it, but I do trust you and know that you are trying to do the right thing. I want to be helpful and don't want to hold anything back from you, but some things are..."

Raven smiled, came around and sat on the edge of the desk. He looked down at her and nodded reassuringly. "You're a good woman, Sister, and we appreciate very much what you're going through. Yes, we need to know everything. Please."

She drew a very deep breath, pursed her lips and finally said, "While one of them was copulating with me, another started to slowly pull the cord out and... I... I... I found myself responding. I forgot the circumstances and allowed my passion to come forth. They were all laughing. I'm so ashamed, so ashamed." She started to cry, holding her face in her hands, her elbows on her knees.

"You just sit here and pull yourself together, Sister," Raven said, touching her shoulder. He motioned for Higgins to follow him out of the room.

When they returned, she was calm and composed. They had one more very important question to ask her, and that was whether, in her experience, the dialog from one of the assailants about going to confession was accurate and real. Could it have come from someone who had once been a priest?

"Yes, definitely," she answered. "It was very real, very legitimate."

Later, after Sister Watts was gone, they listened to the tape. They'd left it running while they were out of the room, and it was filled with her sobs, and her pleas to God for forgiveness. Not too many things about the job caused Raven to lose sleep, but this was one of them.

Now that the interviews with previous victims were completed, Raven expanded on his original list. It read:

Description of perpetrators—
Three unknown males, one priest, one cop, one person wearing blue work suit, possibly gas station attendant.

One unknown—one white male, strong, blond hair, very hairy and with large pecker.

Place of occurrence—Van Cortlandt Park, Bronx, New York— always in the evening—couple most always making love when assaulted.

Distance—twenty-thirty minute ride from Van Cortlandt to unknown location.

Location—unknown—house with cellar, eight steps down, thirteen steps to second floor—chains and bench in basement— wooden planks leading into location set into ground—green tiles in bathroom—no lights on stairs—locked door in basement and slanted table in upstairs room—wooden floor in upstairs room.

Objects—scissors (shears)—golf balls, marbles, Coke bottles, cord with knots, rope, sand, all placed into females' openings.

Vehicle—one red Plymouth Fury, one Willis Jeep with bad clutch and standard transmission.

The stakeout at Van Cortlandt Park by Smith and Bowers had been uneventful and unproductive. Raven's only consolation at that point was that at least he was working indoors.

Eight

Raven and Higgins kept a tiny studio apartment on 207th Street, in the Bronx, where they sometimes slept overnight while on round-the-clock investigations. It also came in handy when one of them scored and needed a place for an afternoon affair. But it had many uses beyond social. They found it a convenient, quiet place in which to map strategy on an important case, away from the chaos of the precinct, and it afforded them the freedom to pursue avenues of investigation that might be frowned upon by higher-ups.

The bottom of a closet contained a secure storage area for sophisticated wiretapping and surveillance equipment they often used in a telephone company truck they kept parked in a nearby garage. The department had purchased it, but Raven and Higgins had outfitted it themselves, complete with a toilet, stove, air-conditioner and an elaborate video setup. They'd installed four microphones—two in the front and two in the rear—which were capable of picking up conversations within a wide radius of the vehicle. An array of heavy batteries enabled them to run a heater in the rear without turning on the engine. They also kept a supply of good whiskey to help pass the lonely hours of a prolonged surveillance.

They met at the apartment the following day to lay out what they had so far on the Lamps case. After pouring themselves drinks and putting away all the materials they'd collected from their previous narcotics case, they posted a large map of the city on a wall and marked off a radius, defining those areas that could be reached by driving 50 mph for thirty minutes from Van Cortlandt Park. They then spread out the notes made during the interviews of previous victims and spent most of the day listening to the tapes of those sessions.

"None of them said they stopped," Higgins said, "and the trips all seemed pretty smooth. No bumps. Major roads, right?"

Raven nodded. He picked up a computer print-out that had come from N.Y.P.D.'s Information Bureau. On it was listed all registered red Plymouth Furies, and all Willis Jeeps in New York City and surrounding suburbs. The list was too long to begin cross-checking with owners in the hope they'd come up with one who had a previous record for sex crimes.

A list of gas stations within the general area of Van Cortlandt Park was also long and extensive. Raven had considered the possibility of checking each one out to determine which employees wore blue coveralls, but decided it wasn't worth it. Maybe later.

"Everybody we interviewed talked about a slanted table," he said. "Has to be a draftsman's table. Let's get a list of all known architectural offices in the area." Higgins made a note of it in a pocket pad while Raven went to the map. He stared at it intently for a few moments, then said, "Lee, if you had to pick one likely location for all of this, what would it be?"

There was no hesitancy on Higgins's part. He said, "That major construction area. Construction means architects, and the one broad talked about wooden planks set in the ground. Junk yard my ass." He joined Raven at the map and pointed to an area in which major construction had been underway for more than two years.

"Let's go out there tomorrow," Raven said.

* * *

They reported to Lieutenant West by phone at five that afternoon. "What's up?" he asked.

"We're making progress, only it's slow. We have a pretty good idea of where these rapes might have taken place. We'll check it out tomorrow."

"Good. I know I told you guys that I was giving you a long leash and I meant it, but I'm starting to get some flack from downtown."

Raven laughed. "So, what else is new?"

"Easy for you to say because you're not getting it. Look, Raven, I'd like to meet with the two of you tonight."

Raven looked at Higgins as he repeated, "Tonight?"

"Yeah, the stake-out team picked up something last night you might be able to use."

"Like what?"

"Like some guy standing in the bushes up on a hill in the park looking down on Lovers' Lane. They questioned him and he said he was out for a walk. His name's Ferris, Nathan Ferris, from Rye—male, white, 190 pounds, stocky, black hair, dark eyes, 38 years old, drives a red Plymouth Fury, New York plate 9998-RE.

"A red Plymouth Fury?"

"Right. That means something to you?"

"Could be," Raven said, his voice not reflecting the excitement he felt at hearing the description of the car. "Where do you want to meet? Your office?"

"No, let's keep it out of headquarters." He named a restaurant in Manhattan, Antolotti's, on East Forty-Ninth Street. "Friends of mine own it. Meet me there at eight."

Raven hung up and told Higgins what the plans were, and about the man in the park who owned a red Plymouth Fury. Higgins smiled. "Can't be that easy, Freddie."

"Why not? We're due."

Raven picked up the phone again and called the "wheel" at the Information Bureau, making sure first that no one was on the line. They'd tapped the apartment phone into a public phone in a gin mill down the street, which meant they never had to pay for outgoing calls.

The line was free, and after being connected with the IB, Raven gave the name Nathan Ferris and asked for a rundown of all vehicles registered to that name. He was told to call back in ten minutes. He did, and the satisfaction he'd experienced before was now heightened. Nathan Ferris not only owned a red Plymouth Fury, he owned a Willis Jeep under a corporate name, Stay Cool Air-Conditioning, with offices in the upper Bronx.

The next call was to the Bureau of Criminal Identification. Ferris's name came up negative—no record of arrests.

West was already at Antolotti's when Raven and Higgins arrived. They sat in a small room at the rear of the elegant restaurant and, after they were served appetizers and drinks, Raven told West of the link-up between Nathan Ferris and the descriptions of automobiles used in the abduction and rapes.

"Sounds promising," West said.

"Promising? This is the guy."

West sipped his bourbon. "I didn't figure you for snap judgments," he said.

"Snap judgments, hell," Raven said, picking up a piece of Shrimp Casalinga and devouring it. "Lee and I have been together a long time and our instincts are pretty good, especially when they match up. We were talking coming down here about it and as far as we're concerned, there ain't a doubt in the world between us that this Ferris clown is the one."

West managed a thin smile. He said, "I'm impressed, Freddie, really impressed. Based on your instincts we'll arrest Ferris, charge him with murder and rape and all go downtown together to get our medals. Shit!"

Raven looked at Higgins, who was busy eating and drinking. He said to West, "Feel like laying money on it, Lieutenant? Five hundred says Ferris is the one, and we'll make it stick."

"Good for you, but I think I'll pass on the action. All I want is the goddamn thing wrapped up so we can get back to what we had to drop. I'm stretched thin. I'm pulling Smitty and Bowers off the stake-out."

"Why?"

West opened his eyes wide and extended his hands to Raven as though handing something back to him. "Because you're so goddamn sure that we have the mad rapist of Van Cortlandt Park. Besides, I told you coming in we're short handed. I need them."

Raven drew a deep breath to keep his anger in check, then said, "If you pull 'em out of the park, at least give 'em to us for a few days. We have a lot of checking to do."

West shook his head and ate another shrimp. "No can do, Freddie. This case is yours and you'd better wrap it up yourselves. And please don't drag your ass. I'm tired of the phone calls from downtown."

Raven sat back, shook his head and let out a sardonic laugh. "Shit," he said, "it really is great working for a big-time police department." He sat forward again, his elbows on the table and pointed a finger at West. "All right, just keep the leash loose like you promised and we'll deliver Ferris and make you a big hero. Sound good?"

West motioned for a waiter to refill their drinks and to take their dinner order. When the waiter was gone, West said to Raven, "I heard you guys were cocky, Raven, but I never thought it was this bad. Aren't you ever wrong?"

Higgins stopped eating long enough to laugh. It was almost a giggle. He said to Raven, "Tell him about the dickie waver."

"What are you talking about?" West asked.

"The only time we were ever wrong."

West said, "Yeah, tell me about that. That I would love to hear."

Raven said, "You tell him, Lee."

Higgins mopped up sauce from his plate with a piece of bread and said, "It was over in Brooklyn a couple years ago. A kite comes in about a dickie waver down at a local Catholic grade school. Somebody calls the Cardinal's office and he jumps on the Commissioner and the whole thing ends up a pain in the ass. They finally tell us to get rid of the guy with his cock in his hands, so we go to the school. We know why right away they couldn't nail the guy. The place was wide open—you could see blue coming two blocks away. We talked to a nun, and she tells us this guy shows up in a car when the kids are out on the playground, opens the door, turns sideways in his seat, whips out his dong and shakes it at them.

"So, we go to Con Ed and get a couple of those big wooden spools they store wire on. We get them delivered to the street where the school's located and we stack one on top of the other.

57

The bottom one is full of wire, the top is empty, and there's enough room for a guy to sit in it and watch. We take turns sitting in that fucking thing for three days. On the third day, I'm in the wheel lookin' through the hole we drilled and I see this guy in a late model car pull up during recess. Sure as shit he opens the door, turns sideways and whips out his joint. He gets the girls to look at him and he starts beating his meat.

"Freddie is six blocks away with a walkie-talkie, so I tell him our guy is there and to roll. I stand up, point my gun at the guy and we get him, book him and then the circus starts. It turns out his name is Rodney Charles Remington the third, or fourth or some shit like that, and his old man is filthy rich. This high-power lawyer arrives, takes us aside and tells us that if we change our testimony and let the kid walk there's twenty-five grand in it for each of us. Freddie tells him he's lucky we don't bust him for bribery, but we both know we'd never make that stick. He's shrewd the way he laid it on us. The price eventually goes up to fifty. We tell him to get lost. He says to us, 'You two morons just blew fifty G's. We'll beat you in court anyway.'"

"The case is postponed a year. When it finally comes up the lawyer gives us one more shot at the money. We tell him no dice, so we end up in court. I wired myself so that Freddie could hear my testimony outside. I'm sitting in the witness chair and Freddie waves to me through a window, so I know he's picking up everything. I tell my story to the judge, and the more I talk, the more I think we have this rich son of a bitch nailed to the wall. The case was that strong.

"Now, the kid gets up on the stand and lies his ass off and does a good job of it. His attorney asks the kid how far I was from him when I made the arrest. The kid says a hundred and fifty feet. They call me back up and I agree. They make the point that the courtroom is about a hundred and fifty feet long, so they tell me to go to the back, then they go through a whole lotta shit about lighting conditions and such and I finally agree I can see just about as good as the day I nailed him at the school yard. Now, we get to the good part."

Raven nodded and started to laugh.

Higgins continued: "The kid's lawyer tells him to show the courtroom what he was doing the day he was arrested. I can't believe what I see. The kid reaches down, opens his fly, whips out his joint and starts jacking off in the courtroom. The fucking judge's eyes are bulging out of his head and the whole place starts to laugh. All I can think of is that this lawyer has decided to plead the kid insane and hope they get off with head help. The judge is digging a hole with his gavel and finally he gets everybody to calm down, but the kid is still choking his chicken up there on the stand. The kid's lawyer says to me in the back of the courtroom, 'Detective, please tell the court in your own words what you just saw.'

"Now, I come up to the front and I say that I witnessed the defendant playing with his exposed penis. The lawyer asks me if it's the same thing I saw the day I arrested him. I tell him it is. They asked me a couple of times whether I have any doubts, and I keep looking at the guy like he doesn't row with both oars and telling him that's exactly what happened. So, the lawyer tells the kid to show the judge what he was doing. The kid gets up, still holding his prick, moves his hand and the damned thing comes off. I mean, shit, his dick comes off right in his hand. He lays it on the judge's bench. It turns out it's a flesh-colored rubber doll's leg and the lawyer says that that's what his client was doing by the school, playing with a rubber doll's leg. The kid takes a walk and we look like jerks. We had him dead but the lawyer outbrained us."

The waiter brought three huge seafood platters, and green noodles Bolognese. They dug in.

Raven said to West, "There's more to the story. The Christmas after the trial, I get a package at home. In it's a doll with one leg missing, and there's a tag attached to the other leg. It says, $50,000. I still got that doll at home and everytime I look at it, I see money floating out the window."

West laughed. "So the lawyer beat you, huh?"

"Not really," Higgins said, wiping his mouth. "He may have won the case but we nailed his ass good. We wired his office, picked up on some illegal deals he was doing and drove him out of business. Last we heard he's down in Florida squeezing tangelos."

"Sore loser, too," West said.

"That's right," Raven said.

They left Antolotti's at eleven. As they stood on the sidewalk, West said, "I hope you're right, Freddie. If it is this Ferris, it makes everybody's life easier."

"Yeah, I'm right," Freddie said.

"Just don't set me up with a doll's leg when I hand this over to the D.A."

Raven and Higgins laughed. "That was a hell of a dinner, Lieutenant," Higgins said. "You live good."

"Didn't you ever hear, Lee? It's the best revenge. See you tomorrow."

Nine

They kicked off the next day by calling the telephone company security office. Nathan Ferris had a listed number—RY2-6742. It had been installed ten years ago. A call to the local FBI office resulted in a report that Ferris had been fingerprinted while serving in the U.S. Navy. He served four years and received an honorable discharge.

A check with the Bureau of Motor Vehicles in Albany indicated that Ferris had another car registered to his wife, Ada, a 1969 Volkswagen. Finally, they went through the Better Business and checked out Stay Cool Air-Conditioning. It had been in business for ten years and had a generally good reputation. It dealt mostly with commercial accounts and did very few home repairs. Higgins called an old friend at the Chase Manhattan Bank who called Stay Cool and pretended he was running a credit check on Ferris. Ferris had been employed by the company for two years. The Willis Jeep belonged to Ferris, but he registered it under the corporate name for tax purposes.

At eleven, they left their apartment and went to the large-scale construction site, walked around it until six, drove to Rye and, after getting lost a couple of times, found Ferris's home, a well-kept two-story frame house in a quiet residential neighborhood. Parked in the driveway was a red Plymouth Fury.

"Let's sit awhile," Raven said. They watched the house for a half-hour until a Rye Police Department patrol car pulled up and asked who they were. A neighbor had reported a strange car parked on the block. Raven and Higgins showed their credentials and explained they were checking on a suspect's address. They didn't give details. The Rye cop wished them a good night and drove off.

There were lights on in Ferris's house and occasionally a figure passed one of the windows, but no one came outside.

"Let's go, Freddie," Higgins said. "Nothing's going down tonight."

Before leaving the neighborhood they checked the telephone lines running into the Ferris house. The first junction box was seven blocks away.

They were back on Ferris's block at seven the next morning, just in time to see him leave the house. He was powerfully built, had probably been an athlete at one time in his life. He drove the red Plymouth Fury along major roads to the air-conditioning company on Gun Hill Road where he disappeared inside until nine, then came out wearing a blue work uniform. He climbed into the Willis Jeep and headed off for his first appointment.

"You see what he was wearing?" Raven said.

"Yeah. He looks better all the time."

They dropped the tail until four, then returned to Stay Cool and waited until Ferris came back, got into his car and drove directly home.

"You want to lay in the tap now?" Higgins asked.

Raven shook his head. "Let's pack it in. If I don't get home tonight it'll end up World War III." They made one stop on the way back, a neighborhood tavern. Raven used a pay phone to call the Rockland County district attorney, introduced himself and said that he and his partner wished to interview William Lamps the next day, along with anybody else who could shed light on the case. The D.A. was courteous but cool. He told Raven he would call the warden of the jail in which Lamps was incarcerated and arrange for them to start there. Raven didn't like the D.A. the minute three words were out of his mouth. He had a pinched, nasal voice, very upper-crust, pompous and superior.

"He sounds like some rich Harvard fag," Raven told Higgins when he returned to the car.

"Who does?"

"The D.A. up in Rockland. It's good."

"What do you mean?"

"It's always nice to shove it up the ass of a guy like that, sort of like getting a bonus."

Ten

The warden of Rockland County Jail ushered Raven and Higgins into his office. He was a heavy, moribund man with little wet curls pasted to a balding head. He feigned pleasantness, but his annoyance at having them there created a thick cloud in the room. "What can I do for you?" he asked, falling heavily into his chair.

"For openers, you can find me an ashtray and something to put this coffee on. It's burning the hell out of my hands," Higgins said.

"Oh, sure," he said, pressing a button on his desk. Moments later a uniformed guard came in and was told what was needed.

"Good service," Higgins said.

"Being a warden is a little like being God in your own world. I have the last word on everything. Too bad it doesn't extend to my marriage."

They all laughed. He wasn't the stiff he initially seemed to be.

"Okay, what about this Lamps kid?" Raven asked. "What's your evaluation of him?"

The warden rubbed his nose. "Who is this guy anyway, some political or financial heavy?"

Raven shrugged and said, "Not that we know of. We hear he's just an average guy."

"Then how come all the concern by you guys down in the city?"

"No big deal," Raven said. "Some of our people think he's innocent and they want us to take a shot at proving it. What do you think? You've been with him awhile."

"I think he's a fruitcake," the warden said. "He walks around in a fog, pisses and moans all day and night about his girlfriend being killed and him being blamed for it. Poor bastard, he placed a collect call to her parents and they wouldn't accept it. As far as I know he doesn't have any family, and he isn't represented by an attorney."

"How come?" Higgins asked.

The warden scratched his armpit and screwed up his face. "It's like he's caught in the middle, if you know what I mean. Too much money for legal aid and not enough to get a good lawyer. Nothing new, right? Happens to all middle Americans. I've got a lawyer friend up here who said he'd talk to the kid as a favor."

"How come you're doing favors for the fruitcake?"

"Well, except being weird he's nice enough. I don't think he killed her."

"You tell your D.A. that?"

"Hell, no. He started off looking to get the kid off, but now he's loaded for bear. Election year."

"What's the D.A. got to make his case?" Higgins asked.

"I really don't know. I just run the jail, I don't build cases. You should talk to the cop who brought him in. He says the kid was pretty close to death from exposure. The way I figure it, you've got to have a set of steel balls to come that close to dying trying to fool somebody."

Raven nodded his agreement. "We cased the hospital report on him. He wasn't using shit or drinking that night. I agree with you. You don't play a game and come that close to freezing to make a point."

65

"The kid doesn't know what the fuck is going on," said the warden. "He's confused as hell."

"How's he getting along here," Higgins asked.

He shrugged. "It's a jail. I have him in General Population but I've got my guards keeping an eye on him so he doesn't get fucked up the ass. The other prisoners seem to steer clear of him, so he's been okay so far. I think if he's around too long, though, he could go off the deep end."

"Can we talk to him now?"

"Sure. You can use the conference rooms where the lawyers meet with clients. Tell the guard what you want to eat and drink and you'll get it."

They were led to a room with a conference table and four armchairs. A key turned in the heavy steel lock and the door opened. A guard stood back and allowed William Lamps to enter. He wore green prison clothing that was too big for him, and his laceless shoes flopped on his feet. Prison had taken its toll; he looked ghostly. The guard slammed the door shut and locked it.

"Lamps, I'm Detective Fred Raven and this is my partner, Detective Leroy Higgins. We're from the New York City Police Department."

Lamp's brown eyes darted back and forth between them like two ball-bearings set loose in a gyrating field of liquid.

"Sit down," Raven said.

Lamps hesitated, then sat in a chair on the other side of the table. "Am I getting out of here?" he asked.

Raven smiled. "Depends."

"On what? What do I have to do?"

"It depends on how fast we find the guys who killed your girlfriend."

Up until that moment, Lamps's body was rigid and erect. Raven's words caused it to deflate in the chair, as though someone had pulled a plug behind him. "Shit," he moaned.

"Hey, kid, we're not miracle workers," Higgins said. "We're here to give it our best shot and that's all we can promise."

Raven said, "If you're going to piss and moan, we'll call the guard and have you sent back to your cell. You want us to help, you work with us. What do you say? Are you going to act all grown up or are you going to whine like a baby?"

Lamps continued to look back and forth between them. He finally said in a voice that he obviously was striving to control, "I'm sorry. It's just that...shit, I hate it here. I'll do anything you say. What do you want to know?"

"We've interviewed everybody else who had roughly the same thing happen to them in the park," Raven said. "Do *you* know anybody who had the same thing done to them?"

"I don't think so," Lamps replied, shaking his head.

"Read him the names," Raven told Higgins. Higgins read the list of previous victims they'd interviewed. Lamps affirmed he knew none of them.

"Okay, I'm going to ask you some questions and I don't want any bullshit from you, no hedging," Raven said.

"Why would I bullshit you?" Lamps said.

"Who knows? I just don't want it. Understood?"

"Yes."

"All right, are you Catholic?"

"No."

"What are you?"

"Jesus, I don't know. I don't go to any church. I don't even remember where my mother and father used to take me."

"Fair enough," Raven said. "Do you speak Latin?"

Lamps let out a small laugh. "You mean like the Romans used to talk?"

"Yeah, that's what I mean," Raven said. "Well, do you?"

"No. What does Latin have to do with this?"

"Do me a favor, Lamps. Let me ask the questions."

"Okay."

"So, tell me, do you speak Latin?"

"I don't speak Latin."

"Have you ever worked as a policeman anyplace, or been a volunteer for organizations that do police work, like a neighborhood group?"

"Nope, never."

"Do you wear a uniform when you work?"

"No."

"Do you own a blue work suit, like gas jockeys wear?"

"No."

"You got any buddies who are policemen?"

Lamps smiled. "You mean aside from you."

Raven smiled, too. "Not counting us."

"Nope."

"You have any close friends who are Roman Catholic priests or brothers?"

Lamps shook his head. "No again."

"Do you own, or have you ever driven, a red Plymouth Fury?"

"No, sir, my car is..."

"We know what you drive, Lamps, just answer the question," Higgins said.

"Okay."

"Have you ever driven a Willis Jeep?"

"No."

"Do you have in your house or office a desk that's slanted?"

"Slanted? Hell, no. Why are you asking me that?"

"Never mind, I'll tell you later," Raven said. "Did you kill your girlfriend, Pat, or do you have any idea who did?"

Now, Lamps unraveled again. He sat forward and said, "Shit, no. I told everybody a million times what happened that night. I didn't do it."

"Willing to take a lie detector test?"

"Sure," he said. "I told them to give me one so that they would know that I was telling the truth."

"Okay, calm down, Lamps. What I want you to do now is to tell me what happened that night in the park. I'm going to run a tape, so think before you talk."

"Maybe I shouldn't do this," Lamps said. "Maybe I should have a lawyer before I say anything else?"

"Do you have one?" Higgins asked.

"No, not exactly, but the warden said he might..."

"Lamps, we're not here to nail your ass, we're here to help. You can talk to us, let us put it on tape so we can review it later, or we can walk. Your choice. If you don't want to cooperate, we've got other places to go and things to do." Raven fixed him in a hard stare.

"All right. I'll tell you what happened."

*   *   *

"It's cold," Pat said as she snuggled against Bill Lamps. "Maybe we should turn on the engine."

"No, it's dangerous. I'll warm you up like I always do."

He'd released her bra and his hands eagerly fondled her breasts. She brought her mouth to his ear and her tongue explored it. He felt her nipples grow beneath his fingers, and his erection pressed painfully against the edge of his shorts.

"I love you," he said as he reached down and unzippered his fly. She continued to kiss him. His hand went beneath her skirt. She wasn't wearing panties. They'd been coming to the park a few nights a week for almost a year and she deliberately left them off when going out with him. His fingers groped to part her sexual lips. She was wet, and his middle finger slid up and down the length of her vagina. She moaned as his finger gently began to probe the opening, going progressively deeper until it was fully entered, its tip rotating around the depth of her.

"Take it out, Pat," he said.

She shifted on the front seat, which necessitated his removing his hand, and opened the top button on his jeans. He raised his hips so that his jeans and shorts could be slipped down to his thighs, which released his burgeoning, twitching penis. Her hand went to it and she ran it up and down its length, her fingers occasionally dipping low to cradle his scrotum.

"Let's go to a motel," he said.

"No, Bill, please no. I want to as much as you do but not until we're married. Let's keep doing it this way."

She lowered her head to his lap and kissed the tip of his penis, ran her tongue over it, looked up and smiled. "It's coming out already," she said, mirth in her voice.

He placed his hands in her thick auburn hair and lowered her face again to him. She took the tip of him in her mouth, then slowly took more of it until the sensation of it against her throat brought her to the verge of gagging. He started to groan as she slowly worked her moist lips up and down over his shaft, increasing in tempo until he came in violent spasms.

She pulled back her head, her mouth full of his semen. He

69

quickly handed her a handkerchief with his initials on it. She spit into it. He opened the car window and threw it into the snow.

Now, the second part of the ritual was about to begin. She would lean back on the seat and he would orally stimulate her. She'd assumed the position and he was about to lower his face to her when they were both aware of the presence of others. Each looked in a different direction and each saw a man holding a shotgun.

"What the hell?" Lamps asked as the doors were opened and they were pulled from the car.

"Shut up and you won't get hurt," one of the men said. Suddenly, another man covered Lamps's head with a sack. The same was done to Pat. They heard the trunk of a car being opened. They were led to it and told to get inside. It was slammed shut over them. The engine was started and they huddled against each other until, a half hour later, the car came to a stop. The trunk was opened and they were taken into a building. Neither could see because of the sacks over their heads. They were led down a set of steps.

"Take off your clothes," Lamps was told. He protested. A shotgun was pressed against his stomach. He quickly undressed, and chains were attached to his wrists and strung over what he assumed were pipes in the ceiling. Someone shoved a bench under him and told him to sit. "Just be good and nothing will happen to you," a man's voice said. "Come on, sweetie, you come with us," he said to Pat.

Lamps heard them ascend stairs. He was petrified; he was afraid for his own life and for what was happening to her. He was cold. He tried to free himself but gave up after a few minutes.

He heard Pat scream from someplace in the building, and he yanked at the chains. Nothing gave. He resigned himself to sitting on the bench and waiting for what would happen next.

More than an hour later the men returned, unchained him, and took him to the car. He asked for his clothes but they ignored his request and put him naked in the trunk.

"Where's Pat?" he asked.

"Shut your mouth," one of the men said, slamming the trunk closed. He heard them get into the car. The engine started

70

and they began to move. Forty-five minutes later the car stopped. Lamps was transferred to the trunk of his own car. They started moving. Lamps was aware that another car was following close behind. They stopped. The engine of Lamps's car was shut off. Then, the car slowly, silently slid downhill until it came to an abrupt stop against something solid.

"Oh, shit," Lamps said over and over as he tried to decide what to do next. He was afraid to move in case the men were still there. He waited five minutes, then yanked the sack from his head and felt about in the trunk. His fingers found a book of matches. He opened it; there were two left. He lit one and used its light to survey the interior of the trunk. There was an open-ended wrench. He picked it up and looked at bolts that secured the lock to the trunk. He frantically turned them until the match went out. He lit the other one and continued. It worked. The lock fell free and he was able to open the trunk.

He stepped out into the snow and wrapped his arms about his slender body. He'd never been so cold before. A brisk wind swirled loose snow into his face. His cheeks stung. He shook.

The car was in a clump of trees. He made his way to the passenger side and looked through the window. Pat was on the back seat. Her legs were akimbo and her skirt was up to her waist, exposing her privates. Her head was twisted to one side. Her eyes were open wider than he'd ever seen them, and there was either a smile or a frozen expression of desperation on her mouth, depending upon the way you viewed it. Her right hand rested on her belly. Her left hand dangled onto the floor.

"Oh, God," he screamed. He tried to open the door but it was wedged against trees.

He looked around in desperation. Someone had to help. He made his way up a steep incline to a road. Across from him was a house with lights on. He went to the door and knocked. A fat man answered and expressed his disbelief at seeing an almost frozen naked young man at his door. Lamps started to say something, then pitched forward onto the foyer floor.

* * *

"That's the way it happened, huh?" Raven asked Lamps across the table.

71

"Yes, sir, that's exactly what happened."

Higgins, who'd assumed his usual posture of feigning disinterest, turned and said, "I've got a question for you, Lamps."

"What is it?"

"How come they don't believe a nice kid like you? How come they're charging you with murdering your girlfriend?"

Lamps became animated. "That's what I keep asking. Why me? I didn't kill her. I loved her very much and we were going to be married. I never met a girl in my life I loved so much...and respected. She was good, better than most people. She wouldn't even go to bed with me because she wanted to be a virgin when we got married." Raven and Higgins raised their eyebrows in unison. "I would never kill somebody like Pat, not somebody as good as her. All I wanted to do was make her happy, not hurt her."

"Yeah, but how come they're so convinced you did it?" Higgins asked.

"I don't know." He slumped back in his chair and closed his eyes. When he opened them, he looked at Raven and said, "Maybe you could find out for me."

"Yeah, maybe we can," Raven said. "Look, Lamps, let me give you some advice. Being in this place ain't the easiest thing. The warden says you're kind of frazzled. Ask to see a shrink. They must have one here. Talk this shit out with him before you go off the deep end. Listen to me, kid, I'm talking sense."

"I thought of that," Lamps said. "Maybe I will. Thanks."

Raven and Higgins went to the door and banged on it. Raven turned and said to Lamps, "We'll be in touch. In the meantime, don't do anything stupid. I believe you, Lamps, and we'll take our shot for you, but don't fuck us up. Don't do anything dumb."

Eleven

"Where to now?" Higgins asked after he and Raven had gotten in the car. He laughed. "The kid got me horny. Know any broads in Rockland?"

"Come on, Higgins, you'll dip in some strange stuff and end up having to pull the Dr. Rappaport routine again on Janet. Let's swing by headquarters. I want to talk to the cop who was on the scene that night."

The uniformed patrolman who'd been summoned to the house where Lamps had collapsed, and who had been the first to investigate the car with the dead girl in it, was playing cards in the rear of the station house. His name was Willard Epson. He was small and wiry. His hair was sandy and he'd begun to grow a moustache that looked like a smear of dirt on his upper lip.

"Can we talk someplace out of here?" Raven asked Epson.

"Yeah, I guess so. I'm on my break." It dawned on him that maybe he shouldn't talk to them without clearing it with his chief. He suggested that.

"We don't have time," Raven said. "Besides, we're here at the invitation of the Rockland D.A. We just left the jail. The warden gave us nothing but cooperation." Raven realized he was going to have to come up with some other incentive to persuade Epson. He said, "This case is the hottest goddamn thing we've been on in a long time. My partner here, Lee, is already walking around with his cock in his hand. Nothing but kinky sex, young stuff, the works. You'll love it."

That, combined with every small town cop's fascination with big city detectives, did the trick.

They went to a local coffee shop where Epson was greeted by everyone in the place, sat at a booth with chipped formica and ordered coffee.

"Why'd the kid kill her?" Epson asked after they'd been served.

Raven shrugged, glanced at Higgins, then said, "Maybe she wouldn't give him head, who the hell knows?"

"I heard they used to do it all the time," Epson said. "Shit, if some young broad would do me a couple times a week I sure as hell wouldn't kill her." He laughed. Raven and Higgins joined him, not out of appreciation for what he'd said but because it seemed politic.

Raven said, "You were the one who took the first look at the car, right?"

Epson nodded smugly. "Yup that's right. I was the first one there, the first one to see her dead."

"She have all her clothes on?" Higgins asked.

"Yup, except for panties. She was sprawled out on the back seat. Her mouth was wide open. So were her eyes. I knew the minute I looked she was dead."

"Tell me about it," Raven said.

"Tell you about what?" Epson asked.

"About first coming on the car. What did you do?"

Epson shrugged and grinned. "Well, I started down the hill toward it. It had been snowing like a bitch and there was ice underneath. I damn near fell on my ass. In fact, I did fall once. I reached out and grabbed the rear of the car to catch myself, only the damn thing slid forward six or seven feet."

"Yeah, then what?"

74

"Well, I got up, dusted myself off and went around to the window. There she was, dead on the back seat."

"Then?"

"Then...I come up the hill to call for backup."

"I see," Raven said. "Did you find anything at the scene?"

"Nah. I was even down there with the detectives. They always like to have one of us with them. They found a burnt match and took it with them. We opened the trunk and found a couple things in there, a wrench, stuff like that."

"Anything else?" Higgins asked.

"No, that's about it. Hey, how come you guys are up here?"

"Because the kid says they were fucking in a park in the Bronx. That makes it N.Y.P.D. business."

"Yeah, I can see that, only Lamps is being prosecuted here in Rockland. Doesn't seem to me where they were taken from should matter a hell of a lot."

Raven laughed. "Probably not, but they told us to come up. We follow orders like you, right?"

"Right." He leaned forward and said, "What was goin' on, some kind of kinky sex?"

Higgins said, "Yeah, so kinky I can't stand to talk about it. I got a wife and kids, you know what I mean?"

The disappointment on Epson's face was evident. "Yeah, I'm married, too. These kids get into some kind of wild shit, don't they?"

"They sure do," Raven said. "Look, Officer Epson, we'll keep you right up to date. There are some weird circumstances surrounding this case." He made an overt show of glancing around the coffee shop to make sure no one was listening, leaned across the table and said, "The kid was trying to get her to do him with a firecracker up her ass."

Epson's face was a mask of shock. "No shit," he said.

Raven nodded solemnly. "Fucking perverted, huh?"

Epson sat back in the booth and shook his head. "Sick."

Raven and Higgins stood and Raven picked up the greasy green check. "It's a sick society," Raven said. "Look, Epson, keep this whole conversation to yourself. I wanted to share it with you because we're in the same business, but don't let it go any further than right here. Okay?"

Epson placed his hat on his head. "Oh yeah, absolutely. You can trust me."

Their next stop was the Rockland County district attorney's office. He was as pinched in appearance as he sounded on the phone, and their original dislike for him was enhanced. He wore an expensive, tight blue suit, bright yellow tie with a small knot beneath a gold collar pin, and highly polished Italian loafers.

"Sorry to barge in on you like this," Raven said. "Thanks for seeing us without notice."

"My pleasure," the D.A. said, gesturing toward two antique chairs in his office. "I told your superiors I was delighted to cooperate and I meant it. Coffee? Lunch?"

"No, thanks, we have to get back. Look, all we'd like to know from you is what evidence you're prosecuting Lamps on. The kid tells us a story that makes sense, but we don't know the facts, only what he says. We've read some reports—the hospital, the arresting officer, the arraignment proceedings in the court—but that's it. What are you going with?"

The D.A. examined his fingernails. He was obviously deciding what to tell them and what to withhold. He glanced up at Raven and said, "In the beginning, Detective Raven, I was convinced this William Lamps had nothing to do with the death of his girlfriend. Then, as the facts started to come in, I saw things differently. What stood up as a plausible story in the beginning started to fall apart. The holes grew bigger, like deteriorating old lace. You ever see that? I had an old aunt who was fond of lace, and every time I visited her she'd be playing with a doily, like a child does with a security blanket. The more you rub it, the weaker it becomes until there's very little fiber left to hold on to. That's what happened to my aunt, and it pretty much sums up the problem with Lamps's story. He's a liar. Take my word for it."

"I wouldn't argue with you for a minute," Raven said. "I don't have any trouble with the idea that the kid killed his girlfriend for whatever reason, then came up with this story. It wouldn't surprise me if he was trying to find a place to dump her, ran out of gas and pushed the car down a hill. He shows up at somebody's door naked and cold and everybody takes pity on him. Not bad. You have to give it to him for creativity. By the way, was there gas in the car?"

The D.A. laughed. "Yes, there was. That exact scenario ran through my mind, detective. The only problem with it is what happened to his clothes, but I suppose he could have stripped a long way from here and tossed them in a trash can."

Higgins said, "Maybe he gave 'em to the Salvation Army. Maybe he dumped them in one of those collection bins."

The D.A. said to Higgins, "I never thought of that. It's a very good possibility."

Raven knew the D.A. was being condescending to him and he resented it. He pulled out a pocket memo pad and pretended to be reading from it. The page was blank. He said, "Aside from not buying the kid's story, what hard stuff do you have?"

"Hard stuff?"

"Yeah, stuff to base your prosecution on."

If the D.A. had been disliked earlier by Raven, his manner now could have prompted Raven into physical attack. The D.A. sighed, smiled, raised his eyebrows and looked at Raven as though he'd just broken wind. "We have enough to put Mr. Lamps away for the rest of his life."

Raven struggled to keep his tone civil, finally managing to say, "That's good. What do you have?"

Again, the pontifical posture on the part of the D.A. "Where shall I begin?" He asked. "Mr. Lamps claims that he climbed out of the trunk and walked around the rear of the car. The fact is, our detectives and the uniformed patrolmen discovered a six-foot area behind the car without the trace of a footprint, not even a bird's scratchings. Then, there is the matter of Mr. Lamps's claim that he opened the trunk from the inside with a wrench he claims was there. We found the wrench in the trunk too, and it did not fit the trunk lock. It was too big to turn any of the bolts."

"Makes sense," Raven said, not meaning it. "What else?"

"Mr. Lamps claims he lit two matches. We found one in the trunk."

"That doesn't sound like a big deal," Higgins said

"Big deal? Please, Mr. Higgins, I assume you know cases

are built on small things, a succession of them, not a... 'big deal.'" He looked at Higgins with fatherly disdain.

"Anything else?" Raven asked.

"Do we need more? Lamps told us that his deceased girlfriend had orally copulated with him and had discharged the results of that copulation into his handkerchief. He claims he threw it out the window, in your park. I dispatched two detectives to search the area and they could not find any such handkerchief." The D.A. laughed. "These young people. Amazing. When I talked to Lamps I suggested that he must have been going broke buying handkerchiefs. He told me that usually she carried Kleenex for the task, but had run out of them that night. Do you have children?"

Raven and Higgins looked at each other. "Yeah, we both do," Higgins said.

"I suppose that's one fringe benefit of my job, seeing the scum of this young society in action and realizing how fortunate I am with my own. Have you experienced the same feelings?"

Raven said, "Yeah, I guess we all do. Well, thanks for your time. We have to get back to New York."

"New York? This is New York, Officer Raven. Funny how those in the city fail to realize that we're all part of one state, one system."

There were a lot of things Raven wanted to say, but he majestically controlled himself. They shook hands, and an hour later they were back in their apartment in the Bronx.

Twelve

They grabbed a quick lunch before heading for the house in the Sparkill area where Lamps had arrived the night of the murder. They rang the bell. A sleepy, angry fat gentleman wearing a ratty blue flannel bathrobe over pajamas opened the door.

"Mr. Rhodes?" Higgins asked.

"Who are you?"

"Detectives, N.Y.P.D.," Raven said, flashing his badge. "Sorry to wake you but we have some important questions to ask."

"What, about that pervert?" Rhodes asked through the glass storm door. "I already told everything."

"You didn't tell it to us." Higgins said, adding a nasty edge to his voice. "It'll only take a minute. Besides, it's cold out here."

Rhodes opened the door and allowed them to step into the foyer. "I work nights," he said.

"So do we," Raven said. "We won't keep you up very long, Mr. Rhodes. We read the arresting officer's statement the night

William Lamps arrived here, but that doesn't do us a hell of a lot of good."

"New York City cops?" Rhodes asked, scowling. "What are you doing up here?"

Higgins started to explain the jurisdictional question when Raven cut him off. "You said in your statement, Mr. Rhodes, that the kid arrived here jaybird naked. He had nothing with him?"

"Not unless he hid it up his ass," Rhodes said, enjoying his flip comment and laughing.

Raven and Higgins didn't respond. Higgins said, "Not a thing with him, right?"

"That's right," Rhodes said. "What are you tryin' to do, get me to go back on what I said before?"

Raven shook his head. "All we're trying to do is find out who killed the girl."

"You got him, for chrissake. Just a goddamn freaky dope-head, like the rest of them."

"What about later that night, Mr. Rhodes, or the next day. They found the girl in the car almost directly across the road from you, down that embankment. You notice anything the next day in the sunshine?"

Rhodes shook his head, yawned and stretched, his large belly protruding through a gap in his robe. "Nah, I never saw nothin'. I did find a wrench out on the front walk, sort of buried under the snow."

Raven and Higgins looked at each other. "Was it your wrench?" Higgins asked.

"Nah, I don't think so. I figured maybe one of the cops dropped it. I was going to call and tell them to come and get it but I forgot."

"What did you do with it?" Raven asked.

"Put it in the garage with my other tools."

"I'd like to see it," Raven said.

It was an open-ended wrench, the sort Lamps had described in his previous statements as having used to open the trunk lock bolts. Raven examined it, then stuck it in his overcoat pocket. "I'll take this with me," he said.

"Yeah, sure. I really was going to call about it but I kept forgetting. That's the trouble with workin' nights. I get home and all I wanna do is go to bed."

Rhodes led them back through the kitchen to the foyer. "Thanks," Raven said.

"I always wanna help the cops, always have. Wanted to be one myself once."

Raven and Higgins nodded at him and left the house, got in their car and drove away. "I hate assholes like that," Higgins muttered, popping a breath mint into his mouth. "We going down to the garage where they impounded the car?"

"Yeah. These sloppy bastards up here would never think to look for a second wrench once they saw the one in the trunk didn't fit."

Higgins laughed. "Hey, our own guys who investigated the previous incidents in the park didn't do such a great job, either. Half the stuff we came up with never showed on their Sixty-Ones."

The officer in charge of the Rockland County Police Garage allowed them inside once they flashed their tin. He led them to William Lamps's automobile. The trunk was open. Raven and Higgins looked in it and saw on the floor the wrench that had been found, and the bolts that had been removed from the lock. Raven picked up a bolt with his gloved hand, took the wrench they'd obtained from Rhodes and fit them together. Perfect.

"Thanks a lot," Raven said to the officer in charge as they left the garage and got in their car. Raven turned and looked at Higgins. "The kid didn't do it, Lee, and Nathan Ferris did. Not a goddamn question in the world. You agree?"

Higgins shrugged and popped another breath mint. "Sure, everything looks that way, doesn't it? What about the matches, though?"

"Fuck the matches," Raven said. "What difference does it make whether there was one or two?"

"It'll make one hell of a difference in the D.A.'s case if it ever gets that far."

Raven knew he was right, but wasn't about to start searching for a match in eight inches of snow. The handkerchief was another matter. Lamps had told them he threw the handkerchief out the window after his girlfriend had gotten rid of his semen in it, but the Rockland detectives claimed they couldn't find one on Lovers' Lane in Van Cortlandt Park.

"I'd like to find that handkerchief," Raven said.

Higgins laughed. "Yeah, wonderful, we'll go look for a white handkerchief in a blanket of snow. Christ, Freddie, come on."

"No, it may not be so bad. Maybe it's off-white. Besides, he said he had his initials on it. We'll get a couple of rakes and give it a shot."

Twenty minutes after they started raking the area where they knew Lamps had parked, they came up with the handkerchief. It was off-white, and had embroidered, brown initials "W. L."

They returned to the 50th and requested a lab analysis of the handkerchief. Raven pulled a copy of the autopsy report on Patricia Knees, read it, then placed a call to the doctor whose signature appeared on the bottom of it, Dr. Stanley Glassmein, an assistant Rockland County medical examiner. He was told by Glassmein's nurse that the doctor could not come to the phone. Raven left his name and number. A half-hour later Glassmein returned the call. Raven introduced himself and said he would like a chance to discuss the Patricia Knees case. Glassmein was hesitant at first, then agreed to meet them at ten the following morning at his office.

"I've had it," Higgins said.

"Me, too," Raven said, rubbing his eyes and yawning. "Let's pack it in and meet up tomorrow. We'll go talk to Glassmein."

Before leaving, Raven placed one more call, this one to the Rockland County district attorney. Higgins listened, a satisfied smile on his face, as Raven told the D.A. what they had uncovered that day. When he got off the phone, Higgins asked what the D.A. had said.

"He choked a little, the son of a bitch, told me he was pleased that I called him but said everything would have to be...how did he put it, 'everything would have to be assimilated into the total evidential picture.'"

"Indubitably," Higgins said, affecting a British accent.

"You do a lousy British accent," Raven said.

"Go home and get laid," Higgins said, slapping him on the back. "I hate it when you get lucky and start coming off like a pompous ass."

Thirteen

Dr. Stanley Glassmein sat in the plush velvet interior of his new Cadillac sedan DeVille. He pushed the button on his automatic garage door opener and the doors rolled up at an even pace, while the overhead lights came to life. He slowly backed out into the driveway, hit the button again and, as the doors closed, swung the car into the street and headed for his office at the hospital.

He didn't like meeting with two New York City detectives. After Raven had called, he'd mentioned it to his boss, Frederick Paley, the hospital's director. "I knew there was going to be a problem over that case," Paley said, which set Glassmein on edge. It was things like this that made him wish he'd stayed in the army. Nobody ever questioned an autopsy in the army. It also caused him to wish he and his brother, Benjamin, had switched careers, that he'd become the lawyer and let his brother grapple with all the nonsense of medical ethics and bureaucracy and second-guessing. But their roles had been determined far too early to switch gears. His mother, when asked the age of her children, always replied, "The doctor is ten, the lawyer is eight."

Being a Rockland County medical examiner usually wasn't a stressful job. There were seldom more than five homicides in the county a year, and most of them were pretty clear-cut. But it was times like these when the outsiders came in and looked over your shoulder that you wondered whether the additional income was worth it.

As he continued toward the hospital, he recognized just how on-edge he really was, not only because of having to meet with the detectives that morning but because of so many things that had happened in his life recently—things like his secretary's pregnancy and the abortion he personally performed on her. "Never again," he'd promised himself when it was over. The slight additional pleasure of riding bareback just wasn't worth it.

He came to a halt behind a school bus that was picking up neighborhood children and cursed the slowness with which they boarded. As he sat there, he thought of his own children and the problems they'd been giving him. Beverly had been caught smoking pot in a parked car behind the Nanuet Mall. The only reason she wasn't arrested was that the cop called him before she was booked, and he'd used his position to gain her release.

A month later, she'd been at a party at the home of a neighbor when the police raided it. The mother and father were away in Europe while the high-school-age son stayed home to "catch up on his school work." Drugs of every description had been found at the party. The thing that saved Beverly this time was the fact she wasn't physically in the house at the time of the raid. She was out in the driveway in the back of a "sin bin," a fancy van where she had her legs wrapped around her boyfriend of the evening. That had triggered one hell of an argument, too. Glassmein had finally exploded and screamed at his daughter, "If you don't shape up, I'll sew up your goddamn hole." Everyone in the house was horrified at what he'd said, and his wife insisted he see a psychiatrist, who happened to be a friend. He saw him once, discussed the incident and received a bill for $150. He telephoned the psychiatrist. "Haven't you ever heard of professional courtesy?" He asked.

"I've heard of it but I don't believe in it," he was told. He paid the bill and never went again.

Then, there was his son, Murray, who refused to study for his forthcoming Bar Mitzvah. Glassmein threatened to cancel it, pointing out to his wife and son that he would be perfectly happy to save the $15,000 it would cost to throw the elaborate affair. "I never had a goddamn Bar Mitzvah," he told them, to which his wife replied, "Maybe if you had, Stanley, you'd be a nicer person today."

His mind continued to focus upon his family and its problems as he pulled into the short driveway leading into the physician's parking lot. He never even thought about the skinny red-and-white stick of wood that remained down until a plastic I.D. was inserted into a slot. He went right through, splintering the gate, pulled into a parking space and looked around. No one had seen it happen. He got out of the car and wiped the front of it in case there were paint marks.

Raven and Higgins were in Fred Paley's office when Glassmein walked in. The director introduced them and said, "Stanley, please give them all records they need and extend any cooperation." He said to Raven, "We pride ourselves in cooperating with all law enforcement agencies."

"That's nice to know," Raven said, looking at Higgins, who yawned.

As the four of them went down the hall to Glassmein's office, the director whispered in his ear, "Watch your ass, Stanley. I have a feeling there's going to be some trouble over this."

After they were all seated in comfortable armchairs around a coffee table, Glassmein drew a deep breath to calm himself, smiled and asked, "What can I do for you today?"

"We're here to talk about the autopsy you did on Patricia Knees."

"Patricia Knees," he repeated.

"Yeah, the girl who was murdered. They brought her in from Sparkill. You did the autopsy on her, didn't you?"

"Yes, I did," Glassmein said, thinking back to that day. He'd gotten into work late that morning because he'd made a scheduled stop at a condo complex where one of his nurses lived. He stopped there twice a week for what he thought of as "a cavity stuffing routine," and to which she playfully referred to as "making little ones out of big ones." He got bored hearing her say that, but not as much as what she said every time they finished: "Any day that begins with a fuck can't be all bad."

The body of Patricia Knees had been waiting for him when he arrived. He'd gone into the operating room, more commonly known to others in the hospital as the "deep freeze room," and looked down at the dead girl, who was lying naked on a tilting stainless steel table. His initial thought was that she was attractive and had a nice body, cute breasts, solid flesh.

He turned and opened his lunch box. It was a running gag for years in the hospital that he brought his lunch to work every day. His wife, Sheila, had a thing about preparing lunches for everyone in the family, and he took the box to appease her. Most days, he went to local restaurants for lunch and tossed the contents of the box into a trash can before returning home. This morning, however, he was hungry; he hadn't taken time for breakfast.

He opened the box and saw it contained a peanut butter and jelly sandwich, an apple and a piece of chocolate candy. He didn't understand. Sheila had packed it with everything he didn't like. He then noticed a piece of paper in the box, opened it and read the permission slip she'd written to his son's teacher for him to participate in a field trip.

"Jesus," Glassmein muttered as he realized he'd taken the wrong box. He visualized his son opening the thermos at school and taking a healthy swig of the martini Glassmein always prepared before leaving in the morning. He checked the clock; it was lunch time at school. He called home. The maid told him that Sheila had been summoned to school to pick up Murray, who'd suddenly taken ill.

"Shit," he muttered to himself as he returned to the table holding Patricia Knees, carrying the lunch box with him. He plunked it down next to her body, picked up a fresh scalpel and made a straight cut the length of her abdomen. He then cut across her body, laid the scalpel on the table and thought about Sheila's reaction to the mix-up.

He looked down into the lunch box and noticed that the peanut butter and jelly sandwich had been cut into four equal pieces. He picked one up and popped it into his mouth. He took another, felt less hungry and proceeded to douche the dead girl on the table. When he was done, he picked up the police report that had been tossed on an adjacent steel table. "Damn," he mumbled when he read that they wanted to know if she'd been raped and sodomized or, as the requesting officer put it, "had been sexually abused in any other way." What else was there after rape and sodomy, he thought as he cursed his impetuousness at douching a possible rape victim.

He spent a great deal of time trying to find sperm samples. It was almost impossible to identify them in her vagina because of the water from the douche—like looking for a minnow in the ocean—maybe even harder. Despite his mistake, he did find sperm in her anus, mouth and stomach. Although he did not find clinical evidence of sperm in her vagina, he decided to act on the assumption that it would be there, and noted it on his report.

It bothered him for the rest of the autopsy that he had noted a finding that had not, in fact, been verified, but he rationalized it to himself two ways—if sperm were found in the other areas, it certainly must have been in her primary sexual cavity; and, no one would ever question his findings. This was Rockland County, not the city, and there had never been an official challenge to his autopsy results since he'd been named an assistant medical examiner.

Raven said to Dr. Glassmein, "In your report, doctor, you stated that the victim had semen in her mouth, anus and stomach."

"Yes, that's correct."

"Can you tell us how much you found?"

"Pardon? I don't understand?"

"Can you tell us how much semen was found in each area?" Raven said.

"Where?" Glassmein said.

"In the dead girl. How much sperm was found in her vagina, her mouth, stomach and anus?"

Glassmein's first thought was that they were trying to trap him. Why was the amount of semen important? It never had been in previous cases. He asked Raven why he was asking the question.

Raven shrugged and said, "Listen, I'm not an expert on autopsies, but I always figured that when someone is the victim of a sex crime, you must weigh, or measure, or count or do something where the sperm is involved."

Raven's modest acknowledgment that he didn't know much about autopsies put Glassmein at ease. He smiled and said, "No, Detective, we never do that here in Rockland. The amount of sperm really doesn't have any bearing."

Higgins made his first comment. "The thing that we're looking for, Doctor, is whether there is more sperm or semen than might have come from one guy."

"Why would you care about that?" Glassmein asked.

Raven said, "Doctor, we have a rape and murder case here where the suspect claims he didn't do it. He says she was giving him a blow job but that she never swallowed the stuff, and we believe him. We also think that she was raped and killed by more than one guy, maybe as many as three, guys who have been raping girls for a couple of years now."

"I see," Glassmein said, nodding seriously and lacing his fingers over his chest. "Yes, I see what you're getting at. The problem is, I really can't give you information that would help to determine that. The average male has ten to twelve CC's of sperm ready to be ejaculated at any given time, but I honestly cannot tell you how much she had in any of her body cavities."

"How about a guess?" Higgins said.

"A guess?" He laughed. "That would be terribly unprofessional."

"How much is ten CC's?" Raven asked.

Glassmein screwed his face up in serious thought, then said, "Well, there are thirty CC's in one ounce, so ten CC's would be about a third of an ounce, a third of a regular shot glass."

"That's amazing," Higgins said. "You mean to tell me that a little bit of come like that has ninety-five calories?"

Raven laughed. "How the hell do you know that?" he asked.

"I used to boff a broad who was on Weight Watchers."

Glassmein smiled. He was pleased at the diversion.

Raven brought the subject back to the matter at hand. "If you can't tell us how much sperm she had in her, I guess you can't tell us whether it came from one guy or from different ones."

"Would it help if I could?" Glassmein asked.

"Yeah, maybe. The guy charged with the crime claims she was banged by more than one. I just figured maybe there was some way to determine whether she had two different sperms in her, from two different cocks."

Glassmein shook his head. "Sorry, too late for that now. She's gone and so are the samples."

"We could have the body exhumed," Higgins said.

"No, that wouldn't help a thing. Too much time has passed."

Raven said, "You claimed on the report that the cause of death was her neck being closed off by something that caused her to suffocate."

"Yes, that's right," Glassmein answered, relieved he was back on secure ground.

"Any idea what might have been used?"

Glassmein leaned forward and said, "This is unofficial, gentlemen, but I would say it was not something hard. I also don't think it was anything like a rope or a stocking; they would leave marks around the throat. It was my judgment that something soft was pressed against the front of her neck."

"Come on, doctor, take a guess," Higgins said.

"No, no guesses," Glassmein said, laughing.

Raven asked, "Any chance she died by freezing to death?"

"No, of course not. She was definitely strangled. The evidence was very clear on that. It was obvious to me that she was killed in a warm place. Believe me, freezing played no part in her demise."

Raven said, "Let me put a hypothetical question to you. Suppose Patricia Knees was put in a car, on the back seat, and her neck is pressing against some part of her own body, like her hand or arm. Could she die from being in that position, assuming she was unconscious?"

Glassmein thought a long time before answering. "As a real

89

outside chance, it could be possible, providing that she was unconscious and wasn't able to move, or to sense what was happening to her. I suppose it is theoretically possible."

Raven said, "Let me get back to the question of freezing, doctor. If what you admit is theoretically possible—that Patricia Knees might have been unconscious and, not being aware of what was going on, might have placed herself in such a position that she caused her own strangulation—then I don't understand why, in the kind of weather that we've been having, she wouldn't show some signs of freezing."

"It would depend how long she was exposed to cold weather," Glassmein said.

"And you say that there was no sign of freezing on her body."

Glassmein nodded and said, "Yes, exactly. There are always signs in the organs and skin when a person is frozen. None were present with the deceased."

Higgins said, "In other words, if she was killed in a place with heat, then put dead on the rear seat of a car with a heater on and driven from one point to another, then a few minutes later her boyfriend, who's locked in the trunk, gets loose, calls the cops and they show up pretty quick, there would be no signs of freezing on the body?"

Glassmein frowned as he processed each of the points Higgins made, then said, "That's right."

"Another question about freezing, doctor," said Raven. "How frozen was the accused, William Lamps, when he was brought into the hospital?"

"I don't know. I have had no direct contact with him, nor did I have that night."

"Yeah, I understand that," Raven said, "but you must have been given a report on him."

"Yes, of course. Would you like to see it?"

"Very much."

Glassmein dialed someone within the hospital and a few minutes later, a pretty, pert blond nurse arrived with a folder. Higgins tried to make small talk with her but she gave him a disdainful look and left.

Glassmein surveyed what was in the folder, looked up and

said, "When William Lamps was brought into the hospital, he suffered from exposure due to extreme cold temperatures. His body functions and reflexes had slowed down, and he was in a confused state."

"Did he have frostbite?" Higgins asked.

"No, he did not, but that isn't necessary in order to die from freezing. If parts of a human body are in direct contact with ice or snow, frostbite sets in very quickly, much faster than the normal time needed to freeze to death. His condition at the time would match that of a person having been locked in the trunk of a car during extreme cold weather. I would say, according to the report, that his condition was consistent with the time frame he reported to the police. The minute he was brought into a heated environment, his recovery was rapid. The human body adapts quickly."

"In other words," Raven said, "you're telling us that his body condition fits perfectly with the conditions he claimed he was under at the time."

"Yes, according to these reports, I would say that is true."

"Give me an opinion, doctor. Could he have sat in the car with the doors open, waiting to reach the state he was in when he was admitted to the hospital?"

Glassmein shook his head. "No, I would say that's highly unlikely. First, it would be impossible to reach that state and, as a lay person, still be able to perform physically. In other words, he would not be capable of judging the precise point he'd reached without going over that line. Second, if he'd sat in the car as you suggest with the doors open, Patricia Knees's body would have exhibited different signs, even though she'd already expired."

"How about this," Higgins said. "Could he have climbed the hill, taken off his clothes and waited until he was almost frozen?"

"I doubt it very much, but I see what you're getting at. Let's assume he didn't know anyone in the area. I mention that because unless he was helped in some way, some part of his body would have to be in contact with the elements. If he stood on his feet, his feet would be in worse shape than the rest of him because of their contact with the frozen ground and snow. If he sat up in a tree, his buttocks would have shown more sign of freezing."

Raven said, "In other words, the guy's story pretty much stands up, based upon your physical evidence."

Glassmein nodded, "Yes, I would say that is a fair assumption." The minute he said it he had doubts about the wisdom of going along with them, remembering the director's admonition to "watch his ass." He'd been so anxious to please them to alleviate his own anxiety that he had completely put out of his mind the fact that the district attorney had charged Lamps with the murder, and was forging ahead with the prosecution. What he'd given these detectives ran contrary to the sort of evidence that the D.A. would want from him in the trial. He held up his hands, smiled and said, "But, gentlemen, bear in mind that all of this is opinion. I've been willing to speculate with you, but it has no legal bearing."

Raven and Higgins knew what was behind the statement. Raven said, "Don't worry about it, Doc, nobody's out to stick you with something you can't live with."

When they were gone, Glassmein visibly relaxed, put his feet up on his desk and smiled. "Cops," he told himself. "They come on so goddamn strong but they really aren't very bright." The only thing he'd really had to worry about was the discovery that he'd douched Patricia Knees before conducting the examination, and he reminded himself that no matter what happened, no one could prove that.

He called home; Murray had gotten sick from ingesting gin. "You put it in his thermos, you idiot," Sheila said.

"The hell I did," he said. "I put it in *my* thermos, but you mixed up the boxes. How is he?"

"Better than you. What are you, an alcoholic? You take gin to work every day, you, a doctor?"

"Get off my back, Sheila," he said. "I've had a rough morning."

"What time will you be home for dinner," she asked.

"I . . . I'll be late tonight, a case coming in later."

"What's her name, Stanley?"

"I don't have to respond to that kind of question," he said.

She slammed down the phone.

He hung up, went down the hall and confirmed the date he'd made that night with a redheaded lab technician, who'd recently joined the hospital staff and who'd been flirting with him since the first day.

Fourteen

They met with Lieutenant West in his office the next morning. Raven got right to the point. "Okay, Lieutenant, here's what we have. One, the Lamps kid didn't do it. Two, Nathan Ferris looks better to us all the time. I don't see anything to be gained by digging into Lamps. I want to go all-out on Ferris, and that means round-the-clock surveillance on him. I need Smitty and Bowers back, plus two more."

West moaned and sipped from a styrofoam container of cold coffee. "I told you I don't have enough manpower—"

"Fine," Higgins interrupted, "so release us and we'll go back to the Forty-Sixth."

West finished his coffee and made a face. "Jesus, that's bad stuff. You guys have better coffee?"

Higgins laughed. "Depends on who sticks his dick in it. Lieutenant, let me ask you something."

"What?"

"How come you claim to be so busy up here when every cop in New York knows this is sleepy-time-up-north?"

West's face flashed anger. Then, he smiled and slowly shook his head. "I'd love to get my hands on the prick who started that rumor. The crime rate may not be as high as in some other squads but that doesn't mean we're not up to our ass in shit."

Raven was a little uncomfortable that Higgins had brought it up. He said to West, "Yeah, we know it's not exactly true, and I learned a long time ago not to judge anybody else's problems. The fact is, though, we have a good shot at nailing Ferris, getting Lamps out of jail and tying up thirteen unsolved rapes. I figure maybe it'll take us two weeks to put it together—*if,* we have a little help. How about it, Lieutenant? Let's make the commitment and get it over with?"

West sighed deeply and leaned back in his chair. He looked through the glass in his door and saw Detectives Smith and Bowers drinking coffee at a table in the far corner. He sat forward and looked over a list of personnel, then said, "All right, you can have Smitty and Bower's back, and I'll give you Rogers and Browne, but two weeks, no more. Agreed?"

Raven and Higgins stood. "Sounds good to us," Raven said. "Where do we hook up with Rogers and Browne?"

"They'll be in at noon. We'll meet here."

Rogers and Browne were a couple of clean-cut younger detectives who listened intently as Raven outlined the case and the steps that would be taken to apprehend Nathan Ferris and whoever was involved with him. "We'll tap his home phone and slap a couple of tracking units in his Fury and Jeep. We'll work two twelve-hour shifts, the third team getting a day off every other one. We log everything he does, every place he goes, who he sees and who he screws, how long it takes him to pee, the works."

Later that afternoon, Raven and Higgins made a deal with an old woman who owned a house close to the junction box from which a telephone line fed into Nathan Ferris's home. "We're trying to put some drug pushers out of business who are selling at the local schools," Higgins told the woman. "We'll just need your garage for a couple of weeks."

"You can have it as long as you want," she said with conviction. "Drugs ruin so many young people. I'd kill those pushers myself if I had a gun."

Higgins and Raven smiled. Raven handed her two hundred dollars. "Will this be enough?" he asked.

"I don't even want the money, but things are tight. Much obliged, officer, and you can trust me. I won't say a word to a soul."

"Yes, ma'am, we appreciate good citizens like you."

Higgins climbed the pole and connected one end of a length of black wire into Ferris's telephone pairs in the junction box. He dropped the wire to Raven, who ran it into the garage. Higgins joined him and they hooked the wire into a Penn Register, a device that would print out, in a series of dots, any number dialed out on Ferris's telephone. They then coupled the hook-up into a seven-inch reel-to-reel tape recorder with an automatic start. Every time Ferris's phone was picked up to make a call, or to receive one, the recorder would automatically start and record both sides of the conversation. The tape would hold approximately two days of normal conversations.

"Looks good," Raven said. "I just hope the old lady keeps her mouth shut."

The next morning they drove to the Stay Cool Air-Conditioning Company and found Ferris's red Plymouth Fury parked one block from the plant. They then went to the Four Star Diner a half-mile away where Raven placed a call to Jimmy Bronson, one of the three brothers who operated the Bronson Auto Salvage Company in the Hunts Point Section. The Bronson boys were the best car thieves in New York City, and probably the best mechanics, too. They'd been keeping Raven and Higgins's car in top shape for years in return for heads being turned.

"Jimmy?" Raven said.

"Yeah. How you been, Freddie?"

"Couldn't be better. Listen, Jimmy, I need a favor." He gave Bronson a description of Ferris's car and told him where it was parked. "Lee and I are at the Four Star Diner. Could you pick it up right away and bring it to us?"

"Sure. Half-hour fast enough?"

Raven laughed. "It'll have to do, I guess. Thanks."

Forty minutes later, Jimmy Bronson pulled into the parking

lot driving Nathan Ferris's red Plymouth Fury. Raven and Higgins were just about to order a third cup of coffee. They told the waitress they'd be right back, went outside and told Bronson to pull the car into a secluded corner of the parking lot. Higgins removed two metal boxes from the trunk of Raven's white Chrysler and went to where Raven and Bronson were sitting in the Fury.

"Excuse us," Raven said to Bronson. Bronson vacated the driver's seat and Higgins slid inside. Raven went under the dash and disconnected the antenna wire from the radio. He plugged it into a square, two-inch by two-inch black box that contained a tone transmitter, then plugged another wire from the transmitter into the radio, and hot-wired the whole device to the cigarette lighter, ensuring that it would run off the car's battery. Ferris would never know: He could use his radio normally, never realizing that the antenna was not only pulling in signals from radio stations, but was broadcasting tones from the tone transmitter to a follow car.

"Take it back and park it in the same place," Raven told Bronson. He reached into his pocket and pulled a one hundred dollar bill.

"No way," Bronson said, refusing to take the money. "Always happy to do a favor for you guys. Just keep us posted on what's going down."

"Don't we always," Higgins said.

At midnight, Raven and Higgins broke into the Willis Jeep in Stay Cool's parking lot and installed another tracking device.

"That's it," Raven said as they got into his car and drove away. "Everything is up. Let's go home."

* * *

They tracked Ferris for the next three days. He didn't do anything to arouse suspicion. The only deviation from his routine of going to and from work was to visit his mother in Westchester. He went there twice. Once he was home, he never left again, and the house lights went out between 11:30 and midnight every night.

The only interesting information obtained during that week had to do with Ada Ferris. Raven and Higgins had arrived at the rented garage one evening at about six and listened to all the telephone conversations recorded that day. Every call was either made by or received by her, and when they were finished listening, the conclusion they came to was that she was the town whore.

"She barters her snatch for everything," Higgins muttered. "Food, car repairs, everything except dry cleaning."

Raven laughed. "I guess it doesn't cost enough to clean a suit to make it worth a lay," he said.

One conversation in particular amused them. Twice that week she'd been on the phone with the owner of a fancy local grocery store. She'd order food, and when the owner totaled up the bill, they'd begin negotiations on what kind of sex it was worth. On one occasion, when she ordered a particularly large amount, she agreed it was worth a blow job. The second time, she stood fast and insisted she would only give it to him straight that day. In both instances, she went to the grocery store, and Detective Rogers followed her inside. He reported that she disappeared into the back room with the owner for about a half-hour.

"You know something," Raven told Higgins that evening as they sat in a local restaurant enjoying a couple of drinks and steaks. "You take a flake like Ferris, and you add his slut of a wife and maybe you've got some crazy husband-and-wife team, you know, getting it off together. Maybe we should toss a bug into the house."

"Sure, why not?" Higgins said. "Are we giving away valuable product samples in return for consumer reaction again?"

"Exactly," Raven said. "I still have forms back in the apartment. You want to bring the stuff to her?"

"Hell, no, let's use Rogers. He looks like a door-to-door salesman."

The next day, after stopping at a discount appliance store and purchasing an electric can opener, electric wall clock and a clock radio, Rogers knocked on the Ferris door. Ada answered.

"Good morning, ma'am," Rogers said, flashing her a boyish smile. "I represent the Northeastern Testing and Analysis Service. Your neighborhood has been chosen to participate in a marketing survey that I think you'll want to be part of."

"What's the catch?" she asked.

Again, the big grin. "No catch at all, ma'am. Here, just take a look at this." He handed her a printed form:

NORTHEASTERN TESTING AND ANALYSIS SERVICE, INC.

The undersigned hereby agrees to accept the following items free-of-charge, to be used in a residence located at:

_____

_____.

*Description of items tested:*_____

_____

_____

_____.

At the end of the six-month period ending on _____, *the undersigned agrees that (he, she) will complete this form and return it to* Northeastern Testing and Analysis Service, Inc. *It is further agreed that in consideration for doing this, the person filing this report may keep the items tested free-of-charge.*

Please complete below: (Circle only one please)

I found the _____ *to be*   *Excellent*   *Fair*   *Poor*
I found the _____ *to be*   *Excellent*   *Fair*   *Poor*
I found the _____ *to be*   *Excellent*   *Fair*   *Poor*
in service and in workmanship.

THANK YOU!
Alfred Goodman
President

"You mean all I have to do is use these things for six months and tell you what I think of them?"

"Yes, ma'am, that's all there is to it. Put the clock in your living room, and use the other two devices just as though they were yours because... well, frankly, because they *are*. All we ask is that six months from now you tell us what you thought of them. No strings, no gimmicks." He gave her his biggest smile yet.

She invited him into the house. He placed the clock, can opener and clock radio on her kitchen table, stood back, extended his hands toward them and said, "There you are, Mrs. Ferris. They're all yours. Use them in good health. Use them often because we are really looking for an honest product evaluation. He handed her an envelope on which was printed the name of the phony company and a non-existent address. "Six months from now, all you have to do is fill this out and send it off. I'll even give you the stamp." He took a postage stamp from his pocket, licked it and affixed it to the envelope.

"Looks like my lucky day," Ada said.

Raven and Higgins, who were in the rented garage, could hear every word being spoken inside the Ferris house because they'd installed in each of the products a transmitting device. They chuckled as they heard Ada say to Rogers, "Did anybody ever tell you you're a handsome young man?"

"Well, ma'am, I really don't see myself that way."

"These would make wonderful gifts. Got any more for me?"

Rogers laughed. "No, ma'am, we only give one set to a household."

Ada's voice became seductive. "I'd love to have another five or six sets to give to my friends. I could get them to send back the forms, too. Maybe you'd like to stay awhile and discuss it."

"She's putting the make on him," Raven said.

"Mrs. Ferris, I really appreciate your generous offer but I have to run. Maybe I could come back another day."

"Yes, that would be nice. Just bring me a few more sets, that's all, just as long as you bring them yourself."

Rogers returned to the garage and told Raven and Higgins that she'd rubbed her breasts against his chest.

"Hey, you know, Rogers, you could have stayed."

Rogers laughed. "And have you guys hear everything."

"You could have done it quiet," said Raven.

"She's not so great-looking," Rogers said. "Looks better from a distance."

"Oh, that's why," Raven said. "She looks like one of Lee's girlfriends, huh."

"No, not *that* bad," Rogers said, glancing at Higgins to make sure he hadn't overstepped his bounds.

* * *

Two days later, Nathan Ferris broke his pattern for the first time. He left work, drove to Yonkers and entered a bar-and-grill on Broadway. Smitty and Bowers were following; they joined him at the bar, four stools removed. A few minutes after Ferris had ordered a beer, a young man with blond hair who was roughly six-feet tall and weighed 160 pounds came in and sat next to Ferris. They had a few beers together. Ferris paid the bill an hour later and they left.

Smitty and Bowers were faced with a dilemma—who to follow. They decided there was more to be gained staying with the newcomer. They fell in behind him as he drove to a house at 132 West Street, in Yonkers, watched him park his car and enter the house. A minute later lights came on in the basement.

Bowers called in the plate number and was told the automobile belonged to Jerry O'Connor. The address given was the same as the house.

"Let's check in with Raven," Bowers said.

"Where is he?" Smitty asked as he started the engine and pulled away from the curb.

"At the garage, I think. Either there or home."

Raven and Higgins *were* at the garage near Ferris's house when Smitty and Bowers arrived. Smitty told them of the new contact they'd made.

"A blond guy, huh?" Raven said.

"Yeah, kind of good-looking, one of those California surfer types," Smitty said.

They found O'Connor's listed telephone in the directory and noted it on a piece of paper.

"Let's check with I.D.," Raven said.

"Now?" Higgins asked.

"Yeah, why not. You got a date or something?"

"I got a pissed-off wife is what I got," Higgins said.

"Bring her flowers," Raven said. "Come on, let's go. The rest of you can call it a night."

They drove to precinct headquarters where they put O'Connor's name into the I.D. system. It came back with the following information: He'd been fingerprinted when he'd made an application to become a New York City cop. He'd never been hired. Raven called the police academy and convinced an officer on duty to scout up the background investigation report that was run on O'Connor when he applied to join the force. Raven waited patiently until the officer came back on the line and asked whether he wanted all of it read to him.

"Yeah, go ahead," Raven said, slipping a hard rubber telephone pickup coil over the earpiece of the phone and jacking it into a small portable cassette recorder. "Shoot."

The officer read the material on the report in a monotone. Nothing was of particular interest until he said, "He'd been a seminary student for almost a year."

"I'll be a son of a bitch," Raven said.

"Huh?" the officer at the academy said.

"Nothing. Thanks."

"Christ, how much more do we need?" Higgins asked after Raven told him of the conversation. "One guy drives both cars the victims say were used, and now we've not only got a blond guy, but it turns out he wanted to be a cop *and* spent time studying to be a priest."

"Yeah, I agree, but we'd never get a prosecutor to act on it."

"What I love about it, Freddie, is that we know goddamn well we're not wasting our time. Let's get a tap in this O'Connor's place and wire his car. We'll split time between the two of them."

They decided not to play games getting the transmitting equipment inside O'Connor's place. They waited until he went to work the next morning, and until his landlady, an old Irish woman, left the house to go shopping. They used a pick to go through the back door of the house. The door leading to O'Connor's finished basement apartment wasn't locked. Fifteen minutes later they were back in their car, a bug having been planted near O'Connor's bed, and a transmitting device placed into a white phone on a small table next to it. They chose a six-story apartment building a block away, went to the roof and installed a receiver and a radio.

"Things are looking up, baby," Raven said.

"Yeah, this building's even got an elevator," Higgins said.

Later that night, a tone transmitter was placed in O'Connor's parked car.

Raven and Higgins discovered over the next few days that Jerry O'Connor was an office worker in an insurance company. Each evening after work, he went to the Yonkers bar-and-grill on Broadway where he enjoyed drinks with his friends and inevitably ended up in a game of darts or shuffleboard. He'd leave the bar and go to an apartment building just off the Sprain Parkway in Yonkers where he visited a girlfriend, who lived with her parents. Raven slipped the building super a hundred dollars and they tapped into the girlfriend's phone off a box in the basement, then installed another tape recorder that would activate each time the phone was picked up.

O'Connor met Nathan Ferris the next night at the Yonkers bar. Their conversation touched upon nothing more exciting than routine events, but much later that night—just after midnight—O'Connor placed a call to Ferris's home on his girlfriend's phone. He was staying over, he told Ferris, because her parents had gone to visit a relative overnight. "I can't sleep, Nate," he said. "I'm having those damn nightmares again."

Ferris, who'd been awakened and who'd told O'Connor he would take it downstairs, said to him, once Ada Ferris had hung up the bedroom phone, "Relax, Jerry, get ahold of yourself."

"That's easy for you to say, Nate, but... I'm being followed, I know it."

"Bullshit," Ferris said. "Just hang tight and everything will be all right."

Raven played the tape for the other five detectives on the case and they all agreed they were getting close.

"Yeah," said Raven, "but I want to know what O'Connor talks to his girlfriend about when they're alone. The phone's not enough. Let's slap some bugs inside."

Smitty laughed and said, "Pretty soon you'll have the whole fucking Bronx wired."

"I'd like to," Raven said.

Raven and Higgins arrived at the apartment house the next morning dressed as plumbers. Their instincts told them the appliance giveaway wouldn't work in this instance. They'd considered playing the exterminator game but decided it was too nice a building to convince anyone there was a rampant roach problem. That always worked better in the ghetto.

They gave the super another hundred, and he called the occupant of the apartment directly above the one occupied by O'Connor's girlfriend's parents. "I'm sending some plumbers up to check for leaks."

An elderly man let them in.

"I'll check the kitchen, you check the bathroom," Raven told Higgins. They parted, each carrying a case purportedly holding plumber's tools. Once Higgins was in the bathroom, he closed the door behind him, filled the sink with water and started scooping up handfuls of it, dumping them alongside the pipe that ran up through all six floors of the building. When he'd poured twenty or thirty scoops of water down the pipe, he rejoined Raven in the foyer.

"Thanks," Raven told the man.

They immediately went to the girlfriend's apartment and knocked. Her mother answered. "Ma'am," Raven said, "we're trying to fix a leak upstairs."

She eyed them suspiciously.

"We just want to check whether it's doing any damage to your apartment."

"No, there's nothing wrong in here."

"Well, ma'am, would you check your bathroom. We just want to make sure before we leave the building."

She said she would, closed and latched the door and was gone for a few moments. She returned, opened the door and said, "I'm being flooded. Quick, come in. It's coming through the ceiling."

Raven went into the bathroom and looked up, nodded his head and said, "Yeah, we have quite a problem here."

Higgins said to the woman, "would you show me your phone?"

"Yes, of course, it's in the kitchen."

While Higgins was in the kitchen with her making a phony phone call to report the plumbing problem, Raven quickly stepped into the daughter's bedroom and placed an Add-a-Plug into an electric outlet behind her bed. It had a built-in transmitter that would broadcast all conversations in the room on a pre-set crystal. It took only seconds to install, and he was back in the bathroom before Higgins and the mother returned.

"Let's go back upstairs," Raven said to his partner. "We'll get this squared away right away, ma'am."

"I'm so glad you're here. It takes so long to get a plumber when you call." She opened her purse and handed Raven a five-dollar tip.

"Much obliged, ma'am," he said, shoving it into his coverall pocket.

The results of the efforts to wire O'Connor's girlfriend's apartment were disappointing. The two made love the next night, but all that could be heard by their auditors were moans and groans, nothing to indicate anything kinky was going on. They talked mostly about his job, how much he hated it and how he wanted to find something better.

*　*　*

It was now two weeks since Lieutenant West had agreed to provide the additional manpower.

"Think he'll extend it?" Higgins asked.

"Yeah, I know he will," Raven answered, "but we still have to move fast. You never know when some asshole downtown will decide to drop it. You know what we need, Lee?"

"What?"

"Joannie Big Tits."

Fifteen

"Joannie, this is Freddie Raven."

"Hey, babe, been a long time."

"Yeah, I know. Been busy. You?"

"Getting by. You calling for a date?" She guffawed.

"No, but Lee and I do have a gig for you."

"It pays?"

"Sure it pays. Have we ever stiffed you?"

She laughed and said, "No, at least not so I knew it."

"Why don't you come up to the apartment tomorrow night at eight."

"You sure this is business?"

"Yeah. The joint needs a good cleaning."

It was a low, guttural laugh. "Which joint are you talking about?"

"See you at eight."

She arrived on time. Higgins had an extra dry vodka martini on the rocks with an olive waiting for her.

She took the drink, tossed her coat on a chair, looked around the apartment with her hands on her hips and said, "You weren't kidding, this place is a shithouse."

Raven said, "What difference should it make to you? The only thing you ever see is the ceiling."

She arranged herself on the couch. She was five feet, eight inches tall, a hundred and twenty pounds, big bosom and skinny waist, sort of a Babe Ruth type. Her face showed signs of aging, and of living high, but the results only minimally diminished the overall effect. Besides being a sensual package, Joannie could be trusted. You never had to worry about her shooting off her mouth. She would have made a good cop, Raven often thought.

She kicked off her shoes and said, "Build me another drink and tell me how I bail you out *this* time."

A half-hour later, after Higgins and Raven had briefed her on the case, Raven went to the concealed compartment in the bottom of the closet, took out a cigarette lighter with a transmitter built into it and handed it to her. "You keep this with you and *on* all the while we're working the guy," he said. He handed her a tiny .25 automatic revolver. "Stick this in your pocketbok, Joannie, just in case you need it. It's clean, unregistered."

She looked up at him. "Suppose I have to use it?"

"Go right ahead," Higgins said. "We'll clean up after you."

Her face turned serious. "Do you really think it'll come to that?"

"No," Raven answered, "but you never know. We'd hate to lose you. Good pussy is hard to come by."

Higgins handed her three hundred-dollar bills for expenses and told her there'd be more when they were through. She was instructed to meet them outside O'Connor's favorite bar on Broadway in Yonkers at five the next evening. Raven suggested she bring her sister, Susie, but told her she'd have to ditch her later if the score worked.

Raven and Higgins were sitting in Raven's Chrysler when Joannie and Susie arrived the next night. "Hello, Needledick," Joannie said.

"You set?" Higgins asked.

"Sure am."

"You remember the word."

"Delicious." Joannie said. "I say that and you beep twice."

"You got it," Higgins said. "Now remember, don't lead the guy into any kinky stuff. Let him make the moves."

"I gotcha," she said.

They watched the two girls approach the entrance to the bar. Joannie turned, gave them the finger, then disappeared through the door.

Joannie and Susie walked up to the bartender and asked for enough telephone change to call Connecticut. He took the five-dollar bill Joannie handed him and broke it down into singles and change, his eyes never leaving her chest. She was wearing a silky purple blouse with a couple of buttons open, which exposed the beginnings of her large breasts. She smiled as she noticed how he sucked in his stomach, thanked him and gave the change to Susie. "Call home and have somebody pick us up as soon as possible," she said.

Susie headed for the rear of the bar where the public telephone was located, and Joannie took a seat.

"What can I make you?" the bartender asked. She smiled, inhaled and said, "You can bring us two of anything that's good."

"You look like you already have two good things," he said, leering, his eyes still focused on her breasts.

She looked him in the eye and asked his name.

"Frank."

"Okay, Frank, my sister and I would like two extra dry vodka martinis with olives. That takes care of the drink order. Now, for what's on your mind. I don't blame you for trying, but you should know I only go out with two kinds, one who can lick his eyebrows and the other who's got nine inches and can hurt me. You qualify on either count?"

Frank fumbled for an answer, could only manage, "Two vodka martinis coming up."

Susie rejoined her.

"Did you get them?" Joannie asked.

"Yeah. I think Harry is going to pick us up."

Frank, the bartender, asked what they were doing there.

"Just our luck," Joannie said, launching into the story she'd concocted with Raven and Susie. "Our uncle died and we came down here to Yonkers for the funeral. We hung around too long and by the time we left, we were the last people at the funeral home. We came outside and tried to start the car. Zero. Dead."

"Where did you come from?" Frank asked.

"Connecticut. My sister just called and our brother will pick us up." She laughed and added, "We might as well settle in here and enjoy the stay."

Raven and Higgins had given Joannie a detailed description of Jerry O'Connor, but said they would try to hit the horn a couple of times when they saw him arrive. The girls heard the horn blow, turned and looked toward the front door. O'Connor came through. Joannie turned to Susie and said, "Looks like any other schmobo."

An hour later, after just about every man in the bar had hit on them, they settled into a conversation with O'Connor, which led to a game of shuffleboard. Joannie didn't want to come on too strong, but she let him know she was interested. He waited until Susie went to the ladies' room before inviting Joannie out for something to eat.

"I'd love it."

"What about your sister?"

"Our ride should be here soon. She'll wait for it."

As Joannie and O'Connor were about to leave, Frank, the bartender, leaned over to Joannie and said, "I'm curious, which one is he, the eyebrow licker or the nine inches?"

"Neither," Joannie said, "but he promised to beat me up. I'm into that. Thanks for the drinks."

O'Connor took her to a cheap fast-food steak house. She had the feeling he was the type who would spend a lot of money on a girl if he had it, but didn't.

When they were through eating, he grinned boyishly and said, "My apartment's not far from here. How about it?"

She waited what she considered was an appropriate time, smiled and said, "Sure. You seem like a nice guy."

They left the restaurant. Joannie saw Raven's white Chrysler parked up the street. She looked up at the sky and said, "It's a delicious night, isn't it?"

"Yeah, it's clear," O'Connor said.

Two beeps of the horn came from the Chrysler. They were receiving her. She relaxed.

Raven and Higgins followed at a discreet distance and watched the couple enter the house in which O'Connor maintained his basement apartment. The lights came on downstairs.

"I'd like to see, too," Higgins said.

"You're a fucking pervert," Raven said. "Shut up and listen."

* * *

They heard the initial lovemaking by Joannie and Jerry O'Connor. It was straightforward and dull, which Raven told Higgins was to be expected. "It's a long night," he said. "He won't push the kinky stuff right away."

They heard Joannie tell him how satisfying he was. O'Connor replied, "My lucky night running into you."

She laughed and said, "Hey, knock off that male chauvinist bullshit. I enjoy getting fucked as much as any guy."

They heard O'Connor offer her a cigarette, could even hear the match being lighted. Then, there was relative silence.

"You figure she's okay?" Higgins asked.

"Sure. We're pulling her in loud and clear. It's rest time in the old sack."

Raven and Higgins sat silently, each immersed in his own private thoughts. They'd share many long nights like this together, grueling, mind-numbing nights on stake-out. Usually, one would end up in a talkative mood, which would help pass the time. This wasn't Raven's night, but Higgins eventually started talking, saying, "This fucking case is ending up a grinder, Freddie. It looked like a grounder going in."

Raven snickered and lit a cigarette. "Yeah, I know. Nothing easy about it."

"You know what I was thinking a few minutes ago, Freddie?"

"No."

"I was thinking back to when I first made detective. I was in the Forty-First. Things really changed there. It used to be all Jewish and Irish until the spics and spades came in. My second night on duty I caught a call about a guy getting whacked at

110

some house party. We roll, but by the time we get there, the sector car guys have everybody lined up in the kitchen and bedroom. Right there on the living room floor is some guy named Jose. He's got a .45 slug in his head. The sector tells us that when they responded, the party was still going on. Shit, it was like Jose was just taking up dance floor space. They left him laying there while they all danced whatever the fuck it is they dance to. Anyway, I'm with a guy named Larry who turns to me and says, 'Let me show you how we handle it here, kid. Go in the kitchen and get me a frying pan.'

"I think maybe he's gone off the deep end but who the hell am I to question a big hat in the squad, so I go and get him a frying pan, one of those old black heavy jobs you don't see anymore. I walk back in and give it to him. He says to me, 'Send out one of the witnesses from the bedroom.' I ask him which one he wants. He gets mad and says, 'I don't give a shit, send me anybody.'

"I send this guy out to Larry, who's standing over the body. Larry looks at him and says, 'Hey, *amigo, que pasa?*' He points down at the body. The guy makes all kinds of gestures and says, 'I know nothing, I no see nothing!'

"Larry smiles and swings the fucking pan, hits the guy a shot in the head you could hear in Cleveland. Sounds like Big Ben in London, you know? The guy hits the floor like a shot and on the front of his head is a lump like a basketball.

"Everybody watches what happens but nobody says a fucking word. Then, Larry looks at me and says, 'Send me out another.'

"I pick another guy and send him to Larry. This guy looks down at the body, looks at his friend with the lump on his head, turns and looks into the kitchen and says, 'That's who did it, Miguel. The gun is in the bathroom behind the toilet.'

"That was it, Freddie. Two minutes—what could have been a grinder ends up a grounder."

Raven yawned and stretched. He'd heard the story before but always enjoyed hearing Higgins tell it. Besides, it was conversation. He said, "Yeah, well, it don't work that way anymore."

Higgins laughed. "Yeah. A week after I'm with Larry with

the frying pan, I end up on a call with guys named Russ and Joey. The same shit is going down, a party and nobody gives a rat's ass about the deceased. I start to question a couple of people when Russ says to me, 'Hey, kid, let me show you how we do it in the Forty-First.'

"I say to him, 'You want me to get a frying pan?' He looks at me like I'm a fucking idiot and tells me to get a kitchen chair.

"I get him the chair like he wants. He puts it down next to the body and tells me to get one of the witnesses. I bring the witness out. Russ sits him in the chair and tells him to tell what happened. The guy goes through the same shit, that he doesn't speak English, he doesn't see, hear or know nothin'."

There was a silence. Raven turned and said, "What happened?"

Higgins laughed. "Russ and Larry pick up the chair with the guy in it and toss the fucking thing right through the window. We're on the second story. The guy in the chair disappears. Russ and Larry never even look outside. They just tell me to bring in the next witness. I bring the next guy out and right away he starts babbling about who shot the D.O.A. We pick him up in an hour. Larry asked me later about the frying pan, and I told him the original story. You know what he said to me, Freddie?"

Raven shook his head.

"He told me when in doubt, use the chair. Maybe that's what we should do with O'Connor instead of playing all these goddam games. Maybe we should put the son of a bitch in a chair and throw him out his window."

Raven laughed. "He lives in a basement."

"Yeah, but it still might get his attention."

Raven decided to climb in the back seat for a nap. "We'll take two hours each, okay?"

"Okay." Higgins nodded. Moments later Raven snored as Higgins continued to listen to the steady buzz from the radio. Joannie eventually got the action going again. "What do you like to do, Jerry?" she asked in a seductive voice. "I'm into just about anything, baby."

Higgins silently hoped she wouldn't go too far in leading him on. It evidently didn't matter because O'Connor said, "I just like it straight, sweetie. I just like a good solid fuck. I like the way my cock feels inside."

She did her best, judging from the muttered sounds coming through the radio. She sucked his toes and tried to sit on his face, but he told her he didn't like that.

The next morning, Higgins and Raven watched her leave the apartment. O'Connor had called a cab for her. She got in it. They followed. She had it stop two blocks away, got out, paid the cabbie and joined them in the car.

"Sorry, guys," she said. "I did my best."

"Yeah, we heard," Higgins said. He turned to Raven and said, "Maybe this guy ain't part of it, Freddie."

"Yeah, or maybe he's just smart. Let's give it some more time. You up for it again, Joannie?" When she didn't immediately respond, Freddie sweetened the pot with a couple hundred extra dollars.

Joannie Big Tits met Jerry O'Connor twice more in the evening. Each time they ended up in his apartment in bed, but nothing surfaced that would indicate he was into the sort of kinky sex that characterized the assaults and rapes in Van Cortlandt Park.

"One more shot, Joannie," Raven said. "Make a date with him next Saturday for lunch and get back in bed in the afternoon. Make a drink and slip this into his." He handed her a tiny bottle of chloral hydrate he'd obtained from the precinct medical office.

That Saturday, after O'Connor had been drugged and was dead to the world, Joannie let them into the apartment. They searched it thoroughly but couldn't find anything to link him to the Van Cortlandt rapes. They made an impression of his apartment key, and Higgins took his wallet, address book and telephone bills to a local drug store where he made Xerox copies of everything. Their final act was to fingerprint O'Connor as he slept, using an inkless kit they'd brought with them.

O'Connor woke up at seven that night.

"Gee, honey, you slept like a baby," Joannie said.

"Yeah, Jesus, I feel like I was drugged or something." It occurred to him that maybe he was, and he checked his belongings before Joannie left. She feigned resentment but

113

didn't make too big a deal of it. Her parting words were, "Either I'm the dullest broad in the world or I fucked you into unconsciousness." He laughed and asked when he would see her again.

"Next week. I'll call you."

"Why don't I call you?"

"I told you, Jerry, I've got a very messy situation up in Connecticut. Please, let's keep it this way." She kissed him on the lips and left.

He never saw her again.

Sixteen

It was an Italian restaurant in Queens frequented almost exclusively by cops and wise guys. Raven and Higgins sat with a close friend, Walter Nugent, a plainsclothesman assigned to vice and gambling. They were in good spirits; Raven and Higgins had taken Sunday off and spent the day with their families. Sometimes, those days turned out to be more tension-provoking than they were worth, but in both cases the day had gone smoothly. The kids had behaved, and hassles with their wives had been minimal.

When they left the restaurant that Monday night, they had what they wanted from Nugent—the telephone number and location of a Queens wireroom.

Their funds were running low, not only to support the private side of their investigation into the Patricia Knees rape and murder, but to pay household bills. As they often said, "Nobody can live on a cop's salary." Most of the cops they knew, including each other, didn't even try.

They waited until the following Saturday to use the information Nugent had given them. At ten o'clock that morning, they rolled their telephone truck to Parker Towers, on Queens Boulevard, and parked. Within fifteen minutes they'd installed a radio transmitter bug on the phone line given them by Nugent, and were in a local diner enjoying a large breakfast. They returned to the truck at eleven, tuned in the radio and heard the bug's hum. At 11:05 the first call came in on the line. The phone was picked up on the first ring. "Hello," a man's voice said.

"This is Bob—for—44," a male voice answered.

"Hold on a minute."

Raven and Higgins knew the wireman was searching through his records to see if it was a valid code, and to make sure the bettor wasn't over his limit. He came back on the line and said, "Okay, Bob—for—44, what's your pleasure?"

Bob—for—44 gave him three hundred dollars of bets on various horse races, then asked him to read the pro football line. Once he had it, he bet five hundred dollars on the Giants, giving two-and-a-half points for a total bet of eight hundred dollars, plus fifty bucks for the vig. He hung up. The tape recorder in the truck stopped. The next call came and the tape spun again.

By 12:45 the room had booked more than seventy-eight thousand dollars worth of action on sports and horses.

At 12:50, the wireman called a paint store in Queens that Raven and Higgins were familiar with and reported the total amount bet for the day. He then shut down the wire; Raven and Higgins knew he'd reopen at four for the night action. They entered the building and went to the apartment door. It opened and the wireman stepped into the hallway. They came up behind and pushed him back inside.

"Oh, shit," he said. "Where the fuck are you from, downtown?"

"No."

"Feds?"

"No."

"Then who the fuck are you?"

"Just us," Higgins said pleasantly.

"Fuck it, man, we're on with everybody. Give your boss a call, shithead."

Raven was not so pleasant. "You're not on with us."

"Where are you from?"

"Narcotics," Raven said.

"Narcotics?" The wireman whined. "What the hell are you talking about? There's no shit here."

"We know that."

"So, get the fuck out. You don't belong here. You got no jurisdiction."

"Hey, scumbubble, come here and take a close look at this," Higgins said, holding out his badge.

The wireman read it: "Detective, City of New York."

"So where do you think you are, wise ass, in Russia?" Raven said.

"Hey, look, let's talk, huh."

"Sure."

Twenty minutes later, and after Raven had placed a call from a pay phone on the corner, they were on their way to Coney Island with the wireman in the back of the truck. They pulled up to a motel and banged on the door that said OFFICE. Eventually, the motel owner, whose name was Arthur, staggered to the door, squinted at them through bloodshot eyes, and opened it.

"Jesus, you look like you been hit by a truck," Higgins said.

"Yeah, I tied one on last night," Arthur said in a whiskey voice.

Higgins and Raven glanced at each other and smiled. Arthur always put it as though getting drunk was unusual for him. The fact was, he was a dedicated rummy who hadn't been sober in twenty years.

"Full house?" Raven asked.

"Shit, Freddie, you know nobody stays here this time of year."

"We have a guest for you," Raven said, nodding at the wireman. "He's a Count, Count Yourchange. The Count is going to be a guest here for a couple of hours, only if his boss doesn't do the right thing, he'll be around til Monday. We'll pick him up either way. Please show us your finest room, something suitable for royalty."

Arthur took them to a room on the second floor. They told him to get lost. After he'd closed the door, they pulled the mattress from the bed and laid it on the floor next to the radiator. "Get down on it," Higgins told the wireman. He resisted, and the two of them pushed him to his knees. Raven handcuffed him to the radiator.

"Relax," Higgins said. "Consider it a little holiday. Don't make trouble and you'll be back in business before you know it." Raven added, "Arthur is family. If anything happens to him you're dead. *Capishe?*"

They went downstairs and gave Arthur three hundred dollars. "Feed him anything he wants, Artie, but don't bring in broads no matter how much he offers." Raven handed him the keys to the handcuffs.

At nine that night they sat at a table at the rear of Junior's Restaurant, on Flatbush Avenue, in Brooklyn. A few minutes later the front door opened and they saw Vito come through it. He came directly to their table, sat down and said, "Don't you fuckers have enough money? What the fuck are you looking to do, buy the fucking world?"

Raven smiled and said, "All we're looking to do, Vito, is to buy the house next to you when we retire, and that'll take big bucks."

Vito "The Hat" Perrone was sixty years old. It was rumored that the first bet he heard in his life was in the delivery room when his father bet the doctors it would be a boy. The rest was history—of sorts. At one time, Vito had bought a nag of a horse and run him in a boat race at Aqueduct. He listed his son as the owner. The horse won as expected, which was not all good news for Vito and his kind. They both ended up in front of a Grand Jury for fixing the race. The son handled himself as best he could on the witness stand, which was difficult because he didn't know very much. Then, his father was called to testify.

The prosecutor, a young lawyer straight out of school, glared at Vito as though he, himself, was on the hook to pay off the bets on the horse. After having Vito identify himself for the record, he said, "Isn't it true you own a horse named Big Sally, and that you own it with your son?"

"You might say that," Vito answered.

"And isn't it true that you are known to be the biggest bookmaker in New York City?"

"You might say that."

"And is it not true that you have been arrested for bookmaking more than twenty times, with three convictions?"

"You might say that."

"And is it not true that you entered Big Sally in the fifth race at Aqueduct last month, the North County Handicap?"

Vito repeated the answer he'd been giving all along— "You might say that."

"And is it not true that the odds on your horse were 15 to 1?"

"You might say that."

"Is it not true that this was the first race the horse had ever entered?"

"You might say that."

"And is it not true that the horse in question is six years old?"

"You might say that."

"And is it not true that the horse won and paid over thirty dollars for every two dollars wagered?"

"You might say that."

The young prosecutor smiled smugly, looked at the jury, then said to Vito, "Now, sir, would you be good enough to tell me and the people of the Grand Jury why you never ran this horse before that date?"

Vito looked at the jury and grinned, and said in a loud, confident voice, "Sure. That horse was so fast we had to chase him for six years before we caught him."

There evidently were a few horse players on the Grand Jury because when they were finished laughing, they returned a "No Bill" —legal terminology indicating that they felt there was not enough evidence to indict.

Higgins reminded Vito of that story, which made him laugh. "I'm hungry," he said.

They ordered an array of dishes. Small talk dominated the

table until the appetizers were served. Vito tasted his, grunted and licked his lips in approval, then said, "So, how much to you pricks to buy back the action?"

Raven and Higgins looked at each other and shrugged. "Twenty grand should do it," Raven said.

"Bullshit," Vito said, filling his mouth again. "I'll give you ten."

"We could compromise," Higgins said.

"Yeah, as a special favor to you and because you're such a nice guy, we'll consider fifteen, but no lower," said Raven. They knew they had the upper hand. The minute they put the word out on the street that the wireroom had been taken and the betting slips had been confiscated, every player would put in a claim as a winner. Without having records, Vito stood to lose a lot more than fifteen thousand dollars.

"I have to think about it," he said.

"Take your time, Vito," Raven said. "You've got until dessert."

They left the restaurant fifteen thousand dollars richer, which Vito had peeled off from a wad in his inside coat pocket. Raven and Higgins assured him in front of the restaurant that no one else knew the location of the wireroom, and that they would keep it safe in return for some monthly action. After a few minutes of bickering, Vito put them "on" for a thousand a month. They handed him the betting slips they'd taken that afternoon.

"Hey, Vito," Higgins said, "you really are a good guy. We always knew that, but...just hang on a second, I'll be right back." He disappeared into Junior's, returning minutes later carrying two cheesecakes for which Junior's was famous. He handed them to Vito. "A little gift to a partner."

Vito looked down at the boxes, then up at Raven and Higgins and said, "You're fucking crazy if you think I'll eat cheesecake that cost me seventy-five hundred apiece."

Raven called Arthur at the motel and told him to release the wireman, to give him fifty bucks and to hold onto the handcuffs until he had a chance to get out there again.

Arthur giggled. "Shit, Freddie, it's a good thing it worked out. The son of a bitch is melting. I turned up the heat."

They drove the telephone truck into Queens, went into Gallagher's Bar on Queens Boulevard and called Walter Nugent at home. He met them there and they handed him two thousand dollars in hundred-dollar bills.

They hung around Gallagher's for another couple of hours. Nugent and Raven spent most of the time drinking and talking, while Higgins tried to put the make on a buxom blond barmaid.

Raven and Nugent watched from their table as Higgins went through his usual courtship routine, holding and rubbing her hands and telling her he'd never met such a beautiful woman with such obvious intelligence. He told her fortune by tracing the lines in her palm. He made her feel like Queen-for-a Day.

"He's too much," Raven said to Nugent. "The problem is, when he makes a score, he disappears for a couple of days, and we don't have the time. I'd better bust this up."

They waited until Higgins went to the men's room before Raven went up to the barmaid and introduced himself as his partner.

"I'm Cindy," she said pleasantly. "Your partner is nice."

"Yeah, I know, and I don't want to ruin your night or anything like that, but I should tell you something that'll save you trouble."

Her large eyes widened even further.

"Look, Cindy, I know it's none of my business because I don't even know you, but I saw you holding Lee's hand a few minutes ago."

"So?"

"Well, I hate to tell you this but he's got the clap."

"You're kidding."

"I wouldn't kid about something as serious as that. He's taking shots now at Bellevue. He's got another week to do."

"Oh, shit," she muttered. "Thanks... thanks a lot for telling me."

"I'm just looking to save a nice kid like you some grief, that's all, and I'm not trying to score myself."

"Yeah, I know you're not. Thanks again."

Raven returned to the table and watched Cindy go behind the bar, pour Canadian Club over her hands and rub them vigorously. A few minutes later Higgins returned and went to touch her. She cringed and twisted away. He frowned, spun around on the stool and glared at Raven and Nugent. He came to the table, leaned over and said, "You motherfucker, Freddie, did you give her that V.D. crap?"

Raven adopted his best hurt, surprised expression. "Hey, Lee, sit down and listen to what really happened." Higgins sat heavily. Raven leaned close and said, "Huey, the bartender, came over when you were in the John and told us the kid has the clap. He didn't want to mess with an infected cop walking out of here."

Higgins wasn't sure whether to believe his partner or not. He looked to Nugent for confirmation.

"Freddie's telling the truth, Lee," Nugent said.

Higgins visibly relaxed. He suddenly looked at his hands, held them up as though they'd been dipped in dog droppings and said, "And to think I was rubbing her hands. That little bitch."

They left the restaurant ten minutes later. Nugent thanked them for their gift and walked away. Raven and Higgins held five thousand out of the pot for working expenses and split the rest.

"See you Monday," Raven said.

"Yeah. Damn, I can't wait to get home and soak in a hot tub."

Seventeen

The following week moved slowly. The six detectives assigned to the investigation met often in the hope that an open exchange of information and ideas might trigger a new approach. It didn't. The fact was that although they were positive that Nathan Ferris and Jerry O'Connor were involved, they had not come up with one tangible piece of evidence that could be used to convict them. The recorded conversations resulted in nothing but routine telephone calls, with the exception of Ada Ferris's promiscuous bartering of her body in Rye, New York.

Copies of O'Connor's telephone bills had been given to a friend in the Telephone Security Office, but they hadn't heard back from him yet. The prints they'd taken of O'Connor confirmed only that he was who he said he was. Higgins had given the copy of O'Connor's address book to Bowers and told him to run a check on every name in it to see if it contained someone who'd been arrested for sex crimes.

"Let's face it," Raven said on Thursday. "They never killed anybody before. Now that they have, maybe the game is over. Maybe they'll never do anything out of line again that would help us."

"Bullshit," Higgins said. "We may not be around on the case that long, but one of them will screw up. Ever know it to fail?"

Raven shook his head, but his heart wasn't in agreeing with his partner. He'd reached the bottom of his reserve of optimism, and had considered that morning requesting that he be taken off the case and returned to normal duty.

"I talked to the Twenty-Second," Browne said. The Twenty-Second Precinct covered Central Park in New York City. "They've never had a case with this M.O. It's purely Van Cortlandt."

"Why don't we call that numbnuts D.A. up in Rockland," Higgins suggested. "You know, Freddie, they never went over Lamps's car the way they should have. Let's drag a lab guy from here and take a look."

Raven shrugged. "Sure, why not? He'll probably shit a brick, but so what."

Raven was right. The Rockland D.A. wasn't happy with Raven's request to bring his own lab technician in to examine the car, but he did the only thing he could—he agreed in "the spirit of cooperation." His sole request was that anything they found be discussed with him before being included in the N.Y.P.D. case file. Raven assured him he'd play the game.

Lamps's car had been moved from its original storage at the police garage, and was now housed in a commercial storage facility. When Raven, Higgins and the lab technician walked in, their spirits fell. The car was in a corner of a large warehouse and was buried under tons of sporting equipment.

"Shit," Higgins said as he started tossing the equipment off the vehicle. It took them half an hour. When they'd finally cleared it, they tried to open the doors. They were all locked.

"That's good," Raven said. "At least nobody's been crawling around in there."

They opened the doors with a Slim Jim and told the technician to concentrate on the inside. "Dust the rearview mirror real good, front and back, and the lever that adjusts the seat," Raven told him. "Everybody who drives a strange car always plays with those when they get in. Check the ashtray close, too, and get any dirt from the brake and gas pedals."

While the technician worked inside, Raven and Higgins went up under the car and recovered stones from the front and rear fenders. The technician found some stones on the floor in the front; none were found in the back.

"What'd you get?" Raven asked the technician.

"Three partial prints on the rearview mirror."

"Probably belongs to the cop who drove the thing in here," Raven said disgustedly. "Come on, let's go back."

They reported what they'd found to the D.A. He said, "Sounds like nothing."

"Yeah, you're probably right," Raven told him, hoping all the while that the partial prints might provide some help. He wanted to say what he thought of the sloppy cops and lab boys who worked in Rockland but decided it wouldn't accomplish anything. He thanked him for his cooperation and hung up.

Late that afternoon, the lab technician called. "The prints I got off the mirror belong to your guy Ferris," he said.

Raven held the phone from his ear, looked to where Higgins was sitting on the other side of the detectives' room and yelled, "The prints belong to Ferris. Goddam it, Lee, we got it."

"Hold on, Freddie," the lab technician yelled into the phone.

Raven put it to his ear again and said, "What's the matter?"

"Freddie, it won't work as evidence. You know you need fourteen or more points of any one fingerprint to link it to an individual. Not one of the three prints has fourteen matching points."

"Jesus Christ, then why the hell are you... ?"

"Freddie, I'm telling you that these prints belong to Nathan Ferris. It may not hold up in court, but based upon the way the points match up on all three prints, there's no doubt in my mind that his fingers made them."

"Great, so we have the right guy but we still can't prove it."

"I don't write the law, Freddie, I just dust."

Smith, Bowers, Rogers and Browne left for the night, leaving Raven and Higgins alone in the 50th's detectives' room.

"What are you doing this weekend?" Higgins asked.

"I don't know, Lee. I need to do something, you know, get some R-and-R. I'm burned out. You?"

Higgins shrugged. "I promised Janet I'd take them all to the zoo." He laughed. "I spend my fucking life in a zoo and then I end up there on the weekend, too."

Raven said, "Let's go up to the apartment and sort things out. Maybe that's what's bothering me. I have a feeling everything is getting away from us."

They stopped on the way to pick up tapes from the recorders they'd installed, walked through the door of the apartment and dumped everything on a small table that served as a desk and dining table. Raven made drinks, kicked off his shoes, flopped on the couch and let out a sigh of contentment. He looked over at Higgins, who was at the table labeling tapes. "Hey, Lee, when this thing is over I'm taking off, maybe Puerto Rico, maybe Mexico."

"Just you?"

"You wanna come?"

"I didn't mean that. I mean whether you'll go with the family."

"I'd rather not, but I'll have to. It doesn't matter, just as long as I get out of here. Christ, I didn't know how much this case was getting to me."

Higgins straightened out the concealed compartment in the closet, carefully removing batteries from equipment that would not be used for a while, making sure everything was in its proper box or bag. Raven stayed on the couch sipping his drink.

"Hey, Freddie," Higgins said, standing up and holding a roll of eight-millimeter film. "What are we going to do with this?"

"What is it?"

"That film my friend from Brooklyn, Henry, got us."

Raven sat up. "I forgot we even had that. That stuff ought to go into a safe deposit box."

"Yeah, I know. I'll do it Monday. Want to see it again?"

Raven started to say no, then changed his mind. "As long as it's before dinner. Let's go order up Chinese."

Raven called in the take-out order from a local restaurant while Higgins threaded the film into a projector.

The film had come into their possession a few years back

while they were working a city-wide vice and gambling unit. Higgins's friend, Henry, had called and said he needed help. Henry ran a card game in a hotel near the Brooklyn Navy Yard. He'd started as a numbers runner and worked his way up in a numbers bank until he was sitting one of the better wirerooms in the city. He was making more than six hundred a week for only a few hours work, but kept losing it, and a lot more, at the track, sporting events and anything else he could bet on.

In the beginning, he'd borrowed from his boss until that source was cut off, then ended up into outside shylocks. Eventually, he owed forty thousand dollars, and no matter how he tried, he couldn't make a dent in the debt.

The shys went along with him because they knew he was in the wireroom business, and they knew Henry's boss, but it soon got to the point where they were no longer willing to let the debt ride. They called his boss and told him they were going to collect. He told them to go ahead; he was washing his hands of the problem, and of Henry.

One night, while Henry was at home with his wife in Brooklyn, the doorbell rang. She answered it. The doorway was filled by a huge enforcer known around Brooklyn as "Godzilla." The running joke was that if the Japanese Godzilla had to fight the Brooklyn Godzilla, the smart money was on the Brooklyn species.

"You got the week's money?" Godzilla asked Henry.

Henry started to give an excuse. Godzilla told him to meet him downstairs.

"I can't believe the size of that man," Henry's wife said when he returned to the kitchen.

Henry laughed to ease the tension, but what he really wanted to do was go into the bathroom and throw up. He'd told Higgins that he'd looked at the window and considered jumping out even though it was three stories up. He figured it probably wouldn't kill him, just cripple him for life, which was what he was facing anyway.

He told his wife he had to go out for a few hours, kissed her goodbye, went downstairs and got into Godzilla's car. They took the Brooklyn Queens Expressway to the Queens Midtown Tunnel, and into Manhattan.

They pulled up in front of an expensive high-rise on Third

Avenue and went up to the penthouse. Waiting for them was Nicky Gondlolfo, Little Cat, Big Cat, Benny-the-Gasher and a sexy-looking blonde. The minute they arrived, Nicky told everybody to get lost.

"It's really nice of you to come all the way from Brooklyn, Henry," Nicky said, sounding sincerely appreciative. "You look good. How's the wife and children?"

Henry answered his questions and, for the five minutes they made small talk, actually began to relax and to think Nicky would let him off the hook.

Until, Nicky threw his drink in his face and said, "Where's the fucking money, you shyster?"

Henry dredged up every excuse he'd made over the past month. He even tried to joke— "Maybe I should find some slower women and faster horses," he said.

Nicky did not laugh. He summoned Godzilla back into the room and told him to set up the projector while he made drinks. The lights were lowered and the film began. It was black-and-white and the quality was not very good, but it was clear enough to make the point.

It started with a large refrigerator door being opened by Godzilla. Godzilla, Nicky and Benny-the-Gasher led a fat man into the refrigerator. He obviously didn't want to go. They picked him up, rammed meat hooks through the middle of his hands and hung him from the ceiling. He was screaming but you couldn't hear it; the film was silent. As he was hanging there, Godzilla and Benny stripped him naked. They each took a baseball bat and repeatedly battered his knees.

The next scene started with the fat man waking up. Nicky held a blowtorch. He fired it up, walked close to the hanging fat man and directed the flame under his right arm, brought it down his side, across his stomach, down to his genitals, then back up to his left armpit. He brought it straight across his face, taking in both eyes. The fat man was unconscious again. Benny-the-Gasher came up to him, pulled his head back and held up an icepick to the camera, then shoved it into the fat man's right ear, withdrew it, did the same to his left ear, and then shoved it up his nostrils as far as it would go. The fat man was dead. The film flickered to an end and the penthouse lights came up. Nicky

128

turned to Henry, smiled and said, "It's our version of The Three Stooges. How did you like it, Henry?"

Henry was speechless. He swallowed an icecube and silently wished he could choke to death.

"You know, Henry, hurting people like that is going out of style," Nicky said. "Brings too much heat, but then again... Look, we've been getting complaints about the quality of the film. Some of my business associates think we ought to produce a new one in color and sound, and I'm looking for a new leading man. You interested?"

Henry copped a plea of sorts with Nicky. He gave them everything he had with him at the moment, cuff links, his watch, a gold chain and cross, and every cent in his pockets. While he was doing it, he noticed Godzilla rewind the film, put it in its box and slip it into the blonde's pocketbook.

"I'll do anything, Nicky. Just don't hurt me, huh? I got the wife and kids and I'm real sorry, you know?"

A deal was struck. Henry would pull a series of armed robberies with Little Cat, the proceeds to be used to pay off his debt.

Once Henry was out of debt, he suggested to Higgins and Raven that if they had the film, not only would they have something to hold over Nicky's head in case they needed his cooperation, he'd have some leverage the next time he got involved with Nicky's crowd. Higgins and Raven agreed. They staked out the blonde, arranged for a burglery at her apartment and took the film. They'd been holding it ever since.

"It's a shame," Raven said.

"What's a shame?" Higgins asked as he put the film in its box and into his pocket.

"That Nicky never got any bigger. Wish we could use it against the little prick."

The Chinese food arrived and they ate with enthusiasm.

"I think I'll head home," Higgins said.

"Yeah, go ahead. I will, too, in a while. I just need to unwind a little more."

"You'll be home this weekend?"

Raven smiled. "No, I think I'll do a number. I figure I'm entitled. Enjoy the zoo."

Eighteen

"Leave me alone," Raven said as he tried to pull the pillow over his head.

"Come on, get up," his wife said, continuing to shake him.

He moaned, turned over and looked up into her face. She was fully dressed. He glanced at the clock next to the bed; nine a.m. "It's early," he said.

"Not for me. I'm going shopping in White Plains with Debbie and Alice. Fluffy's sick. Rachel found him in his basket."

"Jesus, you wake me up this early on a Saturday morning to tell me the cat's sick?"

"I just called the vet and he said to bring him right over. He's only there half a day today. Come on, get up and take him."

"Why the hell doesn't Joy get a driver's license. Some maid. I even told her I'd buy her a car if she did."

"She doesn't like to drive here. She's afraid."

Raven pushed himself up to a sitting position. "How long will you be gone?"

"Most of the day. Why?"

"I don't know, I just figured I'd run in to see my mother and father and then take care of some paperwork on this case. Maybe I'll stay downtown for the night, so don't make any plans for us."

She gave him one of her patented "I know you're lying but there's nothing I can do about it, and even if there were I wouldn't bother, you bum" looks. She said, "The kids are up and dressed and they want to go to the vet with you."

"All right, see you later, and don't buy out the goddam store. You got enough money?"

"Yes." She kissed him and left the room. He got up, showered and shaved and, after getting dressed, went downstairs to take a look at the meanest member of the family, Fluffy, the cat.

He and Fluffy hadn't gotten along since the day the cat was brought into the house. If there were any day in his life he remembered, that was it.

He'd gotten up late on a Saturday morning, came downstairs and searched the refrigerator for something to eat. It was empty except for bologna, bread and milk. He made a sandwich, poured the milk and went to the living room to answer the phone. When he returned to the kitchen, a kitten was sitting in the middle of the table licking its chops—it had finished off the sandwich and was lapping up his milk from the overturned glass.

"Who the hell are you?" Raven said. He tried to shoo the cat off the table but it raised up on its hind legs, hissed, took a swipe at his hand with bared claws and caught him just enough on the back of his hand to draw blood.

Raven was furious. He chased the cat out of the kitchen. It scooted behind a chair. He reached behind to grab it; the cat got him again on the hand, digging deeper this time. The cat scooted into the living room and went behind a couch. Raven pushed the couch out from the wall but couldn't grab the animal. It ran into the dining room, then upstairs, leaving behind a trail of rearranged furniture.

They continued the chase through the bedrooms. Raven thought he had him once but the cat managed to dart away and head for the stairs. Raven, still in his pajamas and barefooted, lunged, lost his balance and started to fall toward the stairs. He desperately reached out for a wrought iron collapsing gate he'd installed to keep the kids from falling down the stairs, and the momentum of his weight forced the gate to close on both hands. He kept going; the gate held. He heard the sound of eight fingers breaking, and then the accompanying pain hit him like eight hot irons.

He was about to black out but managed to extract his hands from the gate. He slumped against a wall. All he could think of was revenge. He staggered into the bedroom and came out with his off-duty Detective's Special revolver, descended the stairs and found the cat in the living room. He came as close as he could without sending it into flight again, managed to use his thumbs to steady the revolver against his chest and slowly aimed it. The cat hissed and brought up a paw as though it were about to attack again.

He squeezed the trigger with his thumb, but at the moment of discharge, the revolver slipped. The bullet went through the floor between his legs, narrowly missing his groin.

The front door opened. It was his wife, Mary, who'd just returned from grocery shopping. She looked around the house at the furniture in disarray and screamed, "Oh, my God, what's going on, Freddie?"

Raven looked at her through eyes tearing with pain and said, "The cat ate my bologna sandwich."

That was years ago. Fluffy and Raven had managed to co-exist in the house under terms of an unspoken but understood treaty. They would ignore each other.

Now, he looked down into the basket in the kitchen at Fluffy in his moment of travail. He turned to his three children who were observing and asked what was wrong.

"He just opens his eyes, but then he shuts them again," Laura said.

Raven resisted the temptation to forget the cat and to leave the house. He couldn't do it with the children looking on. "All right, we'll take him to the vet. Laura, you put him in the station wagon but keep him in the back with you. Understand?"

An hour later, they were in an examining room with the vet, Dr. Skinner.

Raven had never met him before but remembered back to the last bill he'd paid; the vet was aptly named.

"You treated Fluffy last summer," Raven said.

"Yes, that was in July if I'm not mistaken. Fluffy had an intestinal disorder."

"Yeah, I remember the bill."

Dr. Skinner smiled. "Where a beloved pet is concerned, cost isn't always that important."

Raven glared at him. "That may be the way you view it, Doc, but I hate this cat. The sooner he dies, the happier I'll be." Skinner started to interrupt but Raven held up his hand. "Let me finish. I don't want any specialist brought in, no operating rooms, no consultations with other cat doctors. The minute this fucking bill goes over thirty bucks, kill the little bastard."

"Mr. Raven, I can't believe you're talking this way. Think of your children and their love for Fluffy."

"Listen, Doc, I can get a million fucking cats off the streets in the South Bronx that never get sick. They're there every day, healthy as hell. Just remember what I said. When the bill reaches thirty bucks, whack him out because I'm not paying more. If you keep him alive after thirty bucks, he's yours. Don't even bother to call."

Raven joined his children in the waiting room. "Fluffy has to stay here a while," he told them. They were heartbroken, but he eased the pain by taking them for an ice cream soda.

They returned to the house where Raven changed into a black Turkish mohair suit, ultra-white shirt, diamond-and-gold cuff-links and an Omega watch he was particularly fond of. He ran a rag over his two-hundred-dollar Bally shoes, put on a red-and-black striped tie and checked himself in the mirror. He liked what he saw, smiled and went to the dresser where he took twenty-five hundred dollars from a pile he'd hidden beneath his shorts. He went downstairs, kissed the kids goodbye and told Joy to take good care of them.

As he drove to his parents' apartment in Stuyvesant Town, he couldn't shake the dream he'd had last night. It was highly sexual: He was in a lavish hotel room with two women. He knew them both, although the women had met each other for the first time that evening. He couldn't resurrect all the details of the dream, just knew that he woke up in the middle of the night with a throbbing erection, considered waking Mary, decided against it, turned over and went back to sleep, his hand firmly holding himself, a beautiful female face framed in honey blond hair licking him all over until sleep finally arrived.

He'd been thinking of that dream since the minute Mary woke him that morning. Raven didn't believe in psychic things, had no use for mystics and astrology, fortune tellers and psychotherapy, but he knew he couldn't dismiss the dream or, more important, the need to turn it into reality.

He was thinking of the beautiful blonde when his mother opened the door. She yelled over her shoulder, "It's Freddie, it's Freddie." She took his hands, led him into the modest apartment and said, "Come, sit, I'll get you something to eat."

"I'm not hungry, Ma."

"Don't be silly. You shouldn't get skinny, not in your job. You need to be strong."

He knew it was useless to argue with her. He sat at the kitchen table with his mother and father and pushed the food around with a fork, taking an occasional bite. He had plans for dinner later that night and didn't want to take the edge off his appetite.

After an hour of small talk, he told them he had to go. He reached into his pocket, took out a thousand dollars and handed it to his mother.

"We don't need this," she said.

"That's okay," he said. "Just hold on to it in case you do. If not, I'll take it back."

The exchange between them had happened countless times before, ever since he was old enough to begin earning money. He discovered a long time ago that his mother kept a black-and-white school book in the piano bench buried beneath sheet music. She recorded in it every cent he'd ever given her. Years ago, when his brothers Frank and Allan were in college, he paid most of their tuition bills. Frankie had attended an Ivy League school and, despite the fact that he'd managed to garner a scholarship, the cost was still high. One time, Raven had peeked into the book and saw that the amount given to his family was over thirty thousand dollars. He'd asked his mother why she'd bothered to keep such records, and she told him, "Someday, Freddie, when your brothers are rich and famous, they'll pay you back." They'd been out of college for a long time now and he'd never seen a cent, although he didn't hold it against them. Chances were they didn't even know he'd picked up so much of their expenses.

"I have to go now, Ma," he said, kissing her on the cheek. He suffered a feeling he always did when he left them, one of guilt. It was especially strong this evening because of the plans he had. If they knew that he was about to indulge himself on a grand scale with women other than his wife—the mother of their grandchildren—they would have been terribly disappointed. No matter, he told himself as he and his father walked out to the car. He was entitled to have a fling now and then, particularly when he felt the way he did about the long and arduous case he'd been spearheading. If letting it all hang out from time to time made him a better cop, then who was to question, including his parents.

He parked his car in an all-night garage in midtown Manhattan, called the Exclusive Limo Service, and told them to send a car to pick him up at the Brasserie on Fifty-Third Street in an hour.

He took a table in the restaurant and ordered pancakes stuffed with ground chop meat. He wasn't hungry but that particular dish appealed to him. "Like a goddamn pregnant woman," he told himself as he ate just enough of it to satisfy his urge.

The limo driver appeared at the top of the stairs. Raven paid the bill, got in the car and went to the Waldorf-Astoria where he registered in a three-room suite that cost $420. He checked his watch. The timetable was progressing nicely. "Drop me off at Forty-Fourth, between First and Second," he told the Limo driver.

The driver waited while Raven went into the Liberty Bar and Grill, stood for a minute until his eyes adjusted to the dim light, then went to the bar and looked around. It was still early;

the Saturday night crowd hadn't arrived. There were twenty girls drinking and dancing together. An hour later there'd be ten times as many.

The bartender was a tall, square girl with close-cropped hair. She looked at him, leaned close and said, "I'm sorry, but we can't serve you. This is for members only, *sir!*"

Raven smiled. "I'd like a dry Canadian Club Manhattan. You've got a public liquor license hanging in your front window, and if you don't give me my drink and do it with a smile, this joint is going to be a shoe store in the morning. Got it?"

The barmaid wasn't sure what to do, and her face reflected it. The manager, an older woman with a very deep voice, came to him and asked what the problem was.

"No problem. I want a drink, that's all. Superdike here says she can't serve me because I'm not a member. Since when did this joint become a club, sweetie?"

The manager said, "Well, it is sort of a private club and..."

"Listen, let's cut out the bullshit. I'm on the job. I work in the commissioner's office downtown and I want to talk to one of the girls here. That's it. I'll have my drink, have my conversation and be gone."

"Is there any trouble?" the manager asked.

"Not yet, but there will be if I don't get my goddamn drink."

The manager motioned to the barmaid to make it for him.

"Let me see you do it," Raven told the girl. He wasn't about to spend the rest of the night unconscious from a Mickey and spending the next day sitting on the John.

She put the drink in front of him. "Thank you very much," he said, picking it up and sipping it. It was good. He swung around on the stool and looked over the place. The girls were staring at him. The word had obviously spread that he was police and was there to talk to someone. It wasn't true. He was actually trying to decide which one to approach. He finally settled on a stunning brunette with a ripe figure, went up to her and said pleasantly, "Could I talk to you for a minute?"

"Gee, I don't know," the girl said, looking around for help.

Everyone stayed where they were and watched. He flashed a big smile. "Come on outside to my limo and give me fifteen minutes. I think you'll be interested in what I have to say."

She stood immobile long enough to cause him to question whether she'd bite. Then, she shrugged and said, "Okay."

They sat in the back of the limo while Raven explained what he was proposing. When he was finished, she laughed and shook her head. "You're a piece of work, Mr. Raven."

He laughed, too. "Should be fun, and call me Freddie. It's got to come off like we're old friends."

"Gotcha," she said.

He pulled three one-hundred-dollar bills from his wallet, tore them, handed her three halves. "You get the other halves later," he said.

"Great. What'll I do, wait here until you call?"

"Exactly, Jennifer. Just hang tight, it won't be long."

His next stop was a public telephone from which he called an old friend, Ernie, who owned a women's clothing firm, and who lived in a brownstone next to his shop. "Glad I caught you, Ernie," Raven said. "I need a favor."

"Shoot."

Raven gave him a list of clothing and sizes and asked him to messenger the clothing to his suite at the Waldorf.

"I'll bring them over myself," Ernie said. "What's the occasion?"

"I guess you could call it preserving the sanity of Freddie Raven. I guess you could call it a lot of other things, too."

Ernie laughed and assured Raven he'd have the clothing within the hour.

The driver took Raven to a fancy bar on Madison Avenue where he had a drink with Angie, the bartender. As far as Raven was concerned, Angie was the best barkeep in town. They'd become friends over the years, ever since Raven and Higgins had bailed him out of a tough situation with a shylock in Brooklyn. The place was virtually empty; Raven had a long conversation with Angie, and filled him in on his plans for the evening.

"You really think it'll work?" Angie asked.

"Yeah, I think it will. If it doesn't, so what? I'll shift gears, but I really think so. You know the background on her from when she used to come in here years ago."

Angie nodded. "Sure, before she married the bigshot lawyer. Best looking broad I ever saw. You never scored with her, huh?"

Raven shook his head and sipped from his drink. "No, but I sure as hell tried. Came close, but there was always that other shit getting in the way." He checked his watch, sighed and said, "Well, I'd better make the call."

"Go use the one in the office."

"Thanks," Raven said, getting up from the stool and disappearing to the rear of the lounge.

"Marta?" he said to the woman who answered his phone call.

"Yes."

"It's me, Freddie Raven. Remember?"

There was a pause on the other end before she said, "Yes, I remember. How are you?"

"Couldn't be better. How about yourself?"

"Just fine."

"How's the husband?"

"He's fine, too."

"Yeah, I keep up with you through him. I was reading this week about his being out in San Francisco handling that big case. Think he'll pull it off?"

"Probably. He's good. Freddie, why are you calling? We haven't seen each other since..."

"Yeah, it has been a long time. Well, Marta, you'll never believe this but I'm calling to ask a different kind of favor then I ever wanted from you before."

"A favor? What could that be?"

"I was going to..."

"Yes, go ahead."

"Well, Marta, it's like this. Hear me out before you say no."

"I'm listening."

"Okay, here's what it's all about. Every year the Honor Legion Society holds a big dinner dance where they give out

138

medals. It's coming up in about a month, and I was wondering if you would..."

"Are you asking me for a date? I'm married. Remember?"

"Hey, I know you're happily married and so am I. I wouldn't think of asking either of us to compromise that situation. No, I don't want a date with you.... Actually, I've never gotten over being in love with you but that's water over the dam. Let me finish. We have this dinner dance and we give out the awards, but there's also a fashion show. Every precinct puts up its own model and chooses the clothes she'll wear. Actually, we do it for the wives at the dance because being married to a cop and going to something like that can be pretty boring."

"I don't think police business is boring," she said.

Raven continued. "The midtown squads always show up with the best-looking models and clothes every year. You know, they work down here where they have the cream of the crop. I'm working up the South Bronx, a real dump, and we never get to come up with a model who wins. My lieutenant told me he's determined to win this year to give the precinct a better name. He asked me to help find the perfect model. I told him I knew her, have for years. I told him her name was Marta. He asked me to give you a call and..." Raven chuckled. "Well, that's what I'm doing."

"You want me to be a model for your precinct?"

"Exactly. It'd be a lot of fun. We're going all out this year. What do you say?"

"Freddie, I really don't know if I could even consider it. I'm not a professional model. I..."

"That's the whole point, Marta. We don't want some skinny pro walking around up there. My lieutenant told me to choose the best-looking woman in the five boroughs and... Hey, look, you know what I think of you. You make every other woman in town look like she's in menopause."

Marta laughed, said, "You know, Freddie, my husband has become very close to the commissioner. In fact, he was at his office about a month ago on business."

"Great. Bring him to the dance and maybe we can arrange it so that you and him sit with the commissioner."

There was a silence as Raven's suggestion sunk in. He was

glad she'd brought up her husband's connection to the commissioner. It should put her mind at rest. She finally said, "You know something, Freddie, I just might do it."

"Hey, that's great. Come on, I'll buy you a drink to celebrate."

"Now?"

"Yeah. I know your husband's out of town, so what's a friendly drink between old friends, huh?"

"Where are you?"

"Around the corner from you in our favorite joint. You remember what that is, don't you?"

"You were pretty damn sure, weren't you?"

"No, nothing like that. I just happened to be in the neighborhood . . . look, Marta, I have to meet my partner a little bit later. I stopped in here for old times, remembered you lived close by and figured this was a good time to call. Come on, just a drink for old time's sake. I'll tell you more about the dinner dance."

She paused. "All right. I'll be there in twenty minutes."

"Great, I'll be waiting."

He passed the time talking with Angie, and told him Marta would be arriving soon. Angie got busy with other customers, which left Raven alone to reflect a little.

He'd met Marta Wallace about six years ago—her name was Marta Syms then—and of all the women he'd met in his life, she had the most potent impact. She was five-seven, and had natural platinum hair she enjoyed wearing in an elaborate chignon.

He remembered the first time he was introduced to her and noticing that even her ears were perfect. Her face was a magnificent cameo of milky white skin stretched over bones that it would take the world's great sculptors to duplicate. Her eyes were green, her lips sensually full but in perfect symmetry with the rest of her.

When they'd first met, Marta had answered his question about what she did for a living by laughing and saying, "I suppose you could say I am nicely kept."

That didn't surprise him. She was the kind of high-class women who attracted money and power. He tried to probe into her personal life during that initial meeting but she'd been playfully discreet, making him think she was revealing herself until he realized later that he hadn't learned a thing about her. It was a talent, one of many she possessed, and he came to appreciate those talents over the course of other meetings that came about through mutual friends.

He'd bumped into her a few times in fancy restaurants— "21," the Four Seasons, places like that. Occasionally, she'd be with an expensively dressed older man, but usually was without male escort, which raised his hopes every time they met.

He'd tried hard to get her to bed but never succeeded. Then, one day, he received a call from her at the precinct. She was in trouble and needed to talk to him. They met, and she told him she was afraid she was going to be indicted as part of a multi-million dollar stock fraud a close friend of her's had gotten involved with. The man was an attorney named John Wallace. Raven knew of him—a high-roller with good connections. This time, according to Marta, his connections wouldn't do him much good and, because of her relationship with him, she was afraid that she, too, was going to be dragged in.

Raven said he'd do what he could. She expressed her appreciation, but when he tried to convince her that she could do better than words, she confided a startling fact to him. He would never forget her words, her eyes, her face when she told him, "I like girls, Freddie."

He followed through on her behalf, talked to the chief investigator into the stock scheme and convinced him to lay off Marta. John Wallace beat the rap on his own. Then, Raven was going through *The Times* one Sunday and read of the marriage of John Wallace to Marta Syms.

Raven did a lot of thinking about it, and came to the conclusion that either she'd lied to him, or had married a man who was willing to give up sex in order to have her on his arm. He finally decided that it didn't matter why anybody did anything, why Marta Syms married John Wallace. He'd given up long ago judging another's sex life.

Except... he had never been able to get Marta out of his mind. She would appear to him while he was driving through town, when he was at bat in an intra-borough softball game, while showering, slapping cuffs on a suspect or making love with his wife.

As the time approached for her to arrive, he felt his excitement level rising, and he fought to control it. He'd been planning such a night for months, playing with the pieces and wondering how he could fit them together to make it work. He finally decided it didn't matter whether it worked or not. It was like formulating and putting into action a sting operation. You wanted it to work, but manipulating the events leading up to it was the real fun, the real challenge. Like sex, he thought. You chase and chase, you score, and then you realize the chase was at least as pleasurable as the orgasm. Well, almost.

She came through the door and all heads turned. Her hair was back and up as he remembered it; her perfect ears had diamond posts in them. A full-length mink coat was open, revealing a gray cashmere sweater and lighter gray wool skirt. Her high heels were white and gray. She looked better than ever.

She spotted him, smiled and came to where he sat at a corner of the bar, extended her hand and said, "Hello, Fred, good to see you again."

He stood and looked her up and down. "Not as good as it is seeing you, Marta." He took her coat and watched as she gracefully settled on a stool. He couldn't take his eyes off her breasts; all he could think of was two puppies fighting under a blanket. Her waist was slim, her legs long and beautifully turned.

He sat next to her and asked what she'd have to drink.

"Martini, very dry, no olive or lemon," she told Angie, who'd greeted her warmly.

They chatted easily during the next twenty minutes. Raven was surprised how fast she finished the drink and asked for another. He was glad to see it. With each sip she became progressively looser, and it kept running through his mind that it might actually work.

When they'd finished the second drink, Raven said to her, "Marta, I have to make a call. Excuse me."

He went into the office, called Jennifer at the Liberty Bar and Grill and told her to go directly to his suite at the Waldorf. He filled her in on a few details, hung up, waited a few minutes, then rejoined Marta at the bar. "I just talked to my partner. He's meeting me at the Waldorf. We have a suite there. There's one of our policewomen there, too. She's in charge of coordinating our end of the fashion show this year." He raised his eyebrows as though a thought had struck him. "By the way, she has a lot of the clothing you'd be wearing. Come on, have some dinner with us and take a look."

She turned away, then looked into his eyes and said, "You know, Freddie, that I meant what I said. I want my husband there if I decide to do this."

"Of course, sure, no question about it. Come on, I have a limo outside."

She smiled and said, "A limo. You must have gotten a raise."

He withheld a comment about what had really raised on him, shifted his legs to accommodate his erection, got up, helped her on with her coat and a few minutes later they were in the rear of the limousine. "The Waldorf," Raven told the driver, inhaling the sensuous scent of her perfume. There was an instant when he considered simply jumping on her, but he resisted. If things went as smoothly as he hoped, he'd do better a few hours from now.

Jennifer opened the suite door when they arrived. Raven introduced her as Sergeant Jennifer Paul.

"Lee called and said he'd be late," Jennifer told Raven.

A few minutes later there was a knock on the door. Raven opened it. Outside was a waiter with three dinners on an elaborately set rolling cart.

"What's this?" he asked Jennifer.

"I ordered dinner for the three of us, you, me and Lee."

"Oh," Raven said. "Well, he'll just have to get his own when he arrives. Hungry, Marta?"

"Yes, I am."

Raven handed the waiter a twenty dollar bill and asked him to serve the meal. They sat around a table and enjoyed Dom Perignon champagne, goose liver paté and caviar, roast duck in a cognac sauce with wild rice and an assortment of perfectly cooked fresh vegetables. For dessert, the waiter served them ice cream with Tia Maria, and freshly brewed decaffeinated coffee. Raven handed him another ten and told him he could leave.

Raven enjoyed the dinner for a number of reasons, most of all observing what went on between Marta and Jennifer. He'd picked right—Jennifer was seductive without being overt. She flattered Marta to just the right extent, saying to Raven more than once how they couldn't lose this year in the modeling contest.

"I still haven't decided whether I'll do it," Marta said. She'd been saying that all night, but each time it sounded less convincing.

Raven stood and said he had to make a couple of phone calls. He suggested that Jennifer show Marta the clothes she'd be modeling, adding, "*If* you decide to do it." He poured from a bottle of cognac into three snifters, picked his up, raised it in a toast and said, "Here's to beating the pants off everybody else this year. Excuse me, I'll be about fifteen minutes."

He went to one of the bedrooms and left the door ajar so he could see the girls in the other room. The clothes Ernie had sent over were on a chaise lounge—mini-skirts were coming back and there was an abundance of them, along with matching tops and pantyhose of various colors. Jennifer went to the pile, picked up a skirt and held it up for Marta to see. "This is a sample of what you'll be wearing," she said.

"Where's the rest of it?" Marta asked, laughing and sipping her cognac.

"They're not really that short once you have them on, they just look short. Here, try it." Jennifer casually threw the skirt to Marta, went to her and took her drink from her hand. "Let me hold this so you don't spill it."

Marta stepped in front of a full-length mirror next to the chaise lounge, undid the snap on the side of her skirt, pulled down the zipper and let it fall to the floor. She was wearing lemon-colored briefs and a garter belt. Raven sat on a bed smoking a cigarette and sipping his cognac. "What a body," he thought as he watched her through the crack in the door.

144

Jennifer picked up Marta's woolen skirt, straightened it and laid it on the chaise. "You can't wear those things with a mini," she said, referring to the garter belt and stockings. She chose a pair of pantyhose and, before Marta knew what was happening, knelt down in front of her and started to unfasten the snaps on the garter belt. She undid the two fasteners on one stocking, put her hands on either side of Marta's leg and started to roll down the stocking. She slowly pulled it off her foot and did the same with the other leg. "There," she said. She reached up and gently took hold of the top of Marta's panties and slid them down. "Can't wear pantyhose on top of panties, can we?" she said.

"I guess not," Marta replied as she bent over to pull on the pantyhose. She put on the mini-skirt and Jennifer helped adjust it. "Now, let's see, what kind of sweater do we wear with that one?" Jennifer muttered. She selected one and handed it to Marta.

Marta took it and removed her own sweater, leaving her wearing only a bra. Raven adjusted his position for a better look. Marta tried on the sweater, but Jennifer said it didn't match with the skirt. She chose another and handed it to her. She also handed her back her cognac. Marta took a healthy drink and looked at herself in the mirror.

While she was standing there holding the drink and sweater, Jennifer came up behind and said, "I think I know what's wrong." She reached around with her left hand and cupped one of Marta's full breasts from the bottom, while her right hand came over her right shoulder and dug down into the bra. "There, that's better," she said. She then adjusted Marta's right breast, stepped back and saw in the mirror that Marta's nipples were hard and thrusting against the thin material. She went to the chaise, chose another pair of pantyhose and a different skirt, returned, knelt down behind Marta and pulled the pantyhose down. "Turn around and put these on," she said.

Marta turned and faced the kneeling Jennifer, whose face was inches from her blond pubic hair. Jennifer held the pantyhose open as Marta stepped into them. Jennifer helped pull them up, allowing her hands to linger as she adjusted them. Marta finished her drink and asked for a refill.

"Let's try a sweater without the bra," Jennifer said, undoing the catch. Marta's breasts swung free. Jennifer helped her on with the new sweater and ran her hands over it. "This one's wrinkled, it won't do," she said. She let her hands dally as they went over her breasts, then knelt down behind Marta again and pulled down her pantyhose. She felt the crotch; Marta was ready; she was very wet.

Marta, her glass in her hands, looked into the mirror. She now wore a sweater with no bra beneath it, and a mini-skirt with no pantyhose. She felt flushed. She couldn't see Jennifer kneeling on the floor behind her, but she felt her hands on her hips. She turned and faced the chaise lounge. Jennifer placed her hand on the small of Marta's back and gently pushed, which caused Marta to bend from the waist and to put one hand on the chaise. The other hand held her glass. The mini-skirt rode up, exposing her bare buttocks.

Jennifer gently placed her hands between Marta's legs and let her know she wanted them spread. Marta took a step to the right as Jennifer ran her fingertips from the top of her spine down across her buttocks and inside her legs, sending chills through Marta's body. Jennifer then ran her hands up inside her thighs; Marta could feel her hot breath on her backside.

Jennifer spread her hands on Marta's behind put four fingers on either side of her buttocks and her thumbs on her anus. She gently opened it, put her mouth to it and traced its exterior contour with the tip of her tongue. Marta moaned; Jennifer felt her muscles tighten. She withdrew her lips and applied more pressure with her fingers to expand the opening. Marta relaxed as Jennifer curled her tongue into a round, hard, straw-like position and inserted it into Marta's anus as far as she could. She withdrew it and licked the outside rim again, then moved her mouth down to Marta's vagina and began to lick it. She found her swollen clitoris and sucked it into her mouth, holding it with her teeth while her tongue rapidly flicked back and forth. She worked her way back to her anus, licking and stabbing with her educated tongue.

Marta's eyes were tightly closed. She felt the drink being taken from her hand, looked up and saw Raven standing over her. He was naked. Jennifer's tongue continued to dart in and out of her orifices and lick her clitoris.

Raven straddled the chaise and sat down, positioning himself under Marta's face. He reached down to his glass on the floor, wet two fingers with cognac and rubbed it on the head of his penis, then placed his hand on Marta's head and pushed down until her lips brushed it. She stuck out her tongue and ran it over the tip, then moved lower and began to suck. While she was doing this, he pulled two pins from her hair, allowing it to fall free over his legs and stomach. He pulled her sweater up around her neck. Her breasts hung straight down, the nipples hard and extended. He took each between his thumbs and index fingers and squeezed. She shuddered as she went into orgasm and, as he pulled straight down on her breasts, she moaned.

A finger tapped him on the shoulder. He turned and saw Jennifer. She, too, was naked. Marta's head was still going up and down on Raven's cock when Jennifer motioned for him to change places with her. He withdrew from Marta's mouth as Jennifer made a mound of clothing on the chaise, sat on it beneath Marta's face, opened her legs, put them straight up in the air, threw back her head and let it hang off the end of the chaise.

Marta started to lick Jennifer as Raven came up behind her and went into her vagina. Her sexual muscles tighted, and she came almost as soon as he entered her. He backed out, then guided his erection into her anus. She gasped, tightened around him and pumped against him until he reached his climax.

Raven went into the other room and got a bottle of champagne and three glasses. He returned and watched Marta suck on Jennifer's breasts while she fingered her vagina.

"Who wants some of the bubbly?" he asked. The women stopped what they were doing and took glasses from him.

After a few sips, Marta asked if she could try on more clothes. They all laughed. "Only this time, lets get comfortable," she said, jumping on the king-size bed. She got on all fours and looked out from between her open legs, her vagina, anus and mouth staring at Raven. "Pick a hole," she said.

He did; Jennifer mouthed another. He used every opening they possessed, and together they performed fellatio that was painful in its pleasure, one on either side of his penis, kissing each other and running their mouths up and down him. When he was about to come, Jennifer started to move her face to his ass but Marta said, "No, let me." She licked him in the rear while he came in Jennifer's mouth.

They went at it for the better part of the night. At four o'clock Sunday morning, he and Jennifer lay awake in bed while Marta slept. She should be tired, he thought. She'd had quite a workout. He motioned Jennifer into the living room. They had a drink and he gave her the other half of the three-hundred dollars, plus an extra hundred as a tip.

"You're good kid, you know your stuff," he said.

"Thanks."

"I didn't know you went both ways."

"With you it's a job," she answered. "With her it's a pleasure."

"That's some classy lady in there," he said. "She's a looker, and so are you."

"I know, I know, it's a shame I'm gay."

"Yeah, something like that."

"That classy lady in there may not be that classy after all," she said. "She has a small tattoo on her asshole."

"You're kidding."

"Why would I kid you? She has two sets of initials there, FY on the left cheek and RU on the right."

"I don't believe it," he said.

"Come on, take a look."

They walked into the bedroom where Marta was still sound asleep. Jennifer rolled her onto her stomach and Raven placed a pillow under her so that her rear end was up in the air. Jennifer spread her cheeks and they looked. Sure enough, there they were, two initials on either side of her anus, FY and RU.

Marta woke up. "What are you doing?" she asked sleepily.

"We're looking at your ass," Raven said. "What do the initials stand for?"

"Oh," she said "they're not initials, they're words."

"Words? What words?"

"They say FOR YOU."

He spread her cheeks again. With her anus used as an O, they spelled FOR YOU. She told them she'd had it done with her boyfriend while dropping acid in a New England college during her "crazy times." Raven spread her cheeks again and

148

read, FOR YOU out loud. "That's what it's there for," she said. "Use it!"

He did, one more time.

* * *

He stood outside the limo in front of Marta Wallace's apartment building later that morning.

"You're a good sport," he said.

She smiled. "Not as good as you are, Freddie. You must have spent a fortune to put that scene together. I'm flattered."

"Just getting rid of a dream, that's all," he said, shaking her hand.

"What about the modeling job at the dinner dance?"

"We'll find somebody up in the Bronx. Hope you don't mind the bullshit story."

She shook her head. "No, I never mind bullshit when it's done so well. Goodbye Freddie. Promise you won't ever call me again."

"I promise, Marta."

He phoned home before leaving the city. His wife was angry, which he expected. She told him Fluffy was ready at the vet and asked him to pick him up on his way home.

An hour later, Raven stood in Dr. Skinner's office. Skinner went to hand the cat to him.

"No, just put him in the case. We don't get along too good."

After Fluffy was securely in its carrying case, Raven asked, "How much do I owe you?"

"Twenty-nine, ninety-nine," Skinner said with a smile.

Raven returned the smile, nodded and said, "You're a class act, Doc. Here." He handed him a hundred-dollar bill, picked up the case, went to his car and put it on the front seat next to him.

"Glad you're better, you little bastard," he said.

He got a loud "Meow" for an answer.

149

Nineteen

Raven felt good when he woke up on Monday morning. His wife had begun talking to him again Sunday night; bringing the cat home healthy contributed to it.

He met up with Higgins and the other detectives at the Fiftieth Precinct at eight-thirty.

"What's first?" Higgins asked.

"First, I call that idiot D.A. up in Rockland and try to find out why his people missed the prints and stones. Why don't you check with our lab and see if they came up with an analysis."

The D.A. wasn't in his office, so Raven called Rockland County's chief of detectives and put the question to him.

His Rockland counterpart didn't seem at all embarrassed at having N.Y.P.D. detectives come into his territory and discover potential evidence overlooked by his own men. In fact, he laughed as he said, "As far as we were concerned, we had the body and we had the murderer. I still think that's the case, but who am I to get in the way of anybody else's game. We had the car towed out of that gully and right into the garage. We never even bothered dusting."

The Rockland chief's easy-going manner caught Raven off guard. He was ready to berate him, but ended up saying, "I understand. I'll keep in touch." It was obvious the Rockland detective didn't care whether he kept in touch or not. He laughed again, told Raven it was good talking to him and hung up.

Higgins said, "They'll have an analysis of the stones by four."

"Good," Raven said. "Anything new over the weekend with Ferris and O'Connor?"

Browne, who'd pulled the weekend detail with Bowers, shook his head and said, "Nothing out of the ordinary. O'Connor hung around his apartment all weekend, didn't even visit his girlfriend. Ferris spent the weekend with his family, you know, a nice together couple of days with the wife and kids. He took them all out for breakfast at McDonald's Saturday morning, took them bowling in the afternoon. They slept late Sunday, went to church and then hung around home."

Raven thought of his weekend and the irony of it. There he was, the saintly detective investigating a sex crime case screwing his brains out with two women in a plush Manhattan hotel suite while the prime suspect, Nathan Ferris, gets the daddy-and-husband-of-the-year award. He asked if anything had come out of a routine check through B.C.I. of the names in Jerry O'Connor's phone book.

Higgins answered. "There's one guy that keeps catching my attention, Freddie. He was in the book, and we have him on tape a number of times talking to O'Connor. His name's Timothy Wells."

"Any sheet on him?"

"Yeah, but only a minor one. There was a Juvenile Delinquent Card made out on him when he was fourteen. His old man came home early one day from work and caught the kid playing doctor-nurse with a local thirteen-year-old girl. The old man blew his stack, called us, and the card was written on the kid."

Raven laughed. "Every teenager gets his hands on some crotch one time or another. Big deal."

"Yeah, I agree," Higgins said, "but there's one other aspect to this Wells that maybe makes it worth checking him out. He's Catholic."

Smith and Bowers laughed. "Since when does being Catholic make you a suspect in a rape-murder case?" Smith asked.

"It doesn't, Smitty, but have you got any better ideas about what to do today?" Raven's voice had a hard edge to it, and Smitty backed off.

Raven told Smitty and Bowers to go back to the construction site in the Bronx and keep checking locations. They'd been doing that on and off over the past months without success. They'd find a slanted table but no bathroom in the building. If they did manage to find a spot with both a bathroom and table, the tiles weren't green, or something else was amiss.

He turned to Browne and Rogers and told them to pick up the tail on O'Connor and Ferris again.

"Which one?" Browne asked.

"Your choice, and change tapes at O'Connor's and the old lady's garage. We'll meet back here at five."

Raven and Higgins did a little more checking on Timothy Wells. He lived with his parents in Yonkers, drove an old car and worked in a manufacturing plant in the upper Bronx. "Let's give it a couple of days," Raven said, "no more."

They found his house and surveyed the neighborhood, then went to the plant where he worked. It was across the street from a Roman Catholic church, St. Raymond's. They put together their game plan and went to the rectory where they found the priest, Father Wilson.

"How may I help you?" Wilson asked.

"Well, Father, we're investigating one of your parishoners, a young man named Timothy Wells. He's up for a possible appointment to a city job and we're making checks of his friends and affiliations to determine whether he's of good character."

Father Wilson didn't ask for their credentials. He was a big, jovial man with red cheeks that shook when he laughed. "Oh, I can tell you that Timothy Wells is above reproach, a fine young man and faithful Catholic. He works right across the street and..."

"Yes, Father, we know," Raven said. "The problem is we don't want Timothy to know that his application for the job has progressed this far. He'd be terribly disappointed if he didn't get it, so we're doing everything we can to keep it from him. I trust you'll respect that and not mention it to him."

"Of course, of course, I wouldn't want to do anything to hurt Timothy. Yes, he is an exemplary young person. I don't think he's missed nine o'clock mass here in more than a year. He arrives at work at eight, which is earlier than he must, in order to be able to take off at nine to attend mass. That's the sort of dedication we don't see very much these days in our young people. Wouldn't you agree?"

"Oh, yes, Father, definitely," Higgins said.

"Tim became a member of this parish a number of years ago, right after his family moved to Yonkers. He was an altar boy—one of my best—and I was very flattered when he decided to enter the seminary to study for the priesthood."

Raven and Higgins glanced at each other before Raven said, "Where was the seminary?"

"Upstate," Wilson said. "I was disappointed when he dropped out, although pursuing the priesthood takes a tremendous amount of dedication and deprivation."

Raven wanted to tell the priest he knew better, but he decided to be discreet rather than valiant. He simply asked him to continue.

"Tim was doing very well in the seminary," he said. "He spoke beautiful Latin and he knew the mass as well as any of my ordained colleagues. This was when that still meant something, of course. Still, it was better that he made his decision when he did, and the experience certainly has done nothing but reinforce his devotion to his faith."

"That's certainly true," Raven said, nodding at Higgins, who returned it half-heartedly.

Raven continued. He knew the interview would fall to him because of his Catholic background. Higgins was always uncomfortable around clergy of any faith, especially Catholic. Raven asked, "What about Timothy's friends, Father?"

"I really don't know too much about them, although I can only assume they are respectable, devout young people."

"Girlfriends?" Raven asked, a hint of a smile in his voice.

153

"Girlfriends? Come to think of it, I don't know of any young woman with whom Tim has been involved. No, none that I can think of."

Higgins uttered his first words of the meeting, and Raven wished he hadn't. Higgins asked the priest what Timothy Wells talked about during confession. Wilson looked at him as though he had two heads, and Raven quickly terminated the conversation by standing, thanking Wilson and leading Higgins out the door.

"Jesus, Lee, you know what's said in confession is private."

Higgins shrugged, "Yeah, I know, but I figured I'd take him off-guard."

They checked the times for confession at St. Raymond's and discovered that two priests heard them from four until six each Saturday afternoon.

"Let's wire them," Raven said.

Higgins guffawed. "Some Catholic you are."

"I'm a cop first, a Catholic second. We'll need four bugs, two for the priests and two for whoever's on the other side of the curtain. Let's go see Manny."

They stopped by the apartment in the Bronx to pick up a thousand dollars in cash before driving to lower Manhattan where the Wireless Musical Company was located. It was run by an electronic genius, Manny Middleman. Manny had been a television repairman years ago. He made friends with a musician who asked him to design a wireless transmitter for his band. He did it successfully and found himself becoming increasingly involved in the design and manufacture of exotic transmitting and listening devices. He kept the music company as a front, but most of his money came from creating custom surveillance equipment for law enforcement officers and agencies.

Manny greeted them and took them into the back to show off his latest creation, a card table. He'd built into the center of it an electromagnet containing a transmitter. A colleague had customed-designed a deck of cards in which the ten through the ace contained a slim strip of magnetic tape. When one of those cards was dealt across the center of the table, a person wearing a small receiver on his leg would receive a mild shock, indicating to him that cards of high value had been distributed.

154

"Sensational," Higgins said. "Give us a receiver and tell us where it's being used."

"Christ, I can't do that," Manny said. "I'd get killed."

"Maybe you get killed if you don't," Higgins said. Higgins could never resist the lure of being in on a gambling scam and beating the cheaters, but Raven didn't want to upset Manny. They needed him for investigations, not to line their pockets. He told Manny what they wanted.

"No sweat, I'll make you up four crystal bugs, each one with a different frequency. I'll give you a scanner that'll pick up the one that's transmitting."

"Good enough," Raven said. "What'll it cost us?"

"Twelve-hundred."

"We only got a thousand," Higgins said.

"Good enough," said Manny. "You can bring me the rest when you pick up the stuff."

They were about to leave when Raven turned and said, "You know, Manny, maybe Lee is right. Where's this table going to be used?"

"Ah, come on, give me a break."

"Hey, Manny, no harm to anybody. Whoever's using it is raking in plenty, right? All we want to do is get some of our money back that we lay out to protect all of you good citizens."

Manny sighed. He told them that the table would be delivered to a social club on Elizabeth Street in Little Italy.

"When?"

"Next week."

"Thanks," Raven said. "Don't worry, Manny, we'll cut you in."

Everyone met up at the precinct at five as planned. Smitty and Bowers had found nothing new in the way of a location that would fit the descriptions provided by the victims. The continuing tail on Nathan Ferris had also come up with nothing.

"Where's the stone analysis" Raven asked. As he was asking it, a lab technician walked into the detectives' room and handed the report to Raven. He read it quickly, looked up at the technician, then read it again. "This is all you assholes can tell me, that they're stones?"

The technician started to say something but Raven cut him

off with, "For Christ's sake, I could give these to my kid and the first thing he'd say to me is, 'Daddy, they're stones.' Goddamn it, we're as bad as those idiots up in Rockland. I wanted to know where they came from, like a golf course or a construction site or something that would help us."

"Look, none of us are rock experts," the technician said, not bothering to mask his annoyance. "We're just cops, for Christ's sake, and if you're so fucking smart go teach college someplace." He spun around and left the room.

It took Raven a few minutes to calm down. When he did, he said to the others, "Let's find somebody who knows something about rocks."

"Kiley, in the Forty-First, has a famous brother-in-law who's a rock expert someplace out west. Maybe he would..."

"Call him," Raven said, handing Higgins the stones. "See if he can get his brother-in-law to take a look at this stuff, unofficially of course.

Raven and Higgins hung around until the other detectives left. Smitty and Bowers would pick up the surveillance on O'Connor that night, with Browne and Rogers having the night off.

Raven and Higgins had decided earlier in the day to spend some time building their arrest sheets. They'd been around long enough to know that even though they were "off-the-charts" on special assignment, it was always safe in the detective division to keep the arrest record up. Regardless of how successful you were on a special assignment, year-end evaluations placed heavy emphasis on the number of arrests you made. They'd known more than one detective who'd been dropped from the ranks because of that magic number.

They had a fast dinner, then stopped in a small stationery store where they purchased a box of poker chips. By eight that night they were at the corner of Simpson Street and Westchester Avenue, within the bounds of the Forty-First precinct. The sidewalk was jammed with prostitutes, and there was a line of cars, each driver making his own deal with one of the girls. "Looks like pussy's about to be rationed," Higgins said.

"Maybe it is," Raven said, laughing. "Well, let's get it over with."

They'd developed a system over the years of using the poker chips to determine which girls would be taken to court. It didn't matter that whoever they brought in would be released within hours. The only thing that counted was having the arrests on their record. The system worked well. The girls liked it because it spread the odds of having to take the rap too many times. They were so appreciative of the fairness it exhibited that they'd become trusting, willing informants whenever Raven and Higgins needed information from the street.

"Hello, girls," Higgins said, "Time to play poker."

Most of the girls laughed as they gathered around. The first hooker reached into the pile of chips and pulled out a red one.

"Red it is tonight," Raven said. "Come on, everybody take one."

A few minutes later, they had twenty whores holding red chips. A few of the girls had exchanged in order to make things more equitable for those who'd had a run of bad luck over the past month. The ones holding the red chips were told to be in the Forty-First squad room in time for night court, which started at nine.

An hour later, every case had been dismissed. Those who had ended up with the red chips met at a Chinese restaurant on Mott Street where Raven and Higgins bought them dinner. It was a tradition.

When everyone had been fed, they were put in cabs and sent back to the Bronx. The bill was over four hundred dollars, but Raven and Higgins always figured it was worth it. They could forget about making arrests for another couple of weeks and concentrate on the Lamps case.

Twenty

The rest of the week moved slowly. On Wednesday, Raven was called in to Lieutenant West's office and told that the chief of detectives was putting on pressure either to satisfactorily resolve the case or to return Raven and Higgins to regular duty. "It's been too long, Freddie," West said.

"Yeah, sure, but you know how investigations like this go. You hang in until somebody fucks up." Raven knew he was wasting his time giving West a lecture on investigations. He laughed, shrugged and said, "We'll put the screws on a little tighter, Lieutenant."

"That's nice," West said.

On Thursday morning, as they sat around the detectives' room in the Fiftieth, Kiley from the Forty-First called. "I got the report on the rocks," he said. "Want me to read it to you?"

"Nah," Raven said, looking across the room and motioning for Higgins to get ready to move. "We'll be down in an hour."

They sat across the desk from Kiley and read the analysis of the stones found in William Lamps's automobile. They were relatively rare, were called Zoroastrian, after a Persian prophet who lived back in 1000 B.C. The prophet's girlfriend hit him on the head with a similar rock, which accounted for it being named after him. It was mined primarily in the central states and, according to the report, was in very limited supply. The firm marketing Zoroastrian was located in Albuquerque, New Mexico—the Albuquerque Stone Company.

"Thanks," Raven said, tucking the report in his pocket.

"Hey, wait a minute," Kiley said. "If this helps break the Lamps case, I want credit. Agreed?"

"Fuck you," Raven said. "Lee and me are making a fucking career out of this case and you want credit because you sent a few rocks to an egghead relative? Bullshit."

Kiley flared up and became very animated as he told Raven and Higgins what he thought of them and of their sense of ethics and fairness. They didn't bother debating it with him. They left his office, got in the car and drove back to their precinct.

Higgins called the Albuquerque Stone Company from the Fiftieth and was connected with a Mr. Dean, who informed Higgins that he would not cooperate in any way unless the request came through proper channels. "I have an obligation to protect the identity of my people, to consult with my attorney concerning possible lawsuits and..."

"Look, Mr. Dean, all I want to know is what firms you ship rocks to in our area."

"Perhaps you didn't hear me," Dean said. "I can tell you nothing without appropriate authorization."

"Scumbag," Higgins said as he hung up. "I hope he gets cancer of the eyes."

Raven called a friend at the I.R.S. at 120 Church Street and asked if he could put them on to an agent in New Mexico. He said he'd see what he could do, but when he called back an hour later he said, "No good, Freddie. I don't know any agent that ever went from New York to New Mexico. They either kill themselves first or retire."

"Yeah, well, thanks for trying. Got any goodies down there for us?"

"No nothing you could use, but I always keep you in mind."

Raven and Higgins were always looking for some inside information that would give them a leg-up on the rich and powerful of New York. Sometimes, having that sort of information helped in an investigation, but their primary use of it was to shake down people with something to hide, to sell it to the person under I.R.S. investigation. They'd made some impressive scores over the years, including a leading political candidate once who happily paid so that he could square away his tangled tax situation before it hit the front pages.

Raven's next call was to one of his contacts at the New York City Bureau of the F.B.I. Raven's request was simple.

"I just want the screws put on this Dean so that I can get some fast information out of him on the phone."

Two hours later there was a phone call to Raven from Albuquerque. Dean now sang a different tune. "I'm delighted to cooperate, Detective Raven," he said, almost choking on his words.

"Good, Mr. Dean. What changed your mind?"

Dean laughed. "Nothing, actually, just a re-evaluation of my civic responsibility. What is it that you want to know?"

Raven told him. It took Dean ten minutes to gather the information. "We ship to four firms in the east," he said, "one in Boston, one in Maryland, one in Newburgh, New York, and another in Greenburg, New York."

When Raven got off the phone he discussed what he'd been told with Higgins, they automatically discounted the first two, then ruled out Newburgh and focused in on the firm in Greenburg, the Jason Stone Company.

"I hope they're not distributors for this shit," Higgins said. "We'll end up running all over the place."

"The only way to find out is to go up there and ask," Raven said. "Let's go."

They knew the minute they turned into the road leading to Jason Stone that they'd found the place where the rapes and the murder had taken place. The building sat back on a dirt road and was hidden by tall trees. Wooden planks led up to the front door. As they entered the building, they noted that the executive offices were to the right. To the left was a stairway leading to a cellar. Raven went to it and looked down, counted the steps, turned to Higgins and said, "Eight. Beautiful."

The president of Jason Stone was Mark Dubbin. He reluctantly agreed to see them, and when they were seated across from him in his large, sunny office, he told them that he would not be willing to talk until he confirmed who they were. They'd shown him their badges but that wasn't enough.

"Go ahead, make some calls," Raven said, pulling out a cigarette and sitting back in a comfortable leather chair.

Dubbin called the local police, who said they would confirm the identity of Raven and Higgins. A few minutes later he received the return call informing him that they were legitimate detectives. The officer on the other end of the line obviously asked Dubbin why they were in Greenburg. Dubbin told him he didn't know but was about to find out, hung up, smiled, lit a cigar, touched the grey hair on his temples and said, "All right, why are you here? How can I be of help to the New York City Police Department?"

Raven told him a little about the Lamps case and said that based upon descriptions given by former victims, it was possible that his company has been the site of multiple rapes, one resulting in murder.

Dubbin registered appropriate shock. "Would you like to see the building?" he asked.

"Exactly," Higgins said, standing. "We can't wait."

Dubbin led them down the eight steps to the cellar where there was a long wooden bench next to a steel support column. Chains were wrapped around the column. "We used to have a winch here but it was taken out years ago," Dubbin said.

At the rear of the room was another staircase. Dubbin, Raven and Higgins climbed it. It consisted of eight steps that led to a turn, and then another thirteen steps up to the second floor. The only illumination came from a FIRE EXIT sign at the turn. At the top of the stairs was a steel fire door that opened easily.

They went through the door and were confronted with a slanted wooden draftsman's table. It was covered with blueprints. On top of them was a large pair of scissors.

"Bathroom?" Raven asked.

Dubbin pointed to the opposite side of the room. Raven and Higgins looked inside. The tiles on the floor were green.

"Shit, yeah," Higgins said. There was no need to explain to each other the excitement they were feeling. After all the

161

months of searching, they'd found the place that had ruined William Lamps's life and that had been the last place Patricia Knees ever saw.

"Can we talk privately with you in your office?" Raven asked Dubbin.

"Of course."

They closed the door behind them and took seats. "Okay, Mr. Dubbin, it looks like we've found the spot we've been looking for. We have a pretty good idea who one of the murderers is, although we haven't nailed down his two accomplices. It could be anybody, even you."

Raven and Higgins observed the panic on Dubbin's face. Higgins smiled and said, "Calm down Mr. Dubbin, you're not a suspect...at this time."

"I should hope not," Dubbin said, summoning as much indignation as he could.

"We don't want anybody but you to know who we are and why we're here. If that cop from the local force calls back, you make up some story about us checking out references, whatever, but nobody is to know except the three of us. Got it?"

Dubbin nodded solemnly.

"We're going to go over this building with a fine tooth comb, Mr. Dubbin," said Raven. "I want you to tell your employees that we're from an insurance company and that we're doing a survey of the building."

"Yes, of course," Dubbin said. "My God, I can't believe it! My God!" It was something he would say many times over the course of the next few days.

Raven used Dubbin's phone to call Bowers at the precinct. He told him they'd found the location, but that he was not to share that information with anyone except Lieutenant West and Chief Bratten. "The fewer people who know, the better," Raven said. "And don't call us here."

"Got it, Freddie. Hell, looks like we got the break, huh?"

"Yeah, maybe."

They left Dubbin alone for an hour while they went to a local McDonald's for a fast dinner.

"Should we bring in the lab boys for prints?" Higgins asked.

Raven shook his head. "With all the activity goin' on in there everyday they won't find shit. Maybe later."

When they returned to Dubbin's office, he was on one of two telephones in his office. He quickly hung up when they entered. Raven noticed that the phone he'd been using was a single instrument, nothing like the large phone bank on his desk that contained multiple lines and buttons for automatic dialing, conference calls and other marvels of the electronic age.

"That your private line?" Raven asked.

Dubbin was visibly nervous. He forced a laugh and said, "Yes, yes, it is as a matter of fact."

"Give us the number and we'll use it when we have to get ahold of you," Raven said. "Anybody else have the number?"

Dubbin shook his head. "No, not even the wife and kids. I like to leave it completely free to make outgoing calls."

Raven and Higgins were thinking the same thing, that Dubbin was lying. They'd be willing to bet anything that it was the line he used to talk to a girlfriend. Raven made a mental note to throw a tap on it in the morning. You never knew.

"Okay, let's get down to business," Raven said. "I'm going to mention some names to you, Mr. Dubbin, and if any of them ring a bell, let me know."

"All right."

Raven reeled off the names of other detectives. "Jim Barrett?"

"No."

"Harry Squires?"

"No," Dubbin said.

He went through another three names before he said, Nathan Ferris?"

There was no hesitation on Dubbin's part. "No," he said in the same voice he'd used previously.

"Frank Cuesta?"

"No."

A few more detective names, then, "Timothy Wells?"

"No."

Raven continued throwing names at him, including Jerry O'Connor, but didn't receive a single affirmative answer.

They walked with Dubbin through the building, checking doors and locks. Every door had multiple locks, and there was an electronic security system. Raven figured that whoever came into the building at night had to use three keys—two for the locks on the front door and one to deactivate the alarm.

"Has this alarm gone off recently, say in the past year?" Raven asked.

"No, not that I know of. I don't think we've had a report on the alarm going off for at least five years."

"I need a set of keys for this front door," Raven told Dubbin.

"Well, the only ones I could give you right now belong to me and...no, I do have a spare set in the office." He disappeared, then returned moments later with the extra set. Raven handed them to Higgins and said, "Let's check these against O'Connor's."

Before leaving, they reminded Dubbin of the importance of keeping their investigation confidential. They also asked him to check with the alarm company to see when it had been installed and whether the keys had ever been changed. If they had, that would fix a time frame that would save them a lot of effort. They also asked for a copy of his telephone bills for the past two years to see if anyone had called the suspects from the plant. Like most corporation presidents, Dubbin didn't have any idea where to find the answers but promised he'd have them by the following morning.

As they were leaving, Higgins turned and said, "Does the name William Lamps mean anything to you?"

"Lamps? No, I can't say that it does," Dubbin replied.

"Yeah, well, thanks," Raven said, shaking Dubbin's hand. "We'll see you in the morning. I'm glad you leave that private line open. It may be necessary to get through to you quickly.. Have a good night."

They stopped in for drinks at Sebastian's Bar-and-Grill, drank too much and decided to stay at the apartment instead of going home. They made calls to their respective wives, got to the apartment at midnight and set the alarm for seven. Neither of them fell asleep quickly. The excitement of their discovery wouldn't allow it.

Twenty-one

They called Dubbin at nine and told him they wouldn't be there until noon. "We need a private office for a few days," Raven told him. Dubbin assured him there'd be no problem.

Earlier that morning, Raven had called a black detective from the Forty-First, Joe Marshall, and told him he needed a fast favor. Marshall complained that he'd been up late on a case and that Raven had woken him, but he finally agreed to meet at ten at a diner. "And bring Jenkins with you," Raven said.

When Raven and Higgins walked in, Marshall and Jenkins were seated in a booth and were on their second cup of coffee. Jenkins was a small, wiry man with a full head of tight curls that bordered on red. He was dwarfed by Marshall, who sat across from him and who'd barely managed to squeeze into the booth. Marshall had been a high school football star and was building a big reputation at Grambling College when a severe knee injury wiped out his hopes of a career in the NFL. He'd had trouble passing the N.Y.P.D. physical, and Raven knew that the knee played havoc with him at times, but Marshall never let on. He was tough; Raven had always enjoyed working with him.

"Hello, Nigs," Higgins said as he and Raven slid into the booth.

Marshall laughed, shook his head, looked at Jenkins and said, "Look what we got here, Mr. Jenkins, New York City's finest." He turned to Raven and said, "How come you got me out here so early in the morning, Freddie? You know us spooks only come out at night."

"Yeah, I know," Raven said, slapping Marshall's massive arm. "Like I said, Joe, we need a favor."

Jenkins said, "Shit's up, my man. There's panic on in the streets and we're almost dry ourselves."

Raven shook his head. "We don't need shit this time, we need a hand with a case we're working on and I figured you two junkies could help."

"Do I owe you one, Freddie?" Marshall asked.

"Every day goes by I don't hit you in the knees with a bat means you owe me one, Joe."

A waitress served them coffee in stained mugs. It didn't matter; it tasted good. As Higgins and Jenkins listened, Raven filled Marshall in on what he needed. When he was through, he asked, "Will you do it?"

Marshall looked at Jenkins. "What do you say, Paul?"

"I don't mind. Shit, I used to do that for a living."

* * *

They swung back by the Fiftieth and met with Bowers. Raven told him to continue to monitor the tapes on Ferris and O'Connor for the next couple of days while he and Higgins worked Jason Stone. "Make sure we know right away if either of them get a call from somebody up there."

Raven then called his friend, Leon, who ran Audio Spectra Sound on Madison Avenue at Fifty-Seventh Street. After small talk, he ordered from Leon a Kodak Analyst camera with a night vision device attached to it. The camera cost almost four hundred dollars, and Raven agreed to rent the night-owl infrared unit for three hundred a week. "Do me a favor, Leon, and deliver everything to an apartment in the Bronx." He gave Leon the address. "There's a super downstairs who'll take it in. I'll send you the money tomorrow."

The camera Raven ordered had been developed specifically for surveillance work. It used ordinary movie film but would shoot it at a frame a second, at almost any speed desired up to ninety seconds. With a ninty-second interval between shots, a roll of film would last for days. Although Raven assumed that none of the trio who'd been involved in the rapes would dare use Jason Stone again after what happened to Patricia Knees, he felt it was worth the investment to monitor the front door and put it on film. As he often said, "You never know." Higgins didn't always agree with Raven's tendency to spend money on the off-chance it would produce something in an investigation, but he'd learned a long time ago not to buck his partner. Too often, Raven's extravagance paid off.

Dubbin set them up with a private office, and gave them each a set of blueprints to carry during their trips around the plant to give the look of being on official business.

They talked to Jason employees and learned that the alarm system had been installed more than fifteen years ago, and that the keys had never been changed. At least no one could remember a change.

Later, they sat in the office provided by Dubbin and went over Jason Stone telephone bills covering the past two years. No calls had been made from there to either Jerry O'Connor or Nathan Ferris.

At two that afternoon, Dubbin handed them a list of all previous employees. It was a lot longer than either Raven or Higgins had anticipated, and they knew that they had a long job ahead of them. Each name would have to be run through B.C.I to check for previous records, and they would have to try to match up names on the list with entries taken from O'Connor's telephone book.

"Let's go back to the apartment and get started," Raven said.

Higgins looked around the office and said, "Why?" This is nice."

"I'd just as soon get out of here," Raven said. "We'll order in Chinese again later."

They spent the rest of the afternoon in the apartment drinking vodka and going over the lists. The Kodak camera and night vision device had been delivered, and Higgins spent time playing with it while Raven called for the food. They put on the Six O'Clock News and watched as they ate. Nothing caught their attention until the newscaster said, "Next, the gangland killing of Salvatore "The Barber" Marrone in the Bronx, but first, this message."

They waited until the announcer came back on with the Marrone story. He'd evidently been taken for a ride, shot four times in the head and dumped just inside the Bronx line. There were no witnesses. The newscaster briefly summarized Marrone's career in the organization. He'd risen rapidly from his teenage introduction into the mob to a position close to the top.

Raven turned off the TV and said to Higgins, "I have an idea, Lee. Get on the phone and see who's catching the case."

Higgins made the call, hung up and said, "They gave it to Bubba."

"Great," Raven said. He picked up the phone, tracked down Bubba and asked him what was happening with the Marrone murder.

"Nothing, Freddie."

"What did he have on him?" Raven asked.

Bubba took a moment to find a list, then read it to Raven.

"No phone book?" Raven asked.

"No, I don't see no phone book."

"Bubba, I want you to do me, and us, a favor. No matter who calls you for the next twenty-four hours, you tell them you don't know if there was a phone book or not."

"Why do I do that?"

"Bubba, just do what I say, okay?"

Bubba, who was not known as the brightest detective in the precinct, paused for a long time before saying, "All right, Freddie, but don't fuck me up, huh."

"Trust me, Bubba. Just don't tell anybody that there wasn't a phone book on Marrone. Tomorrow, you can tell the fucking world, but give me some time."

"What's up?" Higgins asked after Raven hung up.

"I figure we could use a little more scratch," Raven said.

They stopped at an all-night newsstand and bought a small looseleaf address book for $1.50, then went to the boro office where they went through files in search of high-rollers in the organization who lived in the Bronx. They took turns listing them on appropriate pages in the address book. Once that chore was done, they drove to the country club area of the Bronx, parked in front of an impressive house, went to the door and knocked. A woman answered.

"Good evening," Raven said. "We're here to see Rick."

Rick Langone appeared behind his wife. He wore a powder blue cashmere robe and he carried a glass of cognac. Langone ran a couple of very successful businesses in the Bronx, but his ties to organized crime were no secret to law enforcement officials. He knew Raven by sight. He smiled and asked, "What's up?"

"We just wanted to talk with you a few minutes, Rick, nothing important."

Langone screwed up his face in thought before saying, "Come in." He told his wife to make them some coffee. "Feel like some good Italian food?" he asked.

"No, coffee will do," Raven said. "We just ate."

"You guys should eat at dinner time." Langone said. "It's not good for your health to eat at odd hours."

When the three of them were alone in Langone's large, handsomely furnished den, Raven said, "Rick, I assume you heard that Sal-the-Barber got whacked tonight."

"Yeah, I saw on TV. No big surprise."

"Yeah, I know. I guess the surprise was that they dumped him in the Bronx."

Langone laughed. "Just returning lost property, I guess. Why do you care? What's it to me?"

Raven looked at Higgins, then said, "We rolled on the call right away. When we got there, he had a small address book in his hand."

"Yeah? So?"

"It was opened to this page." Raven handed it to Langone. He'd opened it to the "L" page.

Langone peered at it, and Raven and Higgins could sense his discomfort. When he didn't say anything, Raven asked, "How do you explain this, Rick?"

"Why should I have to explain it? Shit, why would he have my name in his book? I don't even know the guy, for Christ's sake."

Raven shrugged and took the book from Langone. "Look, Rick, I'm not here to answer those kinds of questions. All I know is the guy gets four in the head and before he dies he opens his address book to this page. I hate to tell you this, Rick, but I figure it'll raise some questions downtown."

Langone started pacing the den. "Damn it, I've been home all night," he said. "You can ask my wife."

"Come on, Rick, you know what your wife says doesn't mean a fucking thing. Look, let's not waste more time. Go upstairs and get dressed and we'll go downtown together."

Langone backed against his desk and held up his hands as though Raven and Higgins held a gun on him. "Hey, fellas, come on, this is bullshit. You know I didn't kill Marrone. I'm a businessman. I don't do killing. I've got nothing to do with those guys."

Raven said, "Yeah, Rick, we know all that, but facts are facts, and we're paid to act on them. We got there first and walked away with this book with your name in it. But, let's talk a little more. Maybe we can work something out."

Rick's wife brought them coffee and left. Fifteen minutes later, Langone handed Raven an envelope containing five thousand dollars. Raven thanked him, tore the page out of the book and gave it to him.

"You guys are nothing but..."

Higgins spun around and fixed Langone in a stare that would melt rock.

"Jesus," Langone muttered as he walked them to the front door.

"Much obliged, Rick," Raven said. "Please say goodnight to your wife. She makes good coffee."

They made other stops that night. By morning, they'd collected slightly more than thirty thousand. It was largely in hundred dollar bills.

"Not bad," Higgins said as they drove to the precinct to find Bubba. He was leaving; they walked him to his car. Raven handed him Langone's envelope with the five thousand still intact.

"What the fuck's this for?" Bubba asked.

"Nothing. We spent the night trying to shake some information out on Marrone but we came up a zero. If anybody calls from now on, you can tell them whatever you want about Marrone having a phone book. Thanks, Bubba. Buy yourself a bottle and a good broad."

Twenty-two

They caught a few hours' sleep on Saturday morning before installing the bugs in St. Raymond's confessionals. The job was finished by two that afternoon. Higgins did the actual installing. Raven stood watch.

They had lunch at Joe-and-Joe's Restaurant on Bruckner Boulevard and were back in front of the church by 3:45. Higgins manned the radio receivers and tape recorder in the back of the truck while Raven slid into a pew and watched the steady succession of men and women arriving to bear their hearts and souls to the two priests hearing confessions that day.

Timothy Wells showed up at 5:30 and went into booth Number Three. Raven quickly left the church and joined Higgins in the truck. They listened together as Wells said, "Bless me Father, for I have sinned. It's been one week since my last confession."

"Yes, my son."

"I've been rude to my parents."

"Yes, go on."

"I've been guilty of impure thoughts."

"Yes, my son."

"I committed an act of impurity on myself, Father, self-abuse."

"How many times, my son?"

"About six or seven... I don't remember exactly."

"What else, my son?"

"That's all, Father."

"For your penance, say ten Hail Marys, and make a good Act of Contrition," said the priest.

"Oh, my God, I am heartily sorry for offending thee..."

As Wells continued with his prayer, Higgins mumbled to Raven, "Jesus Christ, twelve-hundred fucking dollars to hear that he beat his meat six times this week. I can't believe it."

After Wells left, they continued listening to other confessions, and ran their own unofficial poll. Adultery was clearly the first-place sin, with homosexual relationships a close second. There was one case of incest. The father of a teenage daughter told the priest of his continuing sexual advances to her. When the priest started to point out how serious was his sin, the father became defensive and said that if the story of Adam and Eve were true, then somebody way back must have been making it with his own children.

They argued back and forth, with the priest finally asking the man if he were there for the forgiveness, or for an argument. They continued the discussion until the priest, in an obvious fit of anger, said, "Knock it off with your daughter and don't ever come back here and tell me you've done it again."

Higgins and Raven were impressed with the priest's forthrightness. Higgins laughed and said, "The ways things are going with parents and kids these days, incest'll be a thing of the past."

Raven looked quizzically at him. "Why do you say that?"

"Because you don't fuck somebody you're not talking to."

They continued to listen until the last confessor had been forgiven by the priests. They decided that masturbation had become the number one sport in America, based upon the past two hours.

They waited until seven before slipping into the church and removing the bugs, then decided to stop for a drink and a fast dinner at Joe-and-Joe's before splitting up and heading home.

Higgins continued to moan about the lack of information that had come out of the confessionals. The only positive note, as far as he was concerned, was overhearing the intimate sexual confession of a good-looking blonde. Higgins had watched her leave the church and jotted down her license plate number. "I've got to check her out," he told Raven.

"Don't waste your time," Raven said. "I gave up on Catholic girls a long time ago."

Higgins laughed. "You're married to one."

"Yeah, that's what I mean," Raven said.

"I think you're nuts," said Higgins. "I scored with one a couple a months ago. I picked her up at LaSalle Steak House and went home with her."

Raven waited for another comment. When it didn't come, he asked how it went.

"Good. Sure, she started all this shit about how I wouldn't respect her tomorrow."

"What did you say?"

"I told her I didn't respect her now, that I didn't have to wait until morning. When she kept it up, I told her to sleep until noon so she wouldn't have to worry about how she felt in the morning."

The first person they saw when they walked into the restaurant was a former detective, Big Al. Al had been overweight throughout his career as a detective with the N.Y.P.D., and retirement had only caused him to balloon up even bigger. They joined him at the bar and bought him a drink.

Joe-and-Joe's was a popular hangout for cops, and the owners went out of their way to accommodate their whims and needs. A row of four pay phones on a back wall was a good example. Of the four, three had Out-of-Order signs on them, and detectives who were catching cases left the numbers with the precinct in case they had to be reached while drinking and eating.

They killed their first drink and ordered another. The waitress, Theresa, asked if they wanted to order dinner.

"Yeah, but make sure we get clean silverware and dishes," Higgins said. Higgins had a phobia about dirty dishes in restaurants, which always tickled Raven. Higgins had no problem falling into bed with every woman he met, but restaurant dishes were another ballgame.

174

Big Al sipped from his drink and then started to cough and wheeze. He turned beet-red and was on the verge of passing out when he finally managed to control it.

"You okay?" Higgins asked.

Raven slapped Big Al on the back and said to Higgins, "You think this is bad? This son of a bitch was always choking when I worked with him." He turned to Al and said, "Remember that time we had the jumper down on Charlotte Street?" To Higgins: "Al and me take the call and when we get there, there's this banana up on the roof of a six-story building threatening to jump. The street's full of people screaming, 'Jump... Jump... Jump.' There's a bunch of uniformed cops in the street and one of them says to the others, 'Everybody relax now, the detectives are here.'

"Al tells wise-mouth to fuck off and we go in the building, start up the stairs one flight at a time, with Al stopping at every landing and coughing and choking like he's about to die. I tell him to stay down and I'll go up and take it, but he tells me to fuck off and says we'll just take our time.

"We finally get to the roof and we stand looking at the dude who's weaving back and forth on the edge. You know what Al says to me?"

Higgins shook his head.

"Al says to me, 'Let's not rush this guy. He's full of shit, putting on a show. There's two things you got to remember with a jumper. One, when they mean it they always jump in the backyard, never the front. Two...

"It looks to me like the guy is about to go. Then, Al yells at him, 'Hey, José, cut the shit, we're on lunch hour and if you're going to jump, jump now or forget about it.'"

"So?" Higgins said.

"So, the guy takes one more look at us and goes off the edge, six floors down to the sidewalk. While he's going down, the crowd gives a cheer like he just scored a fucking touchdown. You know what happens then?"

"No."

"Al turns to me and says, 'The second rule with a jumper, Freddie, is never to listen to an old detective.'"

Higgins started to giggle, which sent Big Al into a spasm of laughter that soon turned into what everybody at the bar was sure was a terminal attack of choking. But, as usual, he pulled himself together and was soon on his next drink.

They hung around until ten, when Raven announced that he was heading home. "I've got company coming over tomorrow," he said.

"Yeah, so do I," Higgins said.

"I could do without it," Raven said, getting up and throwing money on the bar. "All I want to do is sleep."

"So, sleep," Al said.

"If I cancel them and spend the day sleeping, I'll end up with a kitchen knife in my throat."

"That's the trouble with all you young assholes, you're all pussy-whipped," Al said.

Raven and Higgins left the bar, neither of them defending themselves by pointing out that Al's approach to married bliss had cost him three wives.

* * *

Nathan Ferris had been called into work on Saturday and, much to his annoyance, found himself working into the evening. Finally, when he was told he could leave, he grumbled all the way to his locker where he changed clothes, then stepped out into the night to pull the Willis Jeep into the company parking lot. He went to where he'd parked it on the street across from the plant and was about to unlock the driver's door when Detective Joe Marshall, dressed in shabby street clothes and wearing a red bandana around his head, stepped up behind, held a knife to Ferris' throat and said, "Give me all the shit in your pockets, mother fucker."

To Marshall's surprise, Ferris brought his right elbow into Marshall's gut and grabbed his wrist with strength that Marshall would later term "scary." Ferris's attack was so swift, and the power exerted so great that Marshall was about to have the knife turned on him when Jenkins, dressed in an old army fatigue outfit, stepped up behind Ferris and cold-cocked him with the butt of his gun. As Ferris fell, the knife caught him behind the right ear and left a two-inch gash.

Marshall and Jenkins quickly emptied Ferris's pockets. Jenkins took his key ring and made quick impressions of the keys in the soft, pink putty-like substance used by dentists to take impressions of teeth. They kept the wallet and watch to make it look like a robbery, threw the keys on the ground and disappeared into the shadows.

Marshall called Raven at home later that night and reported that the mission had been accomplished.

"Good," Raven said. "Bring the impression in Monday morning."

"Right," Marshall said.

"Are there any alarm keys on that ring?"

"Nope. Just regular keys."

"Thanks, Joe, I owe you one. I'll lay off the knee for another week."

Twenty-three

Raven's dinner guests Sunday evening were the Goldbergs and the Lucianos. Elliot Goldberg owned a record company with his in-laws, and was about to make a move into the motion picture business. Sal Luciano headed up his own advertising agency and, based upon the lifestyle he and his wife, Vera, led, didn't know what to do with the money. The same could be said for Elliot and Roz Goldberg. A year ago, Roz wanted to throw a lavish New Year's Eve party at their house but complained that there wasn't enough room. Elliot called in the contractors and had an addition built that was bigger than the original dwelling.

They were neighbors. As Elliot Goldberg said to his wife after first meeting the Ravens, "Sure as hell is an eclectic neighborhood."

Their housekeeper, Joy, had fed the kids in the kitchen earlier in the evening. Now, as Raven and his guests sat at the dining room table, the sound of feet running from bedroom to bedroom upstairs, and voices arguing about which of the three color television sets had a better picture, prompted Raven to tell Joy, "Go shut them up. Tell them that if they don't knock it off, all three TV's are going out the window."

Raven said to his guests, "When I was a kid living in the city, my father brought home a wind-up phonograph. Me and my brother saved enough to buy two records, Gene Autry singing *Rudolph the Red Nosed Reindeer*, and Frankie Laine singing *Mule Train*. We played those two records over and over until they were almost worn out. We never got to that point, though, because one day, my old man, who was fed up with hearing those songs for six straight hours, threw the records and the phonograph out the upstairs window." He laughed. "These kids today wouldn't know what to do if the electricity ever got turned off."

Vera Luciano mentioned a story that had been in the papers that morning. A child had vanished on Staten Island while playing next to a pond, and local police were in the process of dragging the bottom in search of the body. Mary Raven looked at her husband and said, "Tell them about the time that kid up in the Bronx disappeared and you and the whole department worked three straight days to find him."

"Ah, that was a long time ago and..."

"Come on, Freddie, tell us," Sal Luciano said.

"All right... Me and my partner were working days and a call comes in from some people on Fox Street who claim they saw a little colored kid get tossed out of a fifth floor window. They said some guy picked up the body and disappeared around the corner.

"Whenever a little kid is missing or is in trouble, we pull out all the stops. The whole precinct gets into the act. Emergency Service was brought in, helicopters with bull horns were used, nothing spared. My partner and me take part in a door-to-door search that expands block by block. We were the ones who went up to investigate the apartment that witnesses said they thought the kid was thrown out of. It's empty. The window facing the street is open. We ask around and nobody knows who lives there. Everybody tells the same story, that a dark kid

179

comes down five stories, hits the street with a splash, is picked up and disappears. We've got every cop in the city out looking for the kid with no success.

"This goes on for two days. Nobody ever shows up at a hospital, and whoever lives in the apartment never shows.

"The next day we're sitting in the squad room and this dirty old guy walks in. We ignore him for awhile, but then my partner asks him what he wants. He tells us he's there to report his missing chimpanzee. My partner laughs and tells me to take the statement, so I do. While he's telling me about it I realize that the address he gives me is the same place on Fox Street where the kid was tossed out the window. I question him a little bit and I nail down that he's the one who lives in that apartment."

Everyone had a sense of what was coming, and the laughter started, low and gurgling at first but building as Raven completed the tale.

"This is the story I get out of this old coot. He says he lives alone in that place and spends a few days every week at his girlfriend's house. He says a couple of days ago he pays his cousin, who's a junkie, to feed the chimp while he's with his girlfriend. While he's gone, his junkie cousin and his girlfriend decide they need a fix real bad, so they plan to steal the chimp and sell him. They try to get him out the door but he hangs in the doorway with all four feet planted. He won't budge. Then, the chimp gets nasty and starts biting and clawing, so the junkie tells his girlfriend to go down to the street and he'll throw the chimp to her through the window.

"She's standing on the street and sure as hell, the chimp comes sailing out the window, only he misses her and hits the sidewalk. Splat! The junkie comes downstairs, picks up what's left of the monkey and the two of them disappear.

"My partner and me get ahold of the junkie cousin and he admits he did it. We ask him where they took the chimp and he says they sold him to a restaurant in the neighborhood. We go to the restaurant, talk to the owner, and he takes us in the back, opens the freezer and there's the frozen carcass of the chimp. I asked him, 'What the fuck did you buy a dead monkey for?' He looked at me like my elevator doesn't reach the top floor and says with a straight face, 'It was only five bucks. Where the hell can you buy a monkey for five bucks?'"

180

By now, everyone at the table was helpless with laughter. Raven, who hadn't broken even a hint of a smile, concluded with, "Typical New York City police case. A million bucks spent to find a goddamn frozen ape."

Joy served dessert, and Raven told her, "Take the rest of the day off." As she left the dining room, he yelled after her, "Sleep late."

The six of them settled in the den where they sank into six cushioned leather chairs around a Florentine marble coffee table. Raven served everyone another drink, and a relaxed feeling of general contentment washed over the room.

Raven asked Elliott how the record business was coming.

"Great," he said, "we've got this big one that's grossed over a half-million in two weeks. Eighty percent of it will stick. It's a real monster."

"How about you, Sal, how's business in the world of advertising?" Raven asked.

"Couldn't be better, Freddie. We just got done designing a label for a big soap company. We did all the research on what colors make people grab for one box over the other and it looks like we scored. We struck a deal with the soap people that's unique. We waived our fee in return for a piece of the profits over a certain amount. The way that soap is selling, I wouldn't be surprised over the course of the three-year contract if we don't make a big score on it."

Now, Elliot and Sal asked Raven how things were going with the N.Y.P.D.

Raven looked at Mary, smiled, and said to his guests, "Things are going real well. With any luck, I'll be up to sixteen grand a year by December."

"Everyone laughed. "You are one funny son of a bitch," Elliott said.

"Yeah, I laugh every time I see my check," Raven said.

They started reminiscing about when the Ravens had first moved into the affluent neighborhood. The developer had built fifty homes on top of a rise overlooking a lake, and the Ravens bought one of three with the best view.

Initially, Raven took great pains to not let his neighbors know what he did for a living. Then, six months after moving in, his picture was on the front page of a couple of New York City newspapers, with the headline, *MURDERER?* It stemmed from an incident in which Raven killed someone in self-defense, but the neighborhood got up in arms and accused him of racism, and brutality. As it turned out, Raven was exonerated, and he and the P.B.A. sued the newspapers for libel. They won, although the judge knocked their eighty-five thousand dollar verdict down to six cents. A big moral victory, but no cash. From that time, of course, everyone in Raven's community knew his occupation.

It was Elliot Goldberg who leaned forward, winked and said in a semi-serious voice, "I know we've talked about this before, Freddie, but I still don't understand how you can live the lifestyle you do on a cop's salary."

Raven laughed. "I told you before, Elliot, that I take what I consider calculated financial risks."

Elliot's wife, Roz, who tended to espouse liberal philosophies without ever seeing the irony of those philosophies when viewed against her capitalistic lifestyle, came up with her usual line: "This has nothing to do with you, of course, Freddie...we all love you...it's just that...well...you see, there's always that question of public servants receiving extra money."

Raven came back with his usual line: "You mean graft."

"I wouldn't call it that..."

"I would," he said.

"I'll make more coffee," Mary Raven said. She knew what was coming, the speech from her husband for Roz Goldberg's benefit, and it always made her uncomfortable when he laced into her.

"Look, Roz," Raven said, "one of these days I'm going to get through to you and everybody like you."

"Here we go again," Elliot Goldberg said, loving it.

Raven continued: "You can't name one profession where 'tips' aren't part of the game. Name one to me that doesn't accept 'graft.'" When she didn't respond, he said, "The Vatican hid Nazi war criminals and sent them on to South America for money. Guys who are supposed to seat you in a restaurant give you a better table for ten bucks. You throw money at the garbage men for Christmas so they won't walk past your trash the next year; you tip the postman so he'll deliver your mail and you lay heavy dinners and gifts on bank officials when you're looking for a loan to finance a new business."

He looked at Elliot, who was sitting back in his chair, a large smile across his face. Raven said to Roz, "Look at your husband, for Christ sake. The word 'payola' was invented for him and his business. You make it sound like anybody puts on a uniform—a cop, or a doctor in his white coat, or a priest in his black robe—is suddenly supposed to not be a human anymore. You think once you put a robe on a priest he doesn't need money to eat and he never gets an erection?"

"That's different," Roz said.

"Bullshit it is," Sal said.

Raven nodded at Sal in appreciation of his support, then continued with Roz. "You take an average guy, you put him in a blue suit, give him a gun and a badge, make him take a dumb oath and send him on the street. This guy comes out of a shitty neighborhood where he had to scramble for money from the opening bell. He manages to finish high school and becomes a cop. How many college grads do you see coming on the force? The guy gets married like everybody else, has a couple of kids and all he can do is hand them a picture of him in his uniform and a copy of the oath and tell his wife to take them down to the grocery store and pick up whatever she needs. Forget it. I need money to run my family just like you need money to run yours, Roz."

Elliot now came to a halfhearted defense of his wife. He said to Raven, "I know what you're saying, Freddie, but I think the real question is how do you get away with it?"

"Get away with what? I'm part of a system, which is no different from any other system. There's no sense owning a Cadillac if you don't have the money to gas it up. What are you saying, Elliot, that I should take whatever money I make on the side and bury it in the backyard so nobody knows? I'm supposed to live in a junkie neighborhood and eat lousy food? Look, Roz, like I've told you before, the P.D. is a bureaucracy like every other bureaucracy. It all runs on paper and oaths. They put every cop in an impossible position and then hope we'll act like knights on white horses.

"I'm walking down the street and I spot this junkie. If I push him up against a wall, search him and find junk in his pockets, they send him back onto the street because it was an illegal search. That's the kind of bullshit legal system we have.

So, you learn. I spot the junkie, I pull out my little memo book that every one of us has to carry to list everytime we take a leak, and I note that when the junkie saw me walking toward him, he took out a glassine envelope containing a white substance and threw it into the gutter. I note in my little book that I picked it up and discovered that it contained cocaine. I arrest him. I go into court and they ask me questions, and I take out my fucking little memo book and I read from it. What's in that book becomes the truth because it's on paper, just like every other stupid goddamn organization. The junkie is convicted instead of being set free. I feel better and there's another scumbag off the street."

"Yeah, but I still don't understand *how* it works," Elliot said, hoping to head off his wife's inevitable nasty comment about the corruption of modern society.

Raven laughed and finished his drink. "When I came into the department, they asked me how much money I had. That's standard. You fill out a statement of net worth. I told them I had a quarter of a mil in cash, stocks and Treasury notes. They asked me where I got so much money, and I told them I married a rich broad. Nobody checked, and as far as they know I scored with a wealthy bitch."

Mary Raven had just returned to the den and said, "There I was, a rich girl and I didn't even know it."

Raven shook his head. "Sure, it shouldn't have to be that way but that's reality, goddamn it, and who the hell am I to change reality? I'll tell you this, though, I am the only cop who ever takes money on the side. I have never known any other policeman who has ever accepted cash from outside sources."

Everyone broke up. "Come on," Sal Luciano said.

Raven raised his hand and looked toward the ceiling. "I swear on my children's eyes."

"But what if some official asks you whether *you've* ever taken graft?" Luciano asked.

Again, the raised hand and eyes rolled toward heaven. "I told you, I married a rich woman."

Mary Raven served coffee, but everyone seemed to prefer another drink. When they'd been served, Raven, who was on a roll, continued. He kept the focus on Roz Goldberg, who was becoming increasingly aggravated at his attack upon her, her face set in a tight angry expression, her fingers drumming on the side of her glass.

Raven brought up a young politician running for local office for whom Roz Goldberg had been donating lots of volunteer time. He said, "Let me ask you about that schmuck you think is so wonderful, the one who's running for office. I read the other day he's spending two hundred grand to get into a job that pays twenty-grand a year, with a Cadillac thrown in. Right?"

"Yes, but..."

Raven looked at Elliot. "Tell me that last time you invested two hundred grand in a singer who you knew was going to return you twenty thousand."

Elliot laughed. "That would be dumb."

Raven turned to Sal Luciano. "What about you, Sal? When's the last time you spent two hundred grand on an advertising campaign and only billed the client a tenth of that?"

"We get the point, Freddie, we get the point," Luciano said.

Raven returned his attention to Roz Goldberg. "You tell me you aren't goofy, Roz, when you vote for a guy whose arithmetic is so screwed up he'll spend two hundred grand to make twenty. It's all bullshit. He knows he'll get ten times his investment back his first year in office because he'll take it on the side, under the table, anyway he can."

Roz drew herself up into a haughty posture in the chair and looked away.

Raven winked at Elliot before saying, "Hey, Roz, just one more question. Where does your friend get the two hundred grand to run for office?"

She snapped her head back and looked at him with the zeal of someone who has just been given an opening. "His family is very rich, Freddie," she said with triumph dripping from her voice.

"Yeah, I know, and do you know where that money came from?"

She started to say something about being in the construction business when Raven cut her off. "Your friend's old man was one of the biggest bookmakers in Brooklyn years ago. They say he made millions from it, and now his son is going to become the voice of the people. The fact is his old man knew people and served them better making book then this shitty-ass son of his ever will."

He turned to Mary. "Hey, babe, where's the fresh coffee?"

Twenty-four

Before heading for Jason Stone on Monday morning, Raven got ahold of Nathan Ferris's report of his Saturday night mugging. He described his assailants to the police as both being black, with one being very big. He judged him to be in his mid-thirties, and gave a description of what he was wearing. He claimed the loss of his wallet, a ring, a watch and $178 in cash.

A comment he made during his interview at the precinct was noted. "If there was only one of them, I would've stuck a knife up that nigger's ass until it came out his ear." There was an additional note that Ferris would review mug shots at a later date.

Raven tossed the report to Higgins and smiled contentedly. "Maybe we should have had Joe waste him," he said.

Higgins grunted and dropped the report on the desk. "We'd damn well better do something, Freddie. I said the other day we could always whack Ferris and deep six him."

"Yeah, but what good does that do us? All we get is a piece of shit off the streets but it doesn't save Lamps, and it doesn't nail the others. The same goes for setting him up for a narc bust. He pulls fifteen in jail and leaves us with the same problems."

Higgins vented his pent-up frustration by kicking a metal wastebasket across the floor toward Raven. "Like I said, Freddie, we have to move fast or these guys are going to walk, which means a lot of other broads might get their asses killed."

Raven rubbed his eyes. He was hung over from his house party the night before, which hadn't broken up until four a.m. He'd been on the verge of nausea ever since he got up, and what he really wanted to do was go to the apartment and sleep for eight hours. He forced himself out of the chair and said, "Let's go. I told Dubbin we'd be there by eleven."

They went directly to the office Dubbin had given them. They'd hooked up a small portable cassette recorder to the tap on Dubbin's private line. The recorder had been modified to give up to eight hours of recording time. It was also voice-activated, which meant the tape rolled only when someone spoke on that phone.

"You listen, Lee, while I go talk to Dubbin," Raven said.

Mark Dubbin greeted Raven cordially, but he had the look of a man whose nerves were frazzled. His secretary brought them coffee. Dubbin settled behind his desk and asked Raven if there were anything new on the case.

"No, not really, Mr. Dubbin, but we're getting ready to make some moves. Let's go over again who has keys to this place."

Dubbin sighed. They'd been over that territory before. He pulled out a list they'd made during one of their earlier meetings and scanned it. "No, I can't think of anyone else to add to this."

"You said there was no night janitor," Raven said.

"Yes, that's right. Harry only works days. You talked to him."

"Uh, huh."

"As I told you, Mr. Raven, I can't imagine that anyone who has keys to this building could be involved in something as heinous as rape and murder."

188

"Yeah, but when you've been in my business as long as I have, you don't make assumptions about anybody." He deliberately fixed Dubbin in a hard stare, which caused him to look away.

"My partner and I have gone over those lists of previous employees you gave us. They go back almost ten years. This place has been in business a lot longer than that. I want to go back even further."

"I'm not sure we keep records going back any further, Mr. Raven. There really isn't any need to, legally, I mean."

"I know that, Mr. Dubbin, but maybe there are some old records laying around someplace, like in personnel or payroll. See what you can do for me."

"All right. Will you be here the rest of the day?"

"Probably. We'll be in the office."

"I hope everything is to your satisfaction there."

"Yeah, it's fine."

Raven rejoined Higgins. The minute he was through the door, Higgins said, "Hey, Freddie, listen to this."

He rewound the tape, checked the digital counter until it had reached the point he wanted, then pushed the "Play" button.

It was a conversation between Dubbin and a woman.

DUBBIN: Carla?

CARLA: Yes. I've been waiting for your call all day. (She sounded angry; her voice was covered with frost.)

DUBBIN: I'm sorry, but I've been involved with a nasty situation that has me very upset.

CARLA: What is it, Mark? Can't you tell me?

DUBBIN: No, they said I couldn't.

CARLA: Who's they?

There was a long pause and an audible sigh from Dubbin.

DUBBIN: They're... police from New York City.

He proceeded to tell her everything that had transpired since Raven and Higgins arrived.

"Cocksucker," Higgins said.

189

CARLA: That's terrible. Are you in trouble?

DUBBIN: No, of course not, but I don't like having them around. They're crude and not too smart. Typical cops. They think the murder and rapes might have been done by somebody from here. My God, the publicity would be dreadful.

CARLA: Poor baby. Why don't you come over here and let me relax you. You sound so tense.

DUBBIN: Yes, maybe... no, I really had better get home. I promised Jane I'd take her to the movies tonight.

A long, pointed silence on the other end.

DUBBIN: Carla?

CARLA: Mark, when are you going to realize where you should be coming home to at night?

DUBBIN: Let's not get into that again, please.

CARLA: Call her, Mark, and tell her something came up. You need *me* tonight.

Higgins and Raven both knew that Dubbin was going through the internal debate that every man with a mistress faces.

CARLA: Mark, when you called, I had just come out of the bath. I'm sitting here in that white negligee you bought me, the one you always ask me to wear because you think it's sexy. Mark, I'm taking it off now. I'm naked underneath.

There was the rustling of a garment being removed. Her voice became more breathy. "There, it's off and I'm nude now. I put your favorite perfume on just a few minutes before you called. I put it between my breasts where you always like to nestle your face.

"Oooooh, I can feel you there now, that little rough stubble of beard as you move back and forth and I hold them tight against your cheeks. I put some on my belly and between my legs, too, You always love the smell of me when you lick my sweet pussy."

She let loose with a long, passionate whine. "Oh, Mark, I want you between my legs. I have my hand there now. My finger is rubbing it, Mark, but I want it to be your finger, your tongue, your cock..."

It worked. Dubbin said he'd call his wife, make an excuse and would be there within the hour.

Higgins shut off the tape recorder and said, "Goddamn it, Freddie, I'm horny as hell. Maybe we should tell Dubbin we know about his broad and go over and interview her. She sounds great."

Raven shook his head. "Let's not fuck things up. Anything else on that tape?"

"No."

"Dubbin is trying to find records that go back further on previous employees."

"I think we're wasting our time going that route."

"You got any better suggestions?"

"You're the so-called genius in this case. You think, and I do the shit work."

Raven sat back in his chair and closed his eyes. I'm beat."

They both closed their eyes and were about to doze off in their chairs when Dubbin knocked.

"Come in," Raven said.

Dubbin entered the office and handed them a sheaf of papers. He noticed the recorder on the desk and his eyes widened.

"How far back do these go?" Raven asked, not bothering to make a move to remove the recorder.

"Another four or five years," Dubbin said.

After Dubbin was gone and had closed the door, Higgins laughed. "He looks like she did him good," he said. "Do you figure he pays for it?"

"Ever know anybody who didn't, one way or the other? Let's forget about her and start going over these names."

They split up the pages and wearily began checking each name for some recognition factor. Later, of course, the names would be run through B.C.I., but now they could only silently wish that a name would pop out at them that would make it all worthwhile.

A half-hour later, Raven said in a voice that was almost inaudible, "Lee."

It took Higgins a moment to realize he'd been spoken to. He looked up, rubbed his eyes and said, "What?"

"It's here."

"What's here?"

Raven slowly, deliberately slid a piece of paper in front of Higgins, and ran his index finger down the list until it stopped at a name in the middle of the page.

Higgins's eyes opened wide and he leaned forward as though to affirm what he was seeing. "Ferris," he said.

"Yeah, Nathan Ferris worked here."

They immediately went to Dubbin, who took them upstairs to the personnel office where an elderly woman sat behind a battered desk. Her name was Agnes, and she'd been friendly.

"Thanks, Mr. Dubbin," Raven said, his voice indicating that he would be just as happy if Dubbin left. The president got the message and departed.

"Agnes, we're interested in this person." Raven pointed to Ferris's name on the list.

She looked at Raven over half-glasses and asked pleasantly, "What does he have to do with your insurance survey?"

Raven had to make a decision whether to admit to her their real mission at Jason Stone. He thought for a moment, leaned close and said, "Agnes, you have been the most cooperative and helpful person at Jason Stone, and I want you to know how much we appreciate it." He glanced around, then said, "Can I let you in on a little secret?"

"Yes, of course you can. I'm very closed-mouthed. All my friends say so."

"I'm sure you are, Agnes. The truth is that this particular person might have been involved in an insurance fraud that cost Jason Stone some money years ago. If we can prove it, and if you help, there's a sizable reward for you."

"Oh, my goodness. That would be... how much?"

"A thousand. Maybe two."

"Oh, my, that would be wonderful." Now she leaned even closer and asked in a conspiratorial voice, "What did he do?"

"Well, Agnes, I really don't want to get into that now. All I want to know is why Mr. Ferris seems to be included on this particular list. It seems to be different from most of the others we've looked at."

"Well... I've been wondering why you have been looking at all the names of past employees. It must be exciting."

"What?"

"To be working as an undercover insurance investigator. My nephew, Harold, is an adjuster with a big insurance company. Maybe you know him."

"Probably not, Agnes. Okay, why is Nathan Ferris on this list?"

She adjusted her glasses on her aqualine nose and wrinkled her brow, looked up at Raven and said, "Oh, yes, this was when we were working two shifts, one during the day and one at night. Business was very good then and we needed to be producing around the clock. Do you see this little code next to Mr. Ferris's name?"

Raven squinted. "Yes."

"That means Mr. Ferris was the foreman on the night shift."

"It says here that he didn't last long, only about eight months," said Raven.

"That's right. We only ran a night shift for eight months, and then Mr. Dubbin let everybody go."

"I see. You say he was the foreman. That would mean he probably had keys to the building."

"I imagine so. All our foremen have keys."

"Of course," Raven said, standing and smiling. He looked directly into Agnes's eyes and said, "I think you've earned at least part of that reward."

"Just for telling you what I did?"

"Yes." He snapped his fingers at Higgins and said, "Lee, how about giving Agnes half of the reward right now."

"Five hundred?"

"Yeah, on good faith. You have that much, don't you?"

"Yeah, but..."

Raven snapped his fingers again and Higgins handed Agnes five one-hundred-dollar bills. She was speechless.

"Agnes, it's very important that you not mention this to anyone, and that means anyone," Raven said. "Not even Mr. Dubbin. Understand?"

"Yes. All my friends tell me how good I am with a secret."

"That's fine, Agnes. Thank you very much."

They returned to the office. Higgins asked, "What do we do now?"

"I think it's time we stopped bullshitting around, Lee, and made our move on these guys."

"Based on what? We don't have prints that'll stand up in court. We can't prove that this place is where it happened, even though we know it is, and we have no hard evidence against any of them."

"And chances are we never will," Raven said. "I think the answer is all-out war. Lee, I think it's stick-it-up-their-ass time."

Twenty-five

They met that night with the four other detectives working on the Patricia Knees case—Jones, Browne, Smith and Bowers. Raven chose a Chinese restaurant for the meeting instead of the precinct station. What he was about to do wasn't in the police procedural manual, and he didn't want anybody killing the idea before he had a chance to implement it.

"We're moving on Ferris, O'Connor and Wells tomorrow," he said after everyone had stuffed themselves with General Tso's chicken, Sha-Cha beef, roast pork, shrimp in lobster sauce and a dozen other dishes.

"Jones and Browne pick up Wells tomorrow. Do it quietly and don't tell him more than you have to. Keep everything vague—he's being brought in for questioning, but don't tell him what about."

Raven looked at Bowers and Smith. "You guys grab O'Connor."

"Where do we bring them?" Bowers asked.

"To the squad room. Get them there by noon. Lee and I will handle Ferris."

Smith wiped up the remains of a brown sauce with his fingers and licked them clean. He asked, "Have you guys come up with something hard on them to make it stick?"

Raven shrugged and motioned to a waiter to bring more tea. "If we wait for the hard stuff, the three of them'll piss on our graves. No, we're going to play a little game I learned a long time ago from Big Al. Just trust me and bring them in."

The next morning, Raven and Higgins waited for Ferris to leave his house. He came out on time, got in his red Plymouth Fury and headed down the street, with Raven and Higgins falling in behind. They followed him for a few blocks. "Now?" Higgins asked.

"Might as well," Raven said. "Let's not take a chance with this guy, Lee. We know he's the one—he's got nothing to lose. He only burns once. If he makes a move, waste him. Remember, this cocksucker lifts four-hundred pound air-conditioners. I'm in no mood to get tossed into traffic."

Raven drew a deep breath and said, "Let's move."

Ferris stopped at a traffic light and Raven pulled up next to him. Raven tapped his horn. Ferris looked at them. Higgins held up his gold shield and motioned for Ferris to pull over. Ferris scowled, then drove on to a grass strip.

Raven and Higgins approached Ferris's car from either side, Raven on the left, Higgins taking the passenger side. "Detectives," Raven said, his hand wrapped securely around his revolver.

"What's the problem?" Ferris asked through his open window.

"No problem. Just turn off the motor and put your hands on the wheel. We want to talk to you."

"Why?"

"Because I said so," Raven said.

Ferris looked at Higgins, then back at Raven. He said nothing; his face was filled with defiance.

Raven slowly shook his head, then said, "Look, motherfucker, the game is over. We both have thirty-eights just dying to go off in the direction of your head. Now. if you think you can outrun a bullet, be my guest, but my advice is to turn off the fucking motor and get out of the fucking car."

Ferris again looked toward Higgins, who leveled his revolver at Ferris's ear.

Ferris narrowed his eyes and took a series of short, rapid breaths. His hand went to the door handle and he slowly opened it. Raven stepped back, his gun drawn. Higgins had come around the rear of the car and positioned himself so that there was no chance of Raven being caught in a crossfire.

"If he moves too fast, hit him," Raven said.

"You got it," Higgins said.

Raven instructed Ferris to place his hands on the hood of the car and to spread his feet. They patted him down for weapons, found none, then cuffed him through his belt with his hands behind his back.

Higgins gave the car a quick search, locked the doors and wedged the keys underneath the rear wheel. They put Ferris in the back seat of their car, drove to a phone booth and called Lieutenant West. Raven described the car to West, gave its location and asked that a unit be dispatched to pick it up.

Ferris asked a few questions as they drove to the precinct, but each received a terse reply from Higgins, who sat in the back with him, his gun resting comfortably on his lap and pointing toward Ferris's gut. "Shut up," was all Higgins would say, and eventually Ferris fell into a sullen, angry silence.

They entered the squad room and went down a hallway leading past a series of small interrogation rooms. Raven made them pause long enough in front of one room in which Jerry O'Connor sat in a straightback chair. Ferris saw O'Conner but didn't indicate it.

The same happened when they paused in front of Timothy Wells's room.

They led Ferris into an empty room. Raven slammed the door and said, "Strip."

"What the fuck do you...?"

"Strip, Goddamn it, or I'll give you an extra hole up your ass."

"What is this all about? I want my lawyer!" Ferris said.

"Look, Ferris, I am in no mood to play games with you,"

Raven said. "Take off your clothes so we can make sure you're clean. Then, you can put 'em back on."

Ferris grumbled as he removed his clothing. Raven made him stand in the middle of the room with his legs spread wide apart, and they patted him down again, checking every possible area where he could conceal a small weapon. When they were satisfied, they told him to get dressed and to sit.

Ferris seemed to decide there was nothing to be gained by belligerence. He softened his approach and asked politely, "I would sincerely appreciate knowing why I'm here."

Raven took a chair across the table from him, smiled and said in an equally courteous voice, "You are here, Mr. Ferris, because we are getting you ready to go to prison for the murder of Patricia Knees."

His directness triggered Ferris back into anger. "I want a lawyer! This is crap!"

Higgins, who'd been standing behind Ferris, said, "What do you think we are, Ferris, fucking children? You're a scumbag who thinks he can go around shoving his dick up every girl he sees and get away with it."

Ferris turned to see Higgins, but Higgins slapped him across the side of the face and snarled, "Keep looking forward. Keep looking at my partner. My partner's a nice guy. I'm not. You turn around one more time and I'll use a lead pipe."

Ferris sat motionless in his chair, his eyes locked on Raven.

Higgins came around the other side of the table and stood next to Raven. "Name?" he asked. Ferris said nothing.

"Name?"

"I want my rights, goddamn it. I got rights," Ferris said.

Higgins stood over Ferris, looked down for a few seconds, then brought his right fist up from behind, catching Ferris on the side of his face. Ferris's head snapped back as though he'd been shot, and he barely managed to keep from falling off the chair. As he straightened up, Raven, who'd come around the other side, hit him with a right uppercut that sent Ferris and the chair sprawling.

Ferris lay on his back, his eyes blazing like a trapped animal, his thick lips pulled back over his teeth. He was stunned, but not out.

"Those are your rights," Higgins said. "You want lefts?"

They pulled him to his feet and put him back in the chair. Raven said, "Okay, Ferris, we're going to start over again. The next time we get a wise-ass answer, we're taking you into the back room to give you some good, healthy exercise." He was referring to what was known as the "Decompression Chamber," where difficult prisoners were, as the saying went around the precinct, "gently persuaded to be cooperative."

"Name?" Higgins said.

"Nathan Ferris."

"Address?"

Ferris gave it.

Higgins and Raven asked him routine questions for ten minutes. Then, Raven said, "Got enough, Lee?"

"For now."

They went to the door. Raven turned and said, "Okay, Mr. Ferris, you just sit tight here awhile." They stepped into the hall and closed the door behind them.

"Who do we do next?" Higgins asked.

"It doesn't matter," Raven said. "Let's take a quick shot with both of them. One of them may turn. You never know."

They went into the room in which Jerry O'Connor was being held. Higgins said, "You have anything to tell us?"

"About what?" O'Connor asked. "What are you talking about? Why am I here?"

Raven sat on the end of the table, which put his face only a foot from O'Connor's. "O'Connor, we don't have much time to play around here today with you or your freaky friends. Your ass is in big trouble. That's number one. Two, murder is fine as long as you don't get caught. Point three, you got caught. Point four, the first one of you guys who talks nice to us and tells us what we want to know gets the big break. Point five, the other two of you assholes take the weight. Can you add?"

O'Connor hung on every word, his mouth opening a little wider with each point. He gulped hard, closed his eyes, began to weave in his chair and said, "I'm going to be sick. I need a bathroom."

Raven and Higgins knew he was telling the truth. They took him into a lavatory where he threw up for ten minutes.

They had a uniformed officer stand outside the bathroom door while they went to see Timothy Wells.

"Hey, kid, the game is over," Raven said. "I'm sure you have a lot to tell us."

Wells expressed the same confusion and disbelief as O'Connor.

Raven looked at Higgins, shook his head and let out an exaggerated sigh for Wells's benefit. He sat on the edge of the table and said in a quiet voice, "Wells, you three shitheads have been arrested for murder and rape. Up until now, it was all fun and games shoving golf balls and sand up girls' twats, but now it's going to be the other way around. You, the raper, are going to become the rapee. You ass is going to be so fucking sore once all the horny lifers get ahold of it in prison that you'll probably slit your wrists. You understand what I'm saying, kid? A nice-lookin' young fella like you is prime meat in prison, filet mignon. You walk in there that first day with that cute little ass of yours twitching and..."

"My God, my God," Wells said, tears forming in his eyes, "what are you talking about? I didn't do anything to anybody."

Higgins started to say something but Wells stopped him with, "I want to talk to Nathan."

Higgins and Raven looked at each other. They were making progress. At least the kid admitted knowing Ferris.

Raven's instincts told him that they would get further with Wells by exhibiting a little kindness. He pulled up a chair while Higgins stood by the window. Raven touched Wells's arm and said, "Tim, we don't think you were the guy that killed that girl up at the Jason Stone place, but you were there, and that can make you as guilty as the one who actually did it. I don't want to frighten you, Tim, but I do want to be honest, for your sake. Jail is bad enough, and that's where you'll end up, but we know what a devout young man you are and...well, I suggest you think about your soul burning in Hell for all eternity. That's worse than jail. Jail stops when you die, but Hell's in business forever."

Wells was trembling now, and openly sobbed. Raven didn't say anything for a minute, then touched his arm again and said, "You're not like them, Tim. If you help us, it will go a long way toward not only easing the legal trouble you'll be in, but it will cleanse your conscience. I know that's important to you."

Wells could barely speak, but managed to say, "I want to talk to Nathan and Jerry."

Higgins came up behind. "No, you talk to us."

"Please, let me talk to them."

Raven started again to play on Wells's emotions when Higgins caught the kid with a solid right to his temple. He fell sideways off the chair and his head hit the floor.

"I got no patience with this God bullshit," Higgins screamed at Wells, who had pulled himself into a fetal position, his body heaving.

"Hey, calm down," Raven said.

"Bullshit," Higgins said, kicking Wells in the ribs.

Wells started to scream, which caused Raven to wince. The door opened and Lieutenant West stepped into the room. "What the hell are you doing to him?"

"Nothing," Higgins said. "He was tired and said he needed a nap."

Raven, Higgins and West left Wells on the floor and went into the hall. "Go easy," West said to Raven. "Don't fuck this up. I know what you're up to and I'm not going to interfere because I figure it's the only way to resolve this thing, but don't blow it."

"Sure," Raven said. He tapped Higgins on the arm and motioned him toward Ferris's room.

Ferris had obviously heard Wells's screams. His face had lost some of its hostility and his eyes moved rapidly between the detectives. Raven pulled up a chair, turning it backwards in case Ferris decided to kick him in the groin, smiled and said, "Okay, Ferris, we're going to give you a second shot. The way I figure it, all you guys ever wanted to do was to get laid. I don't think you intended to kill Pat Knees, and there's a difference between wanting to kill somebody and having it happen by accident. You tell us what we want to know and we'll work with the D.A. to see if we can get you a break. An accidental death is no big deal. Cooperate with us and you'll probably be back on the street before you know it."

"I don't know what you're talking about," Ferris said. "This is a real screw-up." His face indicated that he wondered whether he'd said something that would send Raven and Higgins into a rage again, so he quickly added, "I don't mean you guys screwed up, I mean there is some mistaken identity here. Believe me, I don't have any idea what you're talking about. You got the wrong person."

Raven rolled his fingers on the back of the chair and chewed his cheek before saying, "Would it help you to understand, Ferris, just how much of a case we have against you? We've got your fingerprints on the car. We know about when you worked at Jason Stone and the keys you have to the place, and how you took the girls there. We know everything about you, Ferris, what time you go to the bathroom, the fights you have with your wife, the works." Raven paused then continued, "You wouldn't be here if we didn't have our case already, but I'm always interested in saving the taxpayers some money. There's no sense in a long, drawn out trial when the only thing that will result from it is you getting life instead of a chance to cop a plea and get off easy. I'm being straight with you now, Ferris, but I only have a limited amount of patience."

Higgins jumped in and said, "Guys like you always amaze me, Ferris. Your two buddies in there are already crying like babies and pointing fingers at you. What the hell are you going to do, sit here and be Mr. Macho Man, the strong silent type? Do you know what that'll get you, Ferris? You'll go to the chair and they'll skip out because they were helpful. That's the way the system works, Ferris, and people who don't understand that and won't go by the rules are the ones who get burned every time."

A half hour later, Ferris still maintained his innocence.

"Bring in a tape," Raven told Higgins.

Higgins returned with a portion of tape they'd previously selected for just this occasion. He turned on a tape recorder and the small room was suddenly filled with Ada Ferris's voice. She was on the phone with the local grocer, and they were arguing over whether that day's food order was worth a fuck, a suck, or both.

Ferris's face reflected shock.

"We've got miles of tape like this, Ferris, of your wife humping the whole town," Raven said. He told Higgins to shut off the recorder, then said, "I just don't understand assholes like you. Your wife is the town oink, goes down on everybody—the mailman, the black gas station guy, even a twelve-year-old kid who lives up the block from you. You hang around with two losers, O'Connor and Wells, who spill their guts out because they're perfectly happy to see you end up dead, but you still sit here doing everything you can to fuck yourself up." He paused, then asked, "Want to hear some more tape?"

Ferris shook his head.

They left Ferris again and conferred in the hall. "That got to him," Higgins said.

"Yeah, I know, I almost thought we had him, but he's tough. It'll take a little longer."

Raven said the minute they walked into O'Connor's room, "That does it, O'Connor. You could have saved yourself a lot of grief by telling us you were the one who killed the girl."

O'Connor started to say something but Higgins cut him off with, "You never should have waited for your buddy, Ferris, to break the news. You're dead."

O'Connor turned white and mumbled, "I didn't kill anyone."

"It doesn't matter what you say anymore," Raven said. "Ferris has agreed to testify against you. He's the smart one of this trio. He'll walk. You go up for life."

"I swear, I swear, I never killed anybody in my life," O'Connor said, breaking down and crying.

"Fuck you," Higgins said. "The D.A. is on his way over to take Ferris's statement. Once he does, bye bye baby." Higgins added a laugh.

O'Connor stood and yelled, "I didn't kill anybody."

"No?" Raven said. "Who did?"

"I don't know. I don't even know why I'm here."

Raven shook his head and chuckled. "Boy, oh boy, oh boy," he said. "I hoped it wouldn't come to this. We have a new rule in the department that's a bitch to follow, but I have to do it if I want to keep my job. We have an obligation not only to explain to you your rights, but to explain in detail what happens when you go to prison. The way it works is...ah, shit, I just don't feel like doing this. Lee, you do it, huh?"

Higgins grumbled to indicate his displeasure at being handed the task, then took the chair that Raven vacated, rubbed his eyes, drew a deep breath and said, "When you go to the electric chair, Mr. O'Connor, you start in a special cell. They keep you there for as long as necessary. Sometimes they let you out an hour a day, sometimes not at all. A lot of guys think about killing themselves in there but you can't because there's always a TV camera on you, and the guards never take their eyes off you. You just sit and stare at the door that leads to the death chamber. You probably will have lots of time to look at it because your lawyer will go through all the appeals he can, which means maybe you'll live for years, just sitting there and looking at that fucking door.

"The day of the execution, they take you from the cell and put you into a preparation room, just you and a couple of friendly guards. They treat you pretty good because they know what you're facing. They shave the hair off the top of your head, then they shave your ankles and tape wet sponges on your head where you now have a bald spot, and on your legs. This is where it gets tough, because those guards who have to lead you into the chamber have their jobs on the line. Once you're all taped up with the sponges, they stand you up and they give you three or four hard shots in the kidneys, maybe kick you in the balls a few times. That's so you won't give anybody trouble when you walk through the door. They like executions to be dignified.

"Then, they pull down your pants and put a rubberband around your dick so tight you couldn't piss if you wanted to. Next, they bend you over and shove three pounds of cotton up your ass so that you won't dirty yourself when the two thousand volts hit you in the chair."

Higgins continued with his detailed description of what happens once the condemned is strapped into the chair. He told O'Connor about smoke coming out of the top of his head, about how his body would involuntarily strain against the intense pain that he would feel until the electricity had finally done its job, how...

He didn't get to finish because O'Connor cried out and started throwing up all over himself and the table. Raven, who'd managed to jump out of the way just in time, muttered, "Shit, I almost got my suit dirty." He and Higgins opened the door and looked back at O'Connor, who continued to retch. They closed the door and told Bowers, who was standing outside, to get somebody to bring O'Connor a mop and a bucket so he could clean up after himself.

They went to Timothy Wells's room. Raven said, "Well, Tim, that's it, Nathan and Jerry just told us that it was *you* who killed the girl. Frankly, I can't believe it because you come off to me like a nice kid, not somebody who would hurt anybody, but it's not my job to pass judgments. They've confessed and both have agreed to testify against you, which means they'll get a light sentence while you go to the electric chair... while you go to Hell."

Wells went to pieces. He leaped up and ran for the door. Higgins caught him, spun him around and threw him across the room. Wells fell to the floor screaming at the top of his lungs.

Lieutenant West opened the door.

"He's still napping," Higgins said.

West gave them both a look to reinforce what he'd said earlier, spun around and went up the hall at a brief clip.

Raven and Higgins conferred about their next step, and decided to put two of the suspects in a room together, a room that was permanently bugged. They chose Ferris and Wells, and sat them down side-by-side at a long, scarred table. They immediately left them alone and went to the listening post.

WELLS: "Oh my God, what have you gotten me into?"

FERRIS: "Shut up."

WELLS: "I can't stand this. I'll never be able to..."

FERRIS: "Shut the fuck up, Tim, or I'll shut your mouth for you. Don't say another goddamn word, just sit there and keep your mouth shut."

Ferris's warning obviously impacted on Wells. There was silence from the room for the next forty minutes.

Raven and Higgins discussed their next move. They both knew that unless they could get one of the three to give a full confession, they were losers. Ferris, O'Connor and Wells would walk free, never to be bothered again, and William Lamps would stay in jail for the rest of his life.

"I don't see anything else, Freddie, except to use bats on them."

"No, that won't work. Ferris is tough, and he knows that if they just keep their mouths shut they'll beat it. He's got Wells scared enough to go along with him, no matter what we do, and O'Connor the same. Let's do what we discussed the other night, bring in the ringer."

Higgins screwed up his face and said, "Jesus, Freddie, I just don't think it'll work."

"It worked once before. I know because I was there. What do we have to lose."

"I guess you're right," Higgins said. "Goddamn it, I'm tired. I don't care if they do walk. All I want is a vacation and a good broad."

Raven laughed and slapped his partner on the back. "Sounds good, Lee, but just think of how much nicer it'll be knowing that all this bullshit has paid off and that these pricks will be on a permanent vacation."

Twenty-six

They drove to Guido's Restaurant on Arthur Avenue. Raven ran inside; Higgins stayed in the car with the engine running.

Raven reappeared a few minutes later, jumped in the passenger seat and said, "He's at the club."

When they entered the social club a few blocks from Guido's, twenty card tables were fully occupied. They went to the rear of the room where a heavyset man with a swarthy complexion, pendulous jowls and menacing black eyes sat with three other men. He wore an expensive black silk suit, buff tie and a white-on-white silk shirt.

"Winning, Carmine?" Raven asked.

The man's name was Carmine "Boom Boom" Vasillio. He grinned and said, "Yeah. You guys here to play cards?"

"Just want to talk to you, Boom Boom," Raven said as he and Higgins pulled up chairs. They waited patiently until the hand was played out and Vasillio hauled in his winnings. He motioned to a man standing along the wall to take his place at the table, got up and led Raven and Higgins into a back room. His physical bulk wasn't as evident while sitting. Now, as Raven and Higgins walked behind him, the width of his shoulders and thickness of his neck reminded them that Carmine Vasillio had no peer as a mob enforcer. He'd also had a stint as an actor, appearing in small roles in gangster films over the years, courtesy of a Los Angeles studio head with mob connections for whom Vasillio once worked as a bodyguard.

The room was slightly larger than a closet. Vasillio closed the door, turned to face them and smiled a crooked smile, causing a long, deep scar down the side of his left cheek to join with the corner of his mouth. "What?" he asked.

"We need a favor, Carmine," Higgins said. "Nothing big, but we figured you were the one who could do it."

Raven said, "We need somebody exactly like you, somebody with your thespian abilities to help get some scum off the street."

"Go on," Vasillio said.

Twenty minutes later, Raven and Higgins finished explaining what they needed. Vasillio ran thick fingers with manicured nails up and down his tie and frowned. Finally, he said, "Yeah, all right, I'll do it. What's in it for me?"

"What do you mean?" Raven asked.

"How much?"

Raven said pleasantly, "You're being greedy, Carmine."

Again, the crooked smile from Vasillio as he said, "All right, you don't got to pay cash, but you owe me one."

"Fair enough," Raven said. "Hell, we'll square the account right now. Your girlfriend's phone has been tapped for months. Now that you know, maybe you won't shoot off your mouth with her the way you have been."

"Bullshit," Vasillio said. "Everybody tells me my phones are tapped, so what else is new? I don't have a girlfriend. You still owe me."

Higgins shook his head. "Carmine, your cunt's name is Wanda Cheniniski, Polish, residence 455 Belmonte Avenue, Apartment 3C. The tap is in an old, locked dumbwaiter in the basement. Everytime you're with her you mouth off, enough to put a lot of people away and to have you put to sleep at an early age."

Raven chimed in with, "Last month, you lost ten grand betting the spread with your bookmaker. You want to hear more?"

Vasillio asked, "Who's got the tapes?"

"We do," Higgins said. "We were going to turn them over to the D.A. but..."

"Yeah, yeah, I know, so we're even, but I'm pullin' the fucking tape machine out now."

"Sure, go ahead. As soon as you give an Academy Award performance for us, the tapes get burned."

Higgins grumbled as he and Raven got in their car. "What the fuck did you blow the wire for, Freddie? We didn't have to give him *that*. It took me a lot of work to put that wire in."

"So, what's the difference?" Raven said as he started the engine and joined the flow of traffic. "Now we've got a hundred and ninety-nine taps instead of two hundred. Big deal."

Raven was told as he and Higgins walked into the precinct that a man had called twice but wouldn't leave a name.

"Yeah, thanks," Raven said. He told Bowers and Smitty to put Nathan Ferris by himself in a room at the rear of the interrogation area. The room had a special use; a vent linking it to an adjacent room had been removed years ago, which meant that conversations in one room could clearly be heard in the other. There were times when having a suspect overhear a conversation was productive, and this might be one of them, Raven decided.

They waited until Ferris had been in the room for ten minutes, then went into the adjacent room, sat down and started to discuss the Patricia Knees murder. A phone on the small table between them rang. Raven let it ring another five times before picking it up and saying, "Raven." Although the person on the other end said nothing, Raven conducted a one-way conversation, making it sound as though he were responding to the caller's words. He kept it up for a few minutes, then said, "Look, I'd love to do it that way, but it's out of our hands. Too many people involved." He waited an appropriate amount of time, then added, "Look, it can't be done and that's all there is to it. Calm down, you arrogant prick or I'll have a dozen cops come over and break your balls this afternoon." He paused— "That's better. I'll let you know how it's going." He hung up.

"Who was that?" Higgins asked.

"Boom Boom Vasillio," Raven said, glancing up at the vent.

"What the hell did he want?"

"Catch this, buddy. One of the broads that Ferris and his bunch gang-banged was Boom Boom's daughter. She told her old man but he wouldn't let her report it . . . family honor, that sort of shit. I guess they really fucked his kid up. He says she hasn't been the same since."

Higgins let out a loud, incredulous laugh. "No shit? You mean to tell me those assholes raped the daughter of the mob's best hit man? Beautiful." He laughed louder.

Raven joined him, then said, "Boom Boom offered me twenty-five grand to turn over the three of them. When I told him no, he told me to name my price."

"Maybe we *should* sell them," Higgins said.

"Don't be an idiot," Raven said. "It's too late for that now. Besides, the D.A. is on his way. No, we can't do it, Lee, but it's tempting, huh?"

"You bet your ass it is," Higgins said. "Why don't we work a deal with Boom Boom and give him any one of them at a cut rate, you know, just to satisfy him."

Raven laughed. "Yeah, well we can think about it."

They left the room and went to Lieutenant West's office where they told him what they planned to do with Carmine Vasillio. West said, "All right, but make sure nothing happens to these guys. You know Vasillio, Freddie, he's a fucking psychopath. He comes in here shooting off his piece and maybe he gets carried away. Make sure that doesn't happen."

They rounded up Ferris, O'Connor and Wells and brought them out into the main room of the precinct where the fingerprint board was located. They went over their names and addresses again and started the fingerprinting process.

Raven carefully observed the three suspects. O'Connor and Wells were pale and shaking. Ferris, who'd maintained a taciturn, arrogant posture, looked a little uneasy, too.

They asked them questions as Raven kept his eye on a large wall clock. When it was time, he brought Ferris to the fingerprint board, which was just behind the front desk. The technician started to take his prints when the precinct door flew open and Carmine Vasillio burst through. He came up to the waist-high gate and yelled, "Is this the cocksucker who raped my kid?"

"Jesus Christ," Higgins said as Vasillio pulled a .38 from his belt and aimed it at Ferris.

"Look out!" Raven yelled as he pushed Ferris to the floor. Higgins lunged at Vasillio and grabbed his arm just as he pulled the trigger. The shot blasted a hole in the ceiling. Others joined Higgins as he wrestled Vasillio to the floor and took away the gun.

It took fifteen minutes for order to be restored. Ferris, O'Connor and Wells were led away; Ferris was returned to the room with the open vent.

Raven and Higgins took Vasillio to the adjoining room and sat him down at the table.

"What the fuck is wrong with you?" Higgins screamed. "You gone fuckin' nuts or something? You come into a fucking police headquarters, pull a gun and try to shoot somebody?"

Vasillio said in a highly emotional voice, "I don't give a shit about nothin'. They raped my baby and screwed up her life. They disgraced her and me and my family. I don't care about nothin'. I just want to kill those pricks."

"Yeah, that's smart, Carmine," Raven said. "You get your revenge and you end up in jail for the rest of your life."

"I don't give a shit, Freddie," Vasillio said. "I ain't got that long to live anyway. I got a disease. Terminal. In the belly. All I want before I go is *them.*"

Raven said, "Look, Carmine, I can understand how you feel. I'd kill for my kids, too, but be smart. This whole thing has gone too far for you to get away with it. Look at the mess you're already in by coming in here and putting a hole through the ceiling. That's government property, for Christ's sake."

"I got a license."

"Damn it," Higgins yelled, "what the hell good is a license? It's a license to shoot up a headquarters?"

Raven said, "Give me a minute to think about this."

The three of them were silent until Raven said, "I know how to get you out of here, Carmine, but it'll cost you."

"How much?"

"Ten."

"You got it, Freddie."

"Good," Raven said. "Now, get the fuck out of here. I'll check in with you tonight. Lee, take him out the back. I'll go talk to West."

A few minutes later Bowers poked his head in the room and told Raven that the district attorney was there with a stenographer.

"Shit," Raven said loudly.

Two men entered the room, one carrying a portable steno machine. Raven smiled at them, winked and said, "You're too early. We need more time to make this case."

"Sorry, Detective Raven, but this investigation has gone on long enough," the detective playing the role of the D.A. said.

Raven looked up at the vent and pointed to it. The role-playing detective nodded, turned to the other detective and said, "Let's take a preliminary statement." The detective carrying the steno machine sat at the table and prepared to take down what was said.

"All right, what do you have on these three?"

"Well, let me lay it out for you," Raven said. He gave a few details of what they had learned about Ferris, O'Connor and Wells. When he was finished, the D.A. asked, "Did they make any statements concerning the crime?"

"No."

"Nothing at all?"

"Nothing," Raven said.

Higgins joined them in the room, gently slapped the detective playing district attorney on the back and sat on the edge of the table. Raven said to the D.A., "We don't have a doubt in the world that these are the Van Cortlandt rapists and the ones who killed Patricia Knees."

"It's nice that you're convinced they did it," the D.A. said sarcastically, "but convincing a jury of that is another matter. Did you find the keys or the money bags on them, the bags you say they put over their victims' heads?"

"No."

"Any evidence to tie them to the scene?"

"I told you that Ferris worked there in the past. He was a foreman, which meant he must have had a set of keys."

"That's no good, and you know it. How long have you been a detective?"

"Longer than you've been a D.A."

"Don't get snotty with me. You've been around long enough to know your hunches aren't worth a damn in a court of law. If you want me to proceed with prosecution, you'd better come up with something a lot better, and you'd better do it in the next couple of minutes."

"I told you what we have," Raven said.

"Which means you have nothing. You don't even have enough to justify bringing them in here. Everything you're talking about is circumstantial."

"Bullshit," Higgins said. "We've been breaking our balls on this case for months and we know what we have."

The D.A. looked at his partner and said, "Pack it up." He looked at Raven and said, "Release them and do it now."

Higgins shouted in a near hysterical voice, "What are you, fucking crazy? They killed the girl. They've been raping broads in the park for years."

"I don't care if they killed fifty girls," the D.A. said. "If we can't prove it, knowing it doesn't mean a thing. Frankly, you two are a disgrace to the department. Months on a case and this is all you come up with? You drag three citizens in here and put them through hell because you 'think' they committed a crime?" He said to his partner, "Let's go." They left the room.

Raven and Higgins went through some mumbling before Raven said, "Shut the door and let's talk this out."

Raven said, "The D.A. is a mental case, Lee. He's going to let these bums walk out of here, go back to their families like they were three fucking angels."

Higgins said, "I'll be a son of a bitch if I'll let that happen, Freddie. Five months work, a ton of money and this is the way it ends up? I'll blow my own brains out first."

Raven said, "The kid, Lamps, sits in jail and he'll take the heat for this. His girlfriend's dead, and all those other broads got screwed up because these guys went out for kicks once a month

213

like they were going bowling or something. Yeah, I agree with you, I'd rather turn in the badge and the pension than let these scumbags walk out like winners."

There was silence. Higgins said, "So, what do we do?"

"I'll tell you what we do," Raven said, slamming his fist on the table. "We sell Ferris. He's the ringleader, and he's the one Carmine wants. We tell Carmine when Ferris is coming out and Carmine is there. Ferris pays for the crime, Carmine satisfies his soul and at least we can walk away figuring something good came out of it."

"What about the other two?"

"Carmine can have them, too, if he wants them, but I don't mind seeing those two skip. They're just a couple of assholes who followed Ferris. He's the ringleader, he's the one we give Vasillio."

"No good," Higgins said. "Carmine might want revenge but he's not *that* crazy."

"It's not such a big deal, Lee. He wastes Ferris right away, goes low for awhile and when it blows over, he comes back. The other two don't know who Carmine is, so they're not going to blow the whistle on him. Besides, I figure they'll be so happy just getting out that they won't give a shit what happens to Ferris. They'll piss on his grave."

"Yeah, maybe," Higgins said, rolling his fingers on the tabletop. "You think Carmine will go for it?"

"For Christ's sake, Lee, you saw him in here an hour ago. Of course he'll go for it."

"How much you figure he'll pay?"

"I'll ask for the twenty-five grand."

"What about the Lieutenant?"

"All we're doing is following orders. The D.A. told us to release them, so that's what we're doing. The deal we cut with Vasillio is nobody's business."

"Let's go for it," Higgins said.

Raven started to pick up the phone but Higgins said, "Not this phone, Freddie."

Raven held up his hand. "Don't worry, I already talked to Carmine about how we'd arrange it if we decided to go this route." He dialed a number and Vasillio answered.

"Mr. Vasillio, this is Detective Raven, the one selling the

Cadillac. Go outside and call me back at this number." He gave him the direct line into the phone he was using. Ten minutes later it rang. Raven picked it up and said, "Detectives."

"This is Mr. Vasillio."

"Oh, yes, there's been a change of plans. I've decided to accept your offer for the car."

"Really?"

"Yes, you can buy the Cadillac if you still want to."

"How much are you asking now?"

"Well, we had discussed ten thousand dollars but I think a fair price would be twenty-five. It's in mint condition, just ready for you to use and enjoy."

"Twenty-five thousand. Yes, I think that's a fair price. When can I take delivery?"

"In an hour. I'll have the car in front of the station house exactly one hour from now. We'll send out someone with the keys."

"It's a deal."

"Good. Leave the money with Danny before you come here. When Danny has it in his hands, have him call me at this number. When I get the call, I'll know that the car is yours."

Fifteen minutes later, Danny called. "I got the money for the car," he said.

"Good. We'll be by tonight.

"It's set," Raven said. "Let's go give Ferris some bullshit story now about how we have to keep O'Connor and Wells here until we can verify something about their backgrounds. We tell him anything, but he goes out the door in an hour."

They waited a few minutes before entering Ferris's room. Up until then, Ferris had spent his time sitting placidly. Now, he was pacing, and the sound of the door opening caused him to jump.

Raven slammed the door behind him and said, "Sit down."

"What's going on?" Ferris asked, his voice reflecting his inner turmoil.

"I said sit down, motherfuck." Higgins came around behind and pushed Ferris against the table. Ferris sat heavily and looked up at Raven. Gone was the look of defiance in his eyes. He was a frightened man, and Raven knew that the scenes they'd played out in the next room had had their desired effect.

"The D.A. has ordered us to release you, Ferris," Raven said. "You win this round, but we're going to stay on your ass for the rest of your life, and the next time you get a parking ticket we're gonna treat it like you just shit on the White House lawn. Go on, get the hell out of here."

"Where's Jerry and Tim?" Ferris asked.

"They stay here for a while until we verify some things," Higgins said. "Get lost."

Ferris shook his head, "No, I'll wait for them."

Higgins kicked Ferris in the thigh. "We say you go, you go. You want to wait for them, do it outside. You stink up the place."

"Look, I got rights. You brought me in here and..."

Raven hit him across the face with the back of his hand. Their eyes locked. Ferris said weakly, "All right."

Raven and Higgins watched him slowly open the door and begin to step into the hallway. He stopped and turned, his eyes searching for something.

Higgins laughed and said, "You know, Ferris, we should have told the niggers to cut your throat, not just to steal your wallet and keys."

Ferris mouth slackened, and Raven knew what was going through his mind—that if they would go to the extent of hiring muggers, tapping his phone, beating a suspect and wheeling and dealing big money in order to achieve their desired end, they'd stop at nothing to get him. Was he thinking about Carmine Vasillio, Raven wondered? He answered his own question—of course he was, and the pained expression on his face brought joy to Raven's heart.

Raven and Higgins followed him into the squad room where a dozen detectives sat silently. Ferris was forced to pass between them, a psychic gauntlet. He kept his eyes straight ahead and walked with deliberate, tentative steps, reached the gate from behind which Vasillio had fired the shot, weaved unsteadily on his feet, leaned forward and grasped the rail for support. The squad room remained silent.

Ferris straightened up, turned and said to Raven and Higgins, who were standing a few feet behind him, "Look, I got something I want to tell you."

Twenty-seven

Fred Raven sat across a candlelit table from Mary, his wife of many years. It was a local restaurant. It served standard Italian fare, but the owner was always happy to oblige Raven's love of Fettucini Alfredo made the way his mother used to—with sausage.

The children were all away for the weekend. Mary had arranged it so that she and her husband could have some time alone. There seemed to be so little of that sort of time, and she relished the opportunity.

They'd started the evening with a couple of perfect Manhattans. Mary had raised her glass and said, "Here's to finally finishing that case, Freddie. I don't remember any case taking so long."

He'd grinned and clicked the rim of his glass against hers. "It looked like it was going to become a career," he said.

Now, as they lingered over dessert and coffee, Raven answered some of her questions about the Lamps case. "...just regular guys, buddies, out for some fun," he said. "Funny how something like that happens. The three of them go out drinking one night in a V.F.W. hall off the Thruway, in Yonkers, and they decide they want to get laid. They're all drunk and hit a couple of bars but no luck. They go to the park, get out of the car to take a leak, and see this couple necking in another car. She's going down on the guy, so they interrupt and rape her.

"They meet the next night and they're scared, but as time goes by and there's no report, they get cocky. They figure they might as well do it again. That's how it got started, just that simple, three drinking buddies out for a good time."

"Terrible," Mary said.

"Yeah, but at least we got them off the street. Ferris's confession ran three hours. They're all head cases, Mary. Ferris told us they only grabbed 'pigs.' He saw them that way because every time they took one, they were having sex with their boyfriends. The kid, Wells, who used to be in the seminary, is the real fruitcake of the bunch. He told me how he saved the girls by making them go to confession so they wouldn't lose their soul for eternity, that kind of religious crap. When we asked him how he felt about Patricia Knees dying, he says he knew she was in Heaven because he gave her the last rites in the car while they were driving back to dump her. The son-of-a-bitch was even proud that he put most of her clothes back on before they left the Stone place. It was like he did something decent."

"What about the other one? What was his name, O'Connor?"

"Yeah, Jerry O'Connor. He's no bargain, either. He's the one who told us how Knees died. Ferris was screwing her on the table while the other two held her down, but she was putting up a hell of a fight, kept trying to get up, so Ferris leaned forward and rammed his forearm into her neck. He held her down until he finished. When he got up, the kid was dead. Nobody *wanted* to kill her, but nobody wants a lot of things, huh?"

Mary smiled softly, reached across the table and took her husband's hands. "I don't know how you can spend your life dealing with people like this," she said.

"I don't either. Every time I come off a case like this, Mary, I swear I'm packing it in, telling them to take their pension plan and shove it. But then..." He laughed. "Well, then the next thing comes along and... it's hard to explain, Mary, but you know how I am. If anybody knows what I'm all about, it's you. There's something that draws you in, like a magnet, you know, or a moth flying around an electric light in summer."

She squeezed his hands and nodded. She looked particularly attractive that night to Raven. The flickering candlelight cast a warm glow over her full, pretty face. Her eyes were large and green, and there was always the hint of a smile at one corner of her mouth. "She's aging nicely," Raven thought as he returned the pressure on her hands. She still had a firm, nicely proportioned body, and as those thoughts struck him, his groin responded.

"I'm so glad that poor young man who was her boyfriend won't have to go through any more pain."

"If you mean he won't have to stay in jail, you're right. He's free now, but I wonder what all of this is going to do to his head. Lee and I want to keep tabs on him for a while. We figure he's not going to be the same kid he was before it happened, and maybe we can help him out in some way."

The drive home took only five minutes. They went inside the house and Mary offered to make him a drink.

"Yeah, I'd like another. Do we have any of the good stuff left, the Blantons?"

"I think so."

While Mary was in the kitchen preparing the drinks, Raven headed for the bathroom, almost tripping over Fluffy, the cat. He started to curse, then crouched and offered his hand. Usually, the cat would hiss at any such gesture of friendship from him, but this time she moved close and rubbed her body against him. It was as though the resolution of the case had eased the tension with everyone and everything, including Fluffy. Certainly, Mary was more relaxed. He was glad she'd planned a weekend alone.

He went to the large bathroom off the master bedroom and drew warm water into the tub. He noticed that Joy, who was off for the weekend, had put a small vase of fresh daisies on the vanity. He pulled out a few and sprinkled the petals on the water.

Mary entered the bedroom and handed him his drink. They toasted, sipped, then he kissed her. She had an ice cube in her mouth and she passed it to him.

"I love you, kid," he said as his hands reached for the buttons on her mauve silk blouse.

"You haven't said that in a long time," she said, with no hint of chiding in her voice.

"Yeah, I know, but I've been busy."

He slipped the blouse from her shoulders and kissed the exposed portion of her breasts above her bra. He quickly undid the snap on the front and, as her breasts fell free, he slipped to his knees and kissed them, going from one nipple to the other, then pressing his face between them and using his hands to push the white, soft mounds against his cheeks.

"Are we taking a bath?" she asked, laughing as she dropped her skirt to the floor.

"Yeah, I thought that would be nice."

"We haven't taken a bath together in years, Freddie."

"I know, and I can't wait."

When they were both naked, they stepped into the water and slowly slipped beneath it. He started with her feet, gently soaping each toe and running his fingers back and forth along the arch of her foot. She started to purr, the sound he'd decided years ago was the final one he wanted to hear on his deathbed. He soaped and massaged the length of her, her calves and thighs, her belly and breasts.

They got out of the tub and dried each other. Mary started for the bedroom but Raven grabbed her hand and led her to a small white wicker chair with purple cushions that matched the bathroom decor. She looked at him quizzically as she sat. "Let's start off a little different, hon," he said. He observed the expression on her face and knew what she was thinking, that he wanted something "different" because he was used to it from the other women in his life. He wished, at least at that moment, that it wasn't true.

"Freddie, do you really love me? I mean do you really love and respect me like you did when we first met?"

A lavender wall phone in the bathroom rang with jarring loudness.

"Shit," he said.

"Don't answer it."

"I have to. I'm on call... sort of. We'll get back to this in a minute, baby. We've got all night, all weekend."

He took the phone from its cradle, looked down at her, smiled at the circumstances and said, "Hello."

"Hey, Freddie, it's me, Lee. What are you doing?"

"Nothing much. You?"

"The same, just hanging around home. Mary's there?"

"Yeah."

"Good. Say hello for me."

"Will do, Lee," Raven said.

"The chief just called. You know those two cops who got whacked in Harlem last month?"

"Yeah."

"They want you and me on the case. They've been coming up zero."

"When?"

"He wants us to check in tomorrow morning. I told him I'd call back and let him know if you were around."

"Tell him Monday."

"Okay."

"Tell him I'm coming."

"Huh?"

"Nothing, forget it."

"You said Monday, right? You're coming Monday?"

"Have a good weekend. Give me a call tomorrow night and we'll coordinate." He hung up.

Mary looked up and said, "You're crazy, Fred Raven."

"Which makes you crazy for loving a crazy man. Shall we proceed?"

"Huh? Oh." She smiled. Raven looked down and saw Fluffy sitting in the doorway. He winked at the cat, closed his eyes and enjoyed the beginning of a long, pleasant weekend.